"Brendan, either you learn to respect my position here and do it quickly, or you can sleep in that rocky no-man's-land canyon and not my comfortable bunkhouse. Is that clear?"

Brendan grinned.

"I asked you a question. I'm waiting for an answer. And what are you grinning about, you fool?"

He took a step toward her, then another. She saw the intent in his hot gaze. He meant to kiss her. He'd always crossed from anger to arousal so easily, ending quarrels before their conclusion—one of them winning by default.

Now, before she could decide what she wanted, lightning-quick his mouth was on hers. She tried to resist the leather-and-lime smell of him.

But the battle was lost before it began.

* * *

The Texas Ranger's Heiress Wife
Harlequin® Historical #1163—December 2013

Author Note

I hope you enjoy reading about Brendan and Helena's reconciliation and glimpsing their past, as well as the rich history of the Old West. After all, they've been with us from the beginning in *Questions of Honor*—already fighting like cat and dog and each secretly heartbroken over the loss of the other. The danger to them and to their hearts sparked all the full-length books. What great catalysts they were! I couldn't wait any longer to write their story, although it took a while to create the perfect setting.

The kind of land-grabbing scheme depicted in *The Texas Ranger's Heiress Wife* is typical of stories told and retold from America's westward growth—as is the work of the Texas Rangers. Whether truth or myth, these stories have become part of the lore of the West.

Hopefully I've lived up to our exciting history.

THE TEXAS RANGER'S HEIRESS WIFE

KATE WELSH

Recycling programs
for this product may
not exist in your area.

ISBN-13: 978-0-373-29763-4

THE TEXAS RANGER'S HEIRESS WIFE

Copyright © 2013 by Kate Welsh

All rights reserved. Except for use in any review, the reproduction or
utilization of this work in whole or in part in any form by any electronic,
mechanical or other means, now known or hereafter invented, including
xerography, photocopying and recording, or in any information storage
or retrieval system, is forbidden without the written permission of the
publisher, Harlequin Enterprises Limited, 225 Duncan Mill Road,
Don Mills, Ontario M3B 3K9, Canada.

This is a work of fiction. Names, characters, places and incidents are
either the product of the author's imagination or are used fictitiously,
and any resemblance to actual persons, living or dead, business
establishments, events or locales is entirely coincidental.

This edition published by arrangement with Harlequin Books S.A.

For questions and comments about the quality of this book,
please contact us at CustomerService@Harlequin.com.

® and TM are trademarks of Harlequin Enterprises Limited or its
corporate affiliates. Trademarks indicated with ® are registered in the
United States Patent and Trademark Office, the Canadian Trade Marks
Office and in other countries.

Printed in U.S.A.

Available from Harlequin® Historical and
KATE WELSH

Other works include

Love Inspired

Harlequin Special Edition

**Did you know that these novels are also
available as ebooks? Visit www.Harlequin.com.**

To all my readers.
Thanks so much for all your support.

KATE WELSH

As a child, Kate Welsh often lost herself in creating make-believe worlds and happily-ever-after tales. Many years later she turned back to creating happy endings when her husband challenged her to write down the stories in her head. A lover of all things romantic, Kate has been writing romance for over twenty years now. Kate loves hearing from readers, who can reach her on the internet at kate_welsh@verizon.net.

Prologue

Cautiously, Brendan Kane approached the church, keeping his sister, Abby, behind him. It was soon apparent no one hid in the dark shadows around the building. Once this meeting was over, he'd be on the night train, headed west toward his dream and away from a hangman's noose. Had he known Helena's damned guardian was trying and succeeding in framing him for murder, he'd have left long ago. Then he'd have been away from the torture of watching Helena from afar, knowing she was to marry Joshua Wheaton.

Brendan and Abby crept to the church doors and slipped inside. Odd, he thought. More candles glowed than the little church used for benediction.

In the candlelight, he saw her. His Helena. He loved her so much he'd rejected her, for her own good and his own peace of mind. Brendan hissed a word that shouldn't be spoken in a church. Helena Conwell was an American princess. In the eyes of her world he was nothing but Irish-born scum, a dirt-poor coal miner and now an outlaw to boot.

Dear God. How many nights had he closed his eyes

and pictured her in this church exactly as she was—wearing a beautiful white gown? Now, though, she was really there, standing near the altar talking to Father Rafferty. She turned and put her hand on the old priest's arm, then walked up the aisle toward him and Abby.

"What are you doing here?" Brendan growled.

Hurt entered those bluer-than-blue eyes he so loved. "I'm sorry you aren't glad to see me. I suppose that makes this all the more necessary," she said, as she pulled a pistol from the folds of her elegant dress and leveled it at him.

"Is this all an elaborate trick to snare Brendan in your guardian's trap?" Abby demanded. "I trusted both you and Joshua with my brother's life."

Helena smiled up at Brendan, not sparing Abby a glance. "Oh, no. It's my snare to catch myself a husband. Father Rafferty agreed to marry us, darling, and time is wasting. I'm sorry it has to be this way. I know it's because of me they've gone after you, and I'm sorry. Franklin Gowery was never meant to know about us, but he does and so here we are."

"Your guardian is a bit of a poor loser, isn't he?" Brendan grinned. It was a grin he used often to infuriate adversaries and throw them off their stride. It worked a bit too well this time, for Helena looked as if she wanted to slap it off his face. "Ya won't shoot me, lovey," he told her, living dangerously as always when backed against a wall. Tonight seemed to be ripe for that.

Helena didn't rise to his bait, though. "No, I probably wouldn't." She swung the gun left. Toward Abby. "But I might—just might—shoot your sister," she said in the most scarily calm tone he'd ever heard.

He drew in a sharp breath. Had it all been too much

for her? Had his rejection, compounded by her guardian's insistence she marry Joshua, Brendan's childhood friend, caused her mind to surrender to the strain? "Have ya lost your mind?" Brendan asked. He'd meant to sound demanding, hoping to snap her out of her reckless behavior, but even he heard concern leak into his tone. Question was, had Helena heard it?

He glanced at Ab. She stared at him, her eyes sparkling with delight and not worry as Helena held the gun steadily on her. She'd clearly seen his worry and his love for Helena. "I do believe she means it, Bren," Abby said.

"Father Rafferty won't marry us this way," Brendan stated, trying to interject some sense into the conversation.

"Actually, after I explained how you'd trifled with me, then rejected me, he was happy to agree. It's his gun."

Abby coughed, but only to cover a laugh. Then her eyes flashed with temper when she realized Helena spoke the truth. "After what happened to me, you did the same thing to Miss Conwell?"

"This was different. I only broke it off because she's an heiress."

Abby glared.

"I lost my head?" Brendan added.

"I'd say Miss Conwell lost something a bit less metaphoric. Her virginity," his sister declared. "We'd best get on with this ceremony. You'll be losing one form of freedom this night, brother mine, or so help me I'll geld you myself. And I'll be holding that pistol. Now that you'll be my sister, I'll be looking after your interests, Miss Conwell. A bride shouldn't have to hold a gun on her groom. And don't worry, if he refuses, I'll shoot him where he sits. I suspect that's near to where his brains have been of late." She glared. "I wouldn't kill my own brother, but just now, I wouldn't mind a bit of maiming and knowing his ride out West will be mighty uncomfortable."

Brendan sighed. He had to try one more time, for Helena's sake. He had nothing to offer her. Not even his good name. "Sweetlin', if we marry, you'll be married to and travelin' with an accused criminal. You could go to prison for aidin' and abettin'. Gowery lied and put my name on the list of conspirators. Ab says the Pinkertons manufactured proof I blew Destiny to hell and gone. I wouldn't do that to Joshua. I saved his life, didn't I?"

"I know. Joshua and I have been spying on them to keep you safe. Joshua will see your name is cleared, but if you don't want to get caught and see me swept up with you, we'd better get to it." Helena looked toward the altar and raised her voice. "We're ready, Father."

"Enough stalling, brother mine," Abby said. "Take her hand, walk down that aisle and say the words."

Helena looked up at him, her eyes so full of love it made his heart ache. "It'll be fine. We'll go West and buy that ranch you want so badly. We'll call it Shamrock and raise our children there."

Brendan stared at Helena. All night he'd been in agony, thinking her and Joshua's engagement was to be announced at her birthday party. Would leaving her behind to marry Joshua or any other man be easier for the distance? Out of options, and running out of time to think about that or catch the westward train, he did as Abby ordered and walked toward the altar.

"You can buy the ranch," he told Helena as he walked

at her side toward her doom. "You can call it whatever ya please. I'll never lower myself to take your charity."

"What's mine will be yours in moments, so it won't be charity," Helena said. She didn't wait for a rebuttal, but turned toward the priest and nodded.

"Dearly beloved," Father Rafferty began.

It looked as if Brendan's goose was well and truly cooked. But so was Helena's. He wouldn't touch her and they'd have this farce annulled.

All he had to do was keep his hands to himself. He glanced at his bride. God had better help him or he was a goner.

Chapter One

Heavy hoofbeats resounded through the house, sending spirals of fear shooting through Helena. Her heart started to race. Had the Ghost Warriors finally decided to move on Shamrock? She stood and dropped her needlework as her housekeeper rushed in, her eyes wide with fear.

The horses thundered by along the ranch road, but one rider advanced rapidly on the house. Helena grabbed the loaded shotgun she kept leaning against the fireplace, then moved to the front window. Cautiously, she nudged the curtain aside with the double barrel and peered out.

Anger flooded through her. Or was it really desperate, foolish hope? In the blink of an eye her emotions flipped back to anger.

"Brendan?" she whispered. He'd said he would never set foot on Shamrock. Typical. His word meant everything to him except with her.

He seemed to hesitate, one foot on the step up to the porch.

So, he remembers his vow. "Never is a very long

time, isn't it, Brendan?" she whispered, then cursed his contrary soul. She liked to relax on the porch in the evenings, and didn't want to picture him there. Before he decided to go ahead and invade that special space, Helena threw open the door and marched toward her estranged husband.

He slowly eased his booted foot back to the ground. His emerald eyes were unreadable in the shadow cast by the wide brim of his black Stetson. He glanced down at the shotgun as he pushed the hat back on his head. His left eyebrow arched annoyingly as he looked up, snaring her gaze with the power he still held over her.

He stared for a long, uncomfortable moment, opened his mouth, then closed it, as if unsure what to say.

She managed to look away from his eyes. Oh, how he could make her want him—make her care. Even after he'd left her alone during the darkest days of her life.

When she forced herself to look back, those eyes that had captured her heart and made it his, sparkled with mischief and flicked for a split second back to her shotgun. "And here I was thinkin' you might be glad to see me," he quipped in his slight, musical Irish accent.

She might be glad. She was glad, damn him. But she'd had three years of pain and practice at hiding her feelings. She had her pride, too. She stiffened her spine. He'd never know what she still felt for him. Never.

"W-why? Why would you think I'd be glad to see you?" she asked, and looked down at the gun in her hands. No matter how many times she'd threatened it, she would never want to shoot him. Accidentally or otherwise. She took a moment to break the gun open and gather her composure.

Steadier now, she said, "I seem to recall you telling

me you'd never set foot on Shamrock. I believe it was outside the title office, after we signed the papers for the ranch."

Helena turned to her housekeeper, who'd followed her to the porch. "It's all right, Maria. You can go back inside."

Maria shot a black look Brendan's way, "You are sure?"

Helena nodded, then glanced back at her husband. "Is there something other than rejection and scorn I'm to read from what you said that day, and what you've done the last three years?"

"Things change." He looked suspiciously as if he was choosing his words as carefully as she was. Then his whole countenance changed. He looked…serious suddenly. Weighed down, even. "I've bad news. The raiders struck again. Belleza this time. Don Alejandro, the shepherds and their wives were all killed. Señora Varga and her daughter brought the don's body to town for burial."

Helena swayed and grabbed a porch column. "How on earth did Farrah and Elizabeth survive? The renegades don't leave survivors, do they?"

"They'd been in town," he explained. "They heard the commotion in time for Miss Varga to get off their ranch road. She hid her mother and the carriage, but Miss Varga, bein' who she is, snuck to the hilltop overlookin' the homestead. Thinkin' she could help, apparently."

He shook his head. Grimaced. "She saw them kill her da and was smart enough to know it was too late to help anyone down there. Some of the men from town are out there buryin' the dead. Quinn's gone on by here with a posse, chasin' wild geese again. He's hopin' to track the raiders to their hideout this time 'round."

"I thought the governor sent you here to stop these Ghost Warriors. Why aren't you with Sheriff Quinn and the posse?"

"Because they're wastin' their time. The raiders'll disappear into the hills. Mark my words. When the sun sets, all Quinn and the rest will have are tired mounts and saddle-sore behinds."

She took a step back. It hurt too much to see Bren. Talk to him. She wanted him to go away. Far away, so she'd have a chance to heal from the new wounds his presence here caused. "Well, uh, thank you for bringing me the news. I'll look in on the Vargas tomorrow. Where will they be?"

"The hotel. The house is gone. Burned. You'd have seen the smoke but the wind's to the east today. I didn't stop by just to tell you about Belleza. I'm movin' here." At her gasp, he qualified his statement. "Into Shamrock's bunkhouse."

"No. Absolu—"

"If you're of a mind to try stoppin' me," he interrupted, "remember under the law I've a right to move all the way into your bedroom if I want. And remember, too, it was you who wanted this marriage *and* this ranch."

Holding tight to her control and her expression, Helena put a hand on her hip. "I don't care where you lay your head. I stopped caring long ago. But if you set foot on this porch, let alone in my bedroom, I'll blow a hole in you big enough to read the front page of the *Sentinel* through."

She'd started to turn away, so she could go slam the

door in his arrogant, beautiful face, when he took hold of her arm. He'd always had the most incredible way of touching her. It spoke of an abundance of leashed power behind his gentle touch. She couldn't control the tremor that rushed through her.

Then he said, "As far as the townsfolk and ranchers will know, I'm at Shamrock to stay, and livin' with you."

In shock, she stared at him, her mouth working like a hooked trout. "Why would they think that?" she finally muttered.

"Because it's what I *want* them to think."

"Then I'll let them all know you're only here to— Why *are* you here? Why did the posse ride onto Shamrock at all?" she demanded, her anger growing to the size of her pain.

Brendan, his eyes hooded, once again seemed to choose his words carefully. "I tracked the raiders across your northern border. Word is Shamrock doesn't run cattle up there unless there's a drought. They seem to feel safe takin' that route. They've done it twice that I know of. Now that they've moved to bigger places, Shamrock has to be near the top of their list. I want to catch these bastards in the act, and as you're a citizen, and I took an oath to protect the citizens of Texas, I'm here to protect you."

That certainly stated in no uncertain terms where she stood with him. "You took an oath to love, honor and keep me, but that didn't stop you from leaving."

Fire entered his gaze. "I took that oath at gunpoint. It was your poor wronged princess act that had my own sister holdin' the pistol, and forcin' those promises out of me. And *you* said you'd honor and obey. You broke your vows the minute you got hold of your inheritance.

Did you think I'd be able to hold my head up when folks learned the money for Shamrock came from you?"

She gripped the shotgun until her knuckles turned white. "Joshua bought the bank, so the bank account had both our names on it. Who'd have known?"

Brendan and his pride! It had ruined her life. She stared down at his hand on her arm, then up into those cold green eyes, refusing to remember the way he used to look at her. "You gave up any right to touch me the moment you rode off and left me to deal with hundreds of acres of land alone. I built Shamrock from the ground up, each day hoping you'd be back. One day I realized I'd stopped hoping. From that time forward, Shamrock's success was for me and me alone. You have no place here."

When he let go of her like a man afraid of losing his fingers, she knew he'd believed her lie.

"At the land office that day all I'd wanted to do was give you the life I thought you deserved." She went on as if nothing had changed, because, though he no longer held her arm, he still held her heart. She was afraid he always would, and that made her furious. She wished she could hate him, but so far, she could only pretend.

How could his touch make her want so many things he'd never give her? "I was wrong, but not about buying the ranch. I was wrong about what you deserve. You deserve exactly what you've got, *Ranger* Kane. No place to call home, and whores warming whichever one of their beds you've paid to spend the night in."

He raised that annoying eyebrow and grinned. "Unlike you, at least I'm warm."

Helena's heart clutched at his admission. She wanted to slap that grin off his face, but instead lifted her chin and managed another lie. "What makes you think I'm always alone in mine? Did you really think I'd wait for you to get over your childish snit and decide to honor your vows?"

Brendan's grin faded and his eyes went cold. "Then why haven't you filed for divorce? I've clearly deserted you."

"Because, you ninny, you had to be gone for three years. It would have been three years in June. But now, one month shy of freedom, you've put it about town that you've moved here. That means when you decide to go off again, the waiting period starts all over. Three more years of my life gone to a man who cares only for himself and his precious pride. Once again you've stepped in with a unilateral decision to destroy my future."

"Unilateral? Me? It was you who went ahead, like a spoiled princess, and plunked down the coin to buy the land you wanted. Have you ever done an honest day's work? Do you understand how hard others have had to labor for what you were handed?"

Helena's blood pounded in her head and drained from her face. She'd be damned if she'd tell him just how much hard work on Shamrock had cost her. She wouldn't go there. She couldn't. But she was sick to death of him tarring her and her father with the same brush as the man who'd all but forced Brendan into the mines. Her father had been an honorable man. "Handed? My father took a chance and invested a minor inheritance in all the right places. *Handed?* That man meant the world to me! He was all I had after my mother died. Oh, you're so right. All I had to do to get my hands on his money was watch as he was gunned down in the street, then be left alone in the world with *Franklin*

Gowery as a guardian. I earned every cent of what I inherited in the tears I shed that day and every day since.
Go away, Brendan. I'll take my chances with the renegades. They'll just kill me. Not cut out my heart and
leave me alive and bleeding."

"Helena, I'm—"

"You're *nothing* to me. Do you hear? Get off my land.
You don't want it. You don't want me. And I sure as
hell don't want you around reminding me of the mess
I made of my life because I believed you loved me as
much as I once loved you." This time she made it inside and slammed the door. But her home offered no
solace and never had.

She was done.

She'd put Shamrock up for sale and go back East.
And she'd never love another man. Men just dragged
you from hotel to hotel, with only adults to fill your
life, then left you alone in the world with not a friend
to your name. Or else claimed they loved you, only to
toss that love back in your face.

Helena sank to the floor and, instead of howling out
her pain, stuffed the ends of her shawl in her mouth to
muffle her cries. Tears poured down her face. Oh, she
was done with him this time.

Done!

Brendan watched the door slam. Jaysus, the woman
knew how to hurt him. He nearly took the one step up
onto the porch to follow, but turned away and grabbed
Harry's reins instead, heading for the bunkhouse.
Nothing would come of trying to talk to her now. But
he wasn't leaving. Not with the carnage he'd seen at
Belleza. Whoever the animals were, he was going to

find them and see them hanged. Every last mother's son of them.

He rode to the barn to get Harry settled before heading over to the bunkhouse to find out if there was even room for him there. As he dismounted, he looked farther up the ranch road and saw Sean Mallory, Shamrock's foreman, step out of the cottage he shared with his wife and children. Winchester in hand, Mallory stood staring his way. Brendan ground-tied Harry and walked to the cottage.

"Kane," the foreman said as he approached. "What brings you around?" He didn't sound welcoming. *Loyal,* Brendan thought. That was good. Helena was in good hands, as he'd heard.

"Belleza was hit. Twelve dead, Alejandro Varga included. His wife and daughter were in town, thank the good Lord. The wives of the shepherds weren't as lucky."

Mallory winced and glanced back at the cottage. "I wondered when they'd move on to one of the bigger spreads. We saw Quinn ride through with a posse. Why?"

"We tracked them across Shamrock's northern boundary. I know you don't run the cattle up there, for the most part. Got any idea who else might know that?"

"It isn't a closely guarded secret, if that's what you mean. But no Comanche would know it unless they've been watching us for years."

Brendan paused and frowned. No one was supposed to know he was hunting anyone other than a band of renegades. He and Ryan Quinn had decided to keep their suspicions to themselves, even though it really ate at his gut. Brendan hated that everyone was so damned willing to believe ill of the Comanche. True, the tribe deserved the reputation, but they'd gone down in defeat and were buttoned up on the reservation. Yet all the men conducting these raids had needed to do was scalp their first victims, and everyone ignored all the inconsistencies marking these attacks as other than the work of the tribe.

By going along with the popular view, Brendan and the sheriff hoped they'd lure the ones responsible into making a mistake born of overconfidence. Brendan knew Quinn was new to being a lawman, but he was doing a passable job and was in no way stupid enough to spread their plan about.

So who had let the cat out of the bag about white men being suspect? "What makes you think it's not Comanche?" Brendan asked carefully, eying Helena's foreman with suspicion.

"You know my brother-in-law is foreman at the Rocking R," Mallory said. "He told me their fence was downed and they've lost a few head over the cliff edge up where the R and Shamrock meet up with the canyon that separates both spreads from Avery's Bar A. There were also tracks across that back edge of the spread that disappeared into the canyon. So I went looking up there. Our fences were downed, too. And there were tracks from shod horses. Now there's been another attack and there're more tracks. Can't be a coincidence. I think the fences being downed is supposed to discourage both spreads from running cattle up there. Less chance of our men spotting something odd.

"If you add the tracks to Avery being the only one who's bought land off those who were raided, he's looking mighty guilty."

Dammit. Brendan didn't want loose tongues tipping off the bastard. "He's not the only one who tried. Alejandro Varga offered several times to buy Adara. The last time was the day after it was raided."

"But now Don Alejandro's dead," Mallory said, shifting the Winchester to lean it on his shoulder. "As far as I'm concerned that puts Avery at the top of the list. He hates sheep and now all the sheep ranchers are gone. I sure as hell know Varga's son will sell off what's left of his father's flock."

If Mallory's suspicions were this well thought out, Brendan figured he'd better confide in him. He stooped to pick up a stick, then walked to the edge of the cottage porch and sat. He quickly sketched a crude map in the dirt. Mallory bent down on one knee, his gaze intent.

"The raids look random," Brendan said, "unless ya plot it out from a bird's-eye view. Then it makes sense."

"So far Avery's come off lookin' like a real saint, savin' the poor, desperate and terrified from complete ruin." Mallory nodded.

Brendan drew in the dust as he spoke. "And in the meantime, he's picked off targets here, here and there. He tried to get hold of the Harkens' place here," he said, and drew an *F* on another square he'd drawn. "But he failed, thanks to Joshua Wheaton and Alex Reynolds protecting young Billy's interests. Avery offered for the Oliver place, too, but all he got was the sharp side of that young lady's tongue."

Another *F,* for failed attempt, joined the first, but that property was in the opposite end of the county. "Then these three fell. No survivors usually means family back East mourn and sell." Those squares got an *X*.

"Lump together all these places we think he moved on, now add Belleza. Look at this. They all fall in a horseshoe around the town. Which is why I'm here. The Rocking R and Shamrock stand in his way. Shamrock is either the next to be moved on or he's planning to acquire it another way.

"I've heard he's trying to get to Helena's heart." Brendan hesitated, but decided to hell with what the foreman thought. "I couldn't let that happen. So now that I'm here, he'll move on us eventually. Probably before he thinks I can get Shamrock fortified. What safety measures have you taken?"

Mallory outlined a comprehensive plan of misdirection with regard to the number of men at Shamrock, the quality of their firearms and careful round-the-clock lookouts.

"Do you think Helena would tell Avery what she's armed you all with?"

"She has no idea she bought the best. She lets me order what I want. No use getting outmoded equipment. As far as the wife tells me, Helena and Avery don't talk about ranching.

"And about the boss, let me tell you something. She comes off brave, but she's scared. We can't station anyone inside the house, but we try to see she's safe by posting guards near to it. Woman alone. Folks would talk if someone saw one of us was too close."

Brendan winced. Helena had lied. No man had ever warmed her bed. Mallory wouldn't worry for her reputation, were that the case. Why had Brendan believed her? Clearly, she'd been no more unfaithful than he had.

Because he'd wanted to believe she'd been, that's

why. It had eased his conscience. Made him feel justified in remaining apart from her. But the truth was, she finally needed him, and he intended to be here to protect her.

Chapter Two

Brendan put down the currycomb and gave Harry a pat on his neck. The gelding knocked him backward with a head butt to the chest. "Oh, it's like that now, is it?" Brendan crooned. "You see herself again for a few days and right away I'm playin' second fiddle. And who is it that feeds and brushes you till that black hide of yours shines like satin?"

Harry whinnied and lipped Brendan's cheek. "Ah, but aren't you the sweet talker." Then the big black nuzzled his bulging pocket. "I see how the wind blows, you great phony. Just lovin' me up for a treat."

"I see you still talk to him more like a friend than just a horse," Helena said from outside the stall.

Brendan gave Harry a carrot from his pocket, then stepped out into the aisle, saying, "Hear that? It's 'just a horse,' she called you. Remember that and who it is that butters your bread, Harry m' boy." Then Brendan said, "He *is* a friend. And it was you who named him after your da, and spoiled him with apples all the way West. Do ya know the ribbin' I've taken over a horse named for my father-in-law?" Even prepared to look at her loveliness, Brendan felt his heart speed up when their eyes met.

Helena's smile faded and she sighed. "Were we ever that young and foolish? Where did all the love go?" She shook her head. "No. Never mind. It doesn't matter anymore. We're who we are and they were who they were."

Brendan desperately needed to change the subject before he confessed that he still loved her more than life itself. "Is there something I could be doin' for you?"

She blinked, clearly surprised by his offer. "Have you seen Jimmy about?" she asked. "Oh. Forget it. I asked him to help Al build a fence around the garden. I have to remember to order some of the wire Rhia Varga uses around her chicken coop. If it keeps her chickens safe from predators, it should do the same for ours, and keep animals out of Shamrock's vegetable garden."

She wants to order the wire. Brendan stared at her. He'd quickly come to see that Helena knew what she was doing around the ranch. And had to admit how little credit he'd given her. She knew what it meant to work. And it was damn hard work she'd done and still did.

"I'm sorry for that remark I made about you not knowin' the meanin' of work. It's clear the men respect you and that you often work alongside them."

"Don't be sorry. You'd have been right once. The girl who came here *didn't* know what hard work meant." Her eyes glittered in the sunlight—with tears, he feared. "I'm not that naive, sheltered girl any longer. The truth is, you don't know me and I don't know you. Maybe we never did."

He nearly protested that of course he knew her, but she turned away and went to her mare's stall. Paint Box. The silly name made him smile.

He moved to pat the mare's blaze at the same time Helena did, and his hand landed atop hers. She gasped and pulled away. Sadness nearly overwhelmed him. Once upon a time she wouldn't have shied away. And he'd have never left her alone in her bed, either.

No one understood why he and Helena had gone their separate ways after banding together as they made their way to freedom. It had caused a rift in his family he'd yet to fully repair. Worse of all, Brendan was getting to a place where even he didn't understand what kept them apart. And now it was too late.

He'd thrown away her love in a snit—one he still felt had been justified. But he wasn't sure if feeling justified had been worth what he'd lost. Putting the thought away, Brendan realized he stood with his hand on the mare, staring straight ahead. And Helena was staring at him. "What was it you wanted Jimmy for?" he asked, to cover his discomfort.

"I wanted him to harness the gig. Elizabeth and Farrah Varga decided to bury Don Alejandro privately. Farrah's note said they didn't want to hear a lot of insincere platitudes. I can't blame them. Some of the men at my father's funeral were really more like rivals than friends. It made it so much more difficult sorting out who could be trusted and who couldn't."

Brendan frowned. He'd never met Helena's father, who'd already been killed when she'd stumbled upon Brendan's favorite fishing hole. Putting aside the precious memory of their first meeting, he brought his mind back to what she was saying.

"We decided to give them a tea to see them off. They're going to visit family."

That meant a trip into town. "Who are you takin' with you?"

"With me? No one. I go to town alone all the time."

That wasn't happening again. "You can't go alone."

"You have no authority over me!" Helena declared. "I go where I want, when I want."

As if he didn't know that. "Jaysus, woman. Can we not speak a civil word between us? You could run into the raiders. Suppose that happened? Contrary to what you apparently think, they don't just kill the women they come across on these raids. By time they're done with them, the poor women are probably beggin' for death. At least Miss Varga had the sense to stay hidden."

Helena frowned. "Fine. I'll take Al with me. The garden is the least important thing going on right now. Jimmy can work alone."

Brendan thought about the young buck and his belly tightened with what he refused to call jealousy. Unfortunately, he was at a loss what else to call it. He wasn't staking a claim to her. At least, that was what Brendan told himself. But even as he thought it, his heart protested. "I heard Mallory tell Al to ride out to check for laboring cows after fixing the fence. I'll go along with you to town."

She looked as shocked as he felt, and shook her head. "No. You said you were going to work on strengthening our defenses. You should have suggestions for Mallory about them."

He had a few, but she and the foreman seemed to run a tight outfit. Brendan was here to protect Helena, but didn't want to admit it to her. "I talked to Mallory about a few changes already. He's off seeing to them. Right now I'm at loose ends, so I'm riding with you."

"Fine! I'll go put on riding clothes, and change back into my dress at the store. Just don't talk to me. And when we get into town, go away! I'm sure the ladies at the Garter can keep you occupied."

He summoned up a grin. "They usually do," he lied. Then cursed his contrary nature when he saw hurt enter her eyes. What was it about Helena that made him do and say things he regretted before he could get his big mouth shut?

While she changed, he readied Harry and her mare for the ride into town. By the time they were halfway there, he was mighty sick of Helena's stony silence. He managed to honor her demand, though, afraid that if he didn't she'd sneak out of town for the return trip without him.

It was an hour of torture until they reached the edge of town. After setting a time and place to meet up, he peeled off without another word, hoping against hope she was as miserable as he was.

The Vargas' farewell tea had begun to wind down when Helena said goodbye and slipped out the door. She set out for her sister-in-law's general store to change back out of her dress. Then she'd have to meet Brendan for the ride home.

"Helena, wait!" she heard Patience Reynolds call as she reached the front of the store. "I wanted to talk with you," her friend said, a happy grin on her pretty face.

In the fall of last year she'd married Helena's nearest neighbor, Alex Reynolds, owner of the Rocking R. They were expecting their first child and were deliriously happy together.

Helena fought the disgraceful stab of envy she felt.

It wasn't that she begrudged her friends their joy. She didn't. But it reminded her of all the things Brendan had stolen from her. Envy didn't mean she couldn't be pleased for them, though.

Resigned, Helena walked up the steps with Patience at her side. At the top, her friend stopped and turned to her. "Before I forget, Alex and I wondered if you two would like to come to dinner."

"Two?"

"You and Brendan. We're both so happy for you. Brendan did so much to help me. Alex has tremendous respect for him."

Darn Brendan and his lie! But she trusted her friends and wouldn't lie to them herself. "We aren't back together in spite of what you must have heard. He's moved to Shamrock only because he thinks it may help catch the raiders."

Patience blinked. "But when Alex and I met Brendan he was clearly worried about you. And I know you've regretted the state your marriage was in. I didn't understand then, but when I met him, he was so sweet. And kind."

Brendan? Sweet and kind? *He isn't sweet and kind to me. Not anymore. I can't want him back. I'd be a candidate for Bedlam if I did.*

"He's there to catch the Ghost Warriors," Helena said. "That's all."

"Are you saying it's too late? This could be your chance to show him how good life with you would be. Maybe cook him special dinners. You know, show him how much you love him."

Helena shook her head. "No. I've learned my lesson. I'll never try to manipulate him or anyone else again.

That's all that would be. If he doesn't love me enough to accept me as I am, he isn't for me. I've wasted enough of my life.

"Now let's go see why Abby disappeared from the send-off." It was a worry for Helena.

About a year after Brendan's sister had arrived in town, she'd become the friend Helena had never had. For Abby, she would walk through fire.

She let out a breath she hadn't realized she'd been holding. Since becoming her friend, Helena had come to understand that Abby would have been a comfort after the accident. But by then it had been too late. By then Helena had managed to regroup, and remembered a lesson she'd learned early in her life—how to hide her pain behind false cheer.

She and Patience walked in, but the store was deserted. Helena glanced at her friend's worried frown, then rushed into the back room, tucked behind a curtain. There she found Abby lying on a chaise with her eyes closed and a cloth on her forehead.

Eyes nearly identical to Brendan's opened and widened as Helena hurried forward. Abby was pale as death and looked horribly weak.

Helena sat down on the foot of the chaise. "Abby, sweetie, what is it? You look awful."

"I love you, too."

At least her sense of humor was intact. "You know what I mean," Helena said with a mock frown.

A frail smile tipped Abby's lips. "I don't know what anyone can do. I feel like death itself. I never felt this bad with Daniel."

Helena stared. "A baby?"

Patience let out a little squeal of delight from the doorway and rushed to the other side of the chaise.

Helena did her best to be thrilled for Abby, who'd given up hope of having another child. But inside she felt hollow. Alone.

"Don't tell my brother. He's always been my rock, but he hovers, and I don't want that right now. He's pigheaded and won't take no for an answer when he wants to help."

Helena grimaced. "Rock-headed, you mean."

"Good sweet Lord, are you two still going at it? I thought he'd moved home."

"He made it clear he's only there to catch the raiders. He thinks they may hit Shamrock next. Once he solves the problem of these raids, he'll be gone again. Of course, he's let everyone think he's moved home, he *says* to protect me—"

"But that's sent your desertion claim flyin' out the window," Abby said. "He really is a blockhead, but... but I know he loves you."

A surge of anger blasted through Helena. It was so strong she couldn't hold her tongue any longer. "Has it ever occurred to anyone that *I* might be done with *him?*"

"Oh, you can't mean that," Abby cried. Then she took in a sharp breath and stared for a long moment. "I'm sorry. It's easy to forget how much you've had to deal with all alone."

If she only knew the half of it. Helena wiped away tears she hadn't known were falling. They'd blinded her to the worry and concern in her friends' faces. "I'm fine. Having so much to do at Shamrock has kept me putting one foot in front of the other, with no time to think. It's a strain having him there. I don't need him.

Not anymore. When I did, he was off nursing wounded pride. After he left me standing outside the land office that day, I got home, and all his things were just gone. He left me an object of pity to everyone around here when he disappeared."

Abby's expression brightened, as if she'd made a monumental discovery. "That's why you kept to yourself after Brendan left. Not because you were angry at us."

Helena was so tired of half-truths, but she had no choice; she told another. "He never wrote me, or asked after me when he wrote you. If you hadn't kept in touch with him, and dropped little pieces of information about his life to me, he could have been dead for all I knew."

Abby shook her head. "Brendan is an idiot. But, Helena, he did ask after you—when he finally got in touch. I wasn't to tell you, however.

"You were brave and steadfast in your love for him. Suppose that monster of a guardian of yours had figured out that you and Josh were spying to save Bren? I shudder to think what would have happened. My great, giant, pigheaded idiot of a brother needs a good swift kick in the tail!"

Helena made her excuses after that, changed, then left Abby and Patience to their talk of babies. She retrieved Paint Box from outside the hotel and left Tierra del Verde and Brendan behind. But in the back of her mind, one phrase resounded.

He did ask after you.

Two or so hours later, Helena slogged through knee-deep mud to help her men pull a frightened newborn Texas longhorn to safety. The incessant lowing of the

nervous mama in the background wasn't helping settle the little one. But there was no hope of quieting the
cow, which had probably delivered only the day before.

There was no better mother in the bovine kingdom
than a Texas longhorn. To protect their progeny from
a predator, the cows were known to band together in a
circle with their horns outward, keeping their calves and
heifers safely in the center. Unfortunately, there wasn't
much a cow could do if her curious offspring wandered
into a mud pit that was normally a watering hole.

"It'll be just fine, little one," Helena murmured as
she reached the struggling baby, which went still. Since
her voice seemed to soothe the animal and stop its need-
less struggle, Helena kept up the low, quiet crooning. "I
know you're scared, but we're here to help." Big brown
eyes stared into hers and stole her heart. This one was
a keeper. Heifer or calf, this one would be staying at
Shamrock to help build its future. "You'll be back with
your mama in no time," she went on. "I promise."

Over her shoulder she called, "Toss me a rope," and
her eyes connected with Brendan's. She hadn't even
heard him ride up. Were she not in a life-or-death struggle, she'd have laughed at the nonplussed look on his
face. She saw the exact moment he realized the full im-
port of the men taking instructions from her. A look of
surprise passed over his face and he backed up, bump-
ing into his temperamental gelding. She grinned, then
went back to caring for her endangered stock. But her
thoughts were split.

"You were to tell me when ya were ready to leave
town," he shouted.

The calf balked at the sharp sound of Brendan's
voice, and its skull connected with Helena's chin. This

was the first time she'd really understood the term "seeing stars." She shook her head, managing to catch the rope as it left Hodges's grip and sailed toward her.

Forcing her mind off Brendan's glowering image, she stuffed the end of the rope through the thick mud and positioned it behind the poor baby's front legs. After fishing the rope out on the other side, she tied a bowline knot to keep it from tightening or loosening. All that was left was to toss the end back to Hodges.

"Get ready. When I release the suction the mud has on the calf's front legs, keep a steady pressure on the line till I can free the hindquarters. I'll let you know when to back your roan up and pull us both free."

Once she nodded, it took only a moment. When she felt the rope tighten, Helena curled her toes in her boots so they'd come along for the ride. She felt the deep suction pull at her and the calf, then resistance, more resistance, and then, almost like a cork pulled from a bottle, she and the calf were free. It wasn't a minute later that the mother and baby were reunited, and silence reigned but for the sound of suckling. Hodges dismounted and retrieved his rope.

Wearing a rueful grin, Yates handed Helena her hat. "At least this isn't covered in mud," he said. Then the two men stood there, awaiting her instructions.

A glance at Brendan, who remained tight-lipped, his hands on his hips, made the decision for her. "I'm not sure that calf can make it to the barn on his own, and I want them close so we can watch for any problems over the next few days." She grabbed Paint Box's reins and mounted. "I'll take the calf if you'll hand him to me. No sense in anyone else getting wet and muddy."

Yates, the bigger of the two hands, moved toward the

calf, and laughed when he got close. "You were right, boss. He *is* a calf. How'd you know? He was halfway up his belly in that mud."

Helena chuckled. "Only a hardheaded male would ignore his mama and get into a predicament like that." She rode over to the cow and her baby, on the off chance the mother got riled. But typical of the gentle longhorns Helena ran on her spread, the mama just bawled a little in protest as Yates picked up her babe and stretched the little calf across Helena's lap.

Hodges glanced uncertainly toward Brendan and said under his breath, "You want us to come along, or keep checking this section for any cows having calving troubles?"

"Keep checking. And don't worry about him. He's harmless." Physically, anyway. Emotionally, the man was poison. At least for her.

Yates took a clean bandanna from his back pocket and handed it up to her. "Don't look harmless right now. Your chin's bleeding like a stuck pig, thanks to his big mouth."

Helena pulled off her muddy gloves and stuffed them in her back pockets, then took the cloth. Only now aware of the wound, she pressed it to her skin and hissed in a sharp breath at the burning pain. "Just keep checking the cows. There are less birthing problems with this breed, but there's always a chance of a breech. I'll be fine and so will Joker here."

Hodges laughed. "Joker. Something tells me we're going to have another bull roaming across Shamrock."

She managed a grin, well aware she was being a tad too sentimental for a ranch owner. "I do have some extra time invested in this little guy, after all, and another bull will give us a second bloodline running through our herd. After the way we helped him out today, he'll remember and be as friendly as King and Jack. I'll see you all later. Let me know when you get back, okay?"

Both men nodded and went to mount up.

Uncomfortably muddy and wet, and now in pain, Helena was determined to avoid Brendan for as long as possible. Without a word or a glance for him, she waved to Yates and Hodges, then wheeled Paint toward home. She kicked the mare into an easy trot, but when she checked to see if the mama cow was keeping up, found she was lagging a bit. So Helena pulled back on the reins and settled Paint into a walk, and the cow closed the distance. Brendan had already mounted and was nearly at her side by then. She turned back around and stared straight ahead.

"You left town without me," he accused when he drew even with her.

She'd have laughed at the irony of his complaint, but it still hurt too much. "How does it feel?" she muttered instead.

"If ya were tryin' to teach me some kind of lesson, it was pretty childish to compromise your safety to do it."

Helena bit back what she really wanted to say. Listening to Patience and Abby make plans for their babies, and discuss how their husbands were so protective of them, had been painful for her. Especially since the person she'd thought would protect her had abandoned her in a strange land at the first sign of trouble in their marriage.

Oh, who was she trying to kid? She'd always been alone, until the precious times she'd had Brendan in her life. But those magical times had ended when he'd turned his back on her.

Her anger at him spiked again and she retaliated in kind. "I told you, I don't need you here. Besides that, you don't matter enough for me to go out of my way to teach you a lesson. Particularly one you'll never learn."

"You certainly seem to need someone. Look at ya. That stupid calf hurt you."

She dabbed at the cut with the bandanna Yates had given her. "I don't need you," she lied. She did the same work as the smaller men, but she couldn't say she loved it. She'd rather spend her days riding for pleasure or doing embroidery or tatting, a lace-making skill she was still learning from Julia Hampton.

"I didn't say it had to be me. Hire another hand. You aren't suited to this kind of work."

He couldn't have said anything to anger her more. Who was he to judge her or her abilities? "For your information, this happened because of you. You scared the calf and he caught me where his horns will be in about a month. It could have been a lot worse if he were older. You might have even killed me then."

"Don't put that on me. After you got hurt, you went ahead and put yourself in danger again by helpin' take that calf away from its mother. Suppose she'd turned on you, gored you?"

Helena let out a hefty sigh. "Longhorns are, for the most part, placid and gentle. Big long horns and all. If she wasn't good-natured, she'd have gone to market long ago. I'd never let her breed a nasty disposition into my herd. The first thing I learned about longhorns was that if you can't turn your back on one, it belongs on your table for dinner. Even longhorn bulls aren't by nature mean." That seemed to silence Brendan for a half hour or so.

"I'm sorry I scared it," he said as they approached the home place. "I truly am sorry I got you hurt. I didn't realize I'd startled it. Here." He reached out to hand her a clean handkerchief, then he leaned down and opened the pasture gate.

She thanked him and rode ahead, the cow trailing behind her. Once he'd shut the gate after the lowing mama, Helena stepped out of the saddle, then pulled the calf down. She stumbled under his weight but managed to set him on his feet. Seeing him run to his mama and contentedly nurse made her smile. Then Brendan had to go and spoil the moment.

"Don't put yourself in danger to spite me again. And get that cut looked at. It's still bleeding."

She brushed aside his concern. "I'll be fine. Do you really think worse hasn't happened to me in three years of ranching? As for why I left town, I had work to do out here and you said you had a stack of posters to get through. I didn't have time to waste. This place doesn't run itself. Spiting you was the last thought in my head. I told you, you don't matter enough to influence my decisions."

His lips tightened. "Fine. Just remember, town's off-limits without an escort until we stop these raids."

"You gave up the right to give me orders. You don't tell me where and when I can do anything. You're here at my sufferance, *Ranger Kane*. Try to remember that, and we might get through this without all these senseless arguments."

Chapter Three

Brendan sat deep in his saddle as he and Harry stood atop the hill overlooking Shamrock's ranch buildings. Helena's home place was a neat package. He'd expected the main house would be a shining white edifice with columns soaring several stories high. But no. Not for Helena Conwell. Helena Conwell Kane, he amended, the last name almost, but not quite, an afterthought. He was at all times aware that she remained his wife.

Why the hell hadn't he looked into divorce laws in Texas? Each time he'd stopped in to check with Major Jones he'd expected a packet of ominous-looking legal papers. Now he knew why they'd never appeared. And unless he broke his vows—which he had no intention of doing—it would be another three years before she'd be free to file for divorce.

It was infuriating that the thought of three more years of estranged marriage to Helena settled his contrary heart.

He forced his mind off that confusing thought and back onto Helena's house. It wasn't a palace. Not even a particularly large house. The long, low building formed a U, with a Spanish-style courtyard in the middle. Overlapping clay tiles covered the peaked roof. The walls were whitewashed adobe, with deep windows, and a homey porch ran the whole length, along the front and on both sides.

Helena had ordered him off that porch the day of the Varga raid. That was when he'd realized he'd never get another wink of sleep, worrying about her safety if—make that when—the raiders attacked Shamrock.

They'd been merciless with the wives of the shepherds at Belleza, more animals than men. While Brendan mourned the loss of all those women, at least they hadn't had to live with the memories of what had been done to them. He'd never get that sight out of his head. The thought of Helena being next on the list had scared him right to her front door.

To a place he'd sworn never to set foot.

To protect a woman he couldn't stop caring for.

A woman he couldn't even talk to without a battle breaking out.

He squinted against the glare of the sun and stared at the white house with the red tile roof. She lived there, his Helena did. Slept there. Slept there alone, dammit. And she tempted him.

She'd been alone all the time he'd been gone.

Visions of her asleep in his arms haunted him, and had since the day he'd left her standing outside the land office. He'd assumed memories of their lovemaking would plague him. Those specters of the past *did* visit his dreams, disturbing his sleep. More often than not, he'd wake with an unmerciful hard-on, and memories of her fresh in his mind. He'd force himself to roll over, and hope to keep on dreaming.

But surprisingly, it was memories of her beautiful face as she'd slept, secure in his arms, that often rose unbidden to stalk even his waking moments. They were thoughts only constant danger kept at bay. Which, he supposed, was how he'd gotten his reputation for going into situations even other Texas Rangers shied away from.

Dealing with memories of Helena now led to one he tried to block, but never seemed to manage to for very long. His mind rolled back to the day it all went to hell....

"I have a surprise," Helena said when she rushed out the door of their tiny shack of a house on the outskirts of Tierra del Verde. He'd been gone for two weeks, helping drive supplies. He'd picked up the job when one of the regular freight drivers got hurt in a brawl in the Golden Garter.

Since they'd arrived in the sweet little town of Tierra del Verde, Brendan had been putting in hours at the livery and anywhere else he could make a dollar to support them. If he had a bit left over at the end of the month, he put it aside to save for a small ranch. He longed to be his own boss. Then how hard he worked would have a direct effect on how much money he made. It was a small dream, but it was the Holy Grail to someone raised in Wheatonburg, Pennsylvania, in the shadow of Harlan Wheaton's big house, his mining operation and the town he owned lock, stock and people.

Brendan was bone-tired and not sure he was up to a surprise. Still, he followed her inside, where she led him to the small settee that defined their parlor space. He forced a smile for Helena's sake and took in her happiness. She was like air to a drowning man. He'd missed her so much. She'd given up everything to come West and live as his wife. "Now what is it you have planned?" he asked.

"Joshua, Abby and Daniel are here. They arrived the day you left. They wanted to surprise us."

He'd missed his sister and nephew terribly. Joshua, too. "I've missed two weeks with them? How long will they be here?"

"They aren't visiting. Joshua bought the bank and moved them here. He decided to follow Abby's dream, knowing it was the best thing for Daniel. And speaking of best… Best of all is he *did* it, Bren."

Brendan narrowed his eyes. "What is it my brother-in-law did?"

"Joshua cleared your name. He stood up in court back in Pennsylvania and proved you'd been framed by his father and Franklin Gowery. They were both forced to admit there'd been no evidence to prove you were involved but your badly forged initials in the company store's receipt book."

Brendan blinked, then let out a deep breath he felt he'd been holding for half a year. "He did it? I didn't think he could. I'm free?" She nodded and watched the joy bloom on his face as the realization sank in. "I'm free."

"Even better, Joshua untangled my assets from Franklin Gowery's control. My *guardian* can never touch us again. We're both free. And we're rich."

It was like having a weight lifted from him, only to have that same weight dropped right back on his shoulders again. Brendan's efforts all these months were like a dandelion puff in the wind—weak and powerless. Once again she could buy and sell him.

"No. *You're* rich, Helena. I told you the day we decided to make a go of this marriage you so handily arranged."

She covered his hand with hers and he stared down at it. A hand that had been soft and lily-white was now rough and red with toil. His belly tightened with dread. Her hands now looked like his mother's had. Would this life kill her, as sure as life in a mining town had killed his ma?

He could feel Helena willing him to look at her. When he raised his gaze to hers, he saw worry in her blue eyes. "But I told you I wanted to buy that ranch for us if I got control of my funds in time. That's what the money's for. For us. The ranch house isn't much better than this place, but the *land*, Bren. It's huge. And ours for the taking. We can build Shamrock, just like we planned. The widow woman says her husband had a herd of longhorns. They only need to be gathered in and the steers taken to San Antonio. Our Shamrock is out there waiting for us to rename it and make it into a legacy for our children."

Brendan pulled his hand from under hers and paced to the open door, to stare out at the rolling landscape of the Texas Hill Country. "That's your dream. I never wanted anything so grand. I want to build what you simply want to buy. I won't have it."

He wouldn't live on her father's ill-gotten gains. On what amounted to blood money—blood of men like his own father, who'd left his leg in one of Wheaton's mines. Brendan didn't understand how she could expect it of him.

"It's our chance, Bren." She sounded so reasonable. "We have to take it. An opportunity like this won't come along again. If we don't step up, there's someone else who wants it. The widow doesn't want to have to sell it to him, but she can't wait any longer. She wants to sell to us. You'll see. It'll be a wonderful place to raise a family."

"No," he said flatly.

It hurt to see her anguish and realize she cared more for a piece of land than she did for his self-respect. Didn't she know him at all? He'd told her they'd make it on what he provided. She clearly didn't believe in him; it was as simple as that. He fisted his hand next to his leg. "You have to have everything now. You don't want to work hard for it. You want it handed to you, the same way everything has been your entire life."

She stiffened her spine and raised her chin. "It's too late to back out. I already bought it. They're waiting at the land office for us to sign the papers."

"I won't sign any papers. I won't be bought."

She stared at him, her eyes narrowed in thought or disbelief. He wasn't sure he knew her this way. Maybe he'd never known her at all. "Bought? You think that's what I want to do—*buy* you, like a slave? *Imprison* you?"

He felt the words like a knife slash to his heart. He knew she meant nothing like that, but he couldn't give in on this point. "I won't use that money."

The hurt in her eyes hardened into anger. "Then you're going to stand in the way of my dream, all because you're too egotistical and bitter to see past your small, miserly hopes and goals to care about mine.

Joshua followed Abby's dreams here to the West. Why can't you?"

That was a low blow. "Fine. I'll sign the damned papers, but don't think I'll ever set foot there."

She tilted her head and her lips tipped into a sly smile. "Yes, you will, because that's where I'll be. You'll be here in town. You'll see me all the time. And you'll want me. Then you'll come to me and we'll be happy again. My dream *is* yours—it's just bigger...."

And he'd known she was right. Brendan hadn't dared stay. He'd known it would be just as she'd said: he'd have seen her, given in and gone to her. Then he'd have hated himself every day for the rest of his life, for stooping to use the money of a robber baron. Brendan had heard powerful men like that guardian of hers described that way. Harry Conwell couldn't have been far removed from men like Gowery and Harlan Wheaton. Those men had conspired to frame Brendan, and therefore forced him to flee for his life, leaving his family behind.

He'd looked around the little house where they'd been so happy. Not a cross word had been spoken in the months after they'd arrived there. He hadn't known he would miss it—and Helena—so much, but he had known he'd have to move on and find something to do that would keep him away. Then he'd found a new family, a new love—the Texas Rangers and the law.

Now, with his mind and heart still in turmoil, he watched Helena walk out onto the porch and stroll down the step, to the top of the rise behind the house. He noticed she did that every evening and every morning. She'd cross herself, then stand there, gazing out over the valley in prayer. After endless moments, head bowed, she'd retrace her steps. He'd seen tears in her eyes the one time he'd approached her as she'd returned to the house.

He wondered what she wanted. What was it she asked God for twice a day, every day?

Drawn to her now, he guided Harry down the hill to the home place. It was time to at least talk to her about the measures he'd taken to protect her. And why.

She turned as he approached, and this time she rushed to meet him as he dismounted. "Is something wrong?" she asked, clearly flustered. He couldn't help remembering when the sight of him had had a bright smile blooming on her pretty face.

He shook his head and got back to the here and now. What was in her expression? Worry? Fear? She should be afraid; all her protests to the contrary, Helena was no fool. Look at how ready for a fight her men were.

"Nothing's wrong as far as I know. Not yet, anyway. I still think they'll hit you before they move on the Rockin' R. Shamrock's run by a woman. I doubt he thinks you'd be as ready for them as you are, or as ready as the R is bound to be."

"He?"

Brendan damn near spit out a curse, but that would have made his slip of the tongue all the more noteworthy. "Just a figure of speech, and a boatload of evidence that's more confusin' than trying to follow their trail."

"Oh? What do the Indian agents have to say?" she asked.

"As far as they know, all the Comanche war chiefs and their warriors are on the reservation, and have been."

"Hmm. No matter who might come, Shamrock's men

are spoiling for a fight. But after what Farrah Varga told me…" Helena hesitated, pressing her lips together. Then she huffed out a breath, as if surrendering to an inevitable fate. "Okay. I admit it. I'm terrified, Bren. Those men are killers. I don't want anyone at Shamrock to get hurt. Especially not defending me."

He very nearly asked if that included him, but instead said, "You've a right to be afraid. No matter your feelings about the men, if you hear shooting, you need to duck and run for cover. Hide as best as you can," he added, then waited for her to explode all over him for telling her what to do.

The explosion never happened. Instead, her eyes grew sad, her posture resigned. "That isn't going to keep me safe and you know it. It's as if the success of those early raids has emboldened the raiders. They killed every woman on Belleza. Do you think *they* didn't hide? Farrah and her mother were blessed to be in town."

"Blessed," Brendan agreed, remembering well what had been done to those poor beggars.

"Alex Reynolds taught Patience to shoot as soon as they arrived, because the raids were worsening. He doesn't think size will protect either of our places for much longer. Neither does Lucien Avery. He thinks I should move into town. I won't do that, so I need to learn about guns, the way Patience did."

Brendan pressed his lips together for a moment. The idea of Helena in the middle of gunplay turned his breakfast to stone. Carefully guarding his words, he said, "That they've picked on increasingly larger targets is true. You have a good point. You need to be taught to shoot and you have to be ready to kill whoever you aim at. You should have Mallory teach you."

"Mallory already tried." She shrugged. "I can't hit the broad side of the barn, Bren. If they do come here—"

"Then I guess I'd better get to teachin' you," he interrupted gruffly, flustered by her unconscious use of his nickname as much as by the terror in her voice. "Got any empty cans or mason jars you can do without?"

She nodded. "I'll buy new. This is important."

Brendan bit back the insolent remark that nearly leaped off his tongue. Of course she could just go to town and buy new. She could probably buy out the company that made cans and jars, if she'd a mind. Instead of feeding the fires of discontent the way he seemed driven to do around her, he pointed to a fence off to the left. "Over yonder. Set them up on the top rail." He stepped into the stirrup and swung himself back into the saddle. "I'll go warn Mallory before we take ten years off the man's life when we start shootin'. Don't know why he never managed to teach you."

She blushed adorably. "Um, Bren, Mallory really did try. I'd hate to hurt his feelings."

Brendan forced a smile, trying not to react to her, and cursing himself for being so affected by her sweet blush. Damn the woman. And damn him for his weakness around her. "I'll only say we'll be doin' a bit of target practice. That way you won't be embarrassin' *me* if the fault is with you and not the teacher."

"If you mention me and shooting, you'll have to ignore his laughter."

Mallory didn't laugh, though he did shake his head, consternation written on his sun-baked face. "Great waste of powder, if you ask me. I doubt it's going to do her a bit of good."

Brendan allowed that it wouldn't hurt to try. Then, after handing Harry over to Jimmy, he walked to where Helena had set up the jars and cans, his Winchester balanced on his shoulder. He walked a bit beyond where she stood, to lean the rifle against the porch post.

"Let's try this from the top. Mallory must have forgotten a step. Shootin' a gun is easy if you know what you're about. First hold up your thumb."

She turned and frowned. "My thumb? I need to shoot, not paint."

Brendan sighed, turned to the fence, pulled his Colt out of his holster and fired, sending the middle can spinning into the dusty corral as blue smoke expanded all around them. It dissipated in the breeze as he turned to her.

She stared at the now holstered gun. "How did you learn to do that?"

"I've good reflexes *and* I listened to the one teachin' me. That and practice."

Without a word she turned and held up her thumb.

His point made, Brendan said, "With both eyes open, cover that first can on the left with your thumb. With your left eye closed, is the can covered?"

She nodded.

"Now do the same with the right eye. Did your thumb seem to move?"

Again she nodded.

"Then when you choose what you're aimin' at, close your right eye and sight with your left."

"Mallory just told me to point and pull the trigger.

Thus the shotgun. With buckshot flying, I'd have a better chance of hitting something."

Brendan shook his head. "At least we're gettin' to where you'll have more than two shots, and you've not even picked up the gun. I'd prefer you hit what you aim at. Mind, if you do pick up a gun to defend yourself, you have to be ready to pull the trigger."

"So you said. And I said that I am. I'd have to think of it as him or me, right?"

He gave a sharp nod. "There's no room for guilt with these raiders. They've started this war."

She nodded in turn. "I'd fire. I still have too much to do in this life."

He wanted to ask what, but he'd given up any right to even wonder. And if he was honest with himself, he hated that he had. Wished he was the kind of man who'd be comfortable being kept. But Michael Kane hadn't raised his sons to live off their women. And even if Brendan could get past that, there was the knowledge of where her wealth had come from to torture him. He'd been taught not to hate, too…but his father would have to be disappointed in his son, because Brendan did hate Harlan Wheaton, Franklin Gowery and, though he'd never met him, Harry Conwell by association.

He cleared his throat. "So about the actual shootin'. It's important not to tense up." He showed her how to load and unload his Colt in its half-cocked position. "This is a single action. Meanin' you pull the hammer all the way back, through all four clicks, each time you want to fire." He eased the hammer back and the clicks sounded in the silent clearing. "Now it's ready to fire. You have six shots," he went on, and handed the weapon to her. "Hold it with both hands and sight down the barrel."

She turned to the targets.

"Now squeeze the trigger," he ordered.

She did, but only the good Lord knew where the shot went.

"No. No. Don't jerk it. That sends the barrel up or down. You don't want to be hittin' the bad guy in the foot, or blowing a hole in his hat. You need to keep the barrel parallel to the ground."

He stepped behind her, caged her with his arms, his hands enveloping her small ones so he'd absorb the recoil and she'd see her next shot fly true. "Pull the hammer back," he ordered, his voice suddenly rough. It was her—the rose scent of her—grabbing hold of his senses that was to blame.

Brendan swallowed as Helena readied the Colt to fire. The feel of her warm hands beneath his heated his blood to boiling. And the feel of her back nestled against his chest nearly undid him. He went hard below the belt. Luckily, her round bottom wasn't nestled against him.

Helena went utterly still for a protracted moment. Then, apparently less affected than he, she said, "Now I fire?"

He cleared his throat. "Squeeze the trigger."

The can she'd aimed at flew up into the air, then fell to the earth. He stepped back as she spun to face him, her face filled with delight. "I did it!"

Frowning at the effect her nearness had on him, he all but growled, "Don't ever point a gun at anyone you don't want to dig a hole for."

She looked down at the Colt in her hand, then backed

up. "Oh! Sorry." She pointed the revolver at the ground. "But did you see? It flew up just like yours did."

Brendan couldn't help but grin at her happiness. He nodded. "Deader than a doornail, that dastardly can is. Now try on your own. Be ready to compensate for the kick."

She fired, but a chip tore off the bottom rail. The rest of the cans fell off from the vibration. But the seven jars remained. Her shoulders drooped a bit in defeat.

"That's okay," he told her, trying to be encouraging. "Figuratively, you at least hit the barn this time. Try again," he insisted.

Helena bit her bottom lip, then pressed both lips together as she pulled back on the trigger. And one of the jars shattered. Then two more exploded, one after another. "I did it. Oh, thank you."

Maybe he should start hiring himself out to greenhorns. Or maybe she had one hell of an eye. That or it'd been beginner's luck. "That's good. Really good," he forced himself to say. He took the gun, ejected the empty shells and reloaded it for her, noting her rapt expression as she watched. "There are six jars left standing," he said, and pointed that way with the Colt. "Have at them."

But he had eyes only for her as he heard one after another shatter. He finally looked at the fence and blinked. The fence was clear. *Damn, but that's enough to give a gunfighter a wet dream.*

She sighed loudly and relaxed her tense shoulders. "At least if they do come, I can defend myself. You won't have to worry about me."

And that naive statement had him thumping back to earth double quick. How could she not know that was impossible?

* * *

Helena watched as confusion shadowed Brendan's emerald eyes for a moment. Then he pressed his lips into a hard line. What had she done wrong now?

"Now there's a load off my mind," he all but snarled. "You can practice with a revolver on your own. Just warn the rest of us before you start." He took the gunpowder-stained Colt and spun it into the holster on his right hip. "You do have one, don't you?"

She looked at the gun, which had gone back where it had come from as quickly as it had appeared, and nodded. She'd bought one. Now she knew what to do with it. "Thank you," she told him, bent on ignoring his shifting moods. But really, what had she done now?

"The lesson isn't over," he told her. "A Colt is a good weapon, but it's a close-in weapon. Let's give the Winchester a try."

She looked at it, figuring it must weigh what she did. "But it's so big."

"No bigger than that shotgun you greeted me with. And it'll blow a big hole in an attacker before he gets to your porch, and you'll still have nine rounds to chamber, instead of two with the shotgun. I'd prefer it if you could defend yourself from a bit of a distance, havin' ten full shots at the ready."

She stared at him. He was so different from the man she'd married, yet still the same. She didn't know why, but she had to know how much had changed. Could he finally see who she really was?

"Brendan, where have you been? Abby cagily mentioned whenever she got a letter, and let what you were up to drift into our conversations. But then I think the letters stopped coming, because she stopped doing so."

He raised his left eyebrow, then nodded. "That's a fair question, I suppose." Still, he seemed a bit hesitant as he said, "I spent the last year or so before I came back here posin' as a gun for hire in and around Corpus Christi. In doin' that I managed to infiltrate and shut down a gang of outlaws who'd been terrorizin' the residents in that part of the state. The Lyons gang, they were called. They'd eluded the law for four years before the major put me on their tails. I wired where they'd be on a certain day. Now all but three are in Huntsville Prison. The others are six feet under. They resisted arrest. The hit-and-run tactics Lyons used reminded the major of the raiders here."

Helena tilted her head. "But they aren't the same men—they're in prison, right? And these are Indians. Ghost Warriors."

"There's a big difference between what went on down in Corpus Christi and the trouble here. Here they're killin' indiscriminately. Lyons was a former Confederate officer. He kept his men in check. They *robbed* indiscriminately, but never killed a soul. Nor did they steal horses, which is why they're in prison and didn't swing from a rope."

"And you're here because Sheriff Quinn wired for help."

He shrugged. "Major Jones called me in and told me about these raids that started while I was…gone…and that Quinn had requested help. I have family here, so I came, but because of that I couldn't come here posin' as a gun for hire."

She didn't know why she wanted to know all this, but she did. There was an ache in her chest and she needed to understand what these last years had been about for him. "Why the rangers? It's not what you said you wanted in the West."

"Because of what your guardian tried to do to me."

She frowned. "That doesn't make sense. Franklin Gowery lied to the law. They were going to arrest you because he did. You were completely innocent."

Brendan stared at her, his green eyes narrowed and showing anger. "Why the rangers? Simple. I believe no one. I find out what needs to be discovered. I make sure what's said is true before I put a man in shackles. I work for *real* justice, not some jumped-up little potentate who thinks his money gives him leave to wield power over those with no voice."

Helena straightened her spine and planted her hands on her hips. She'd thought he felt as drawn to her as she was to him when he'd been showing her how to fire the Colt. She was such a fool! The lesson had only been about putting her fate in her own hands again. Nothing more. So once the Winchester lesson was over she'd be on her own.

And he'd once again lumped her in with Franklin Gowery and those like him. "You have a bad habit, Ranger Kane," she snapped, her fury making his look like a child's temper tantrum. "You forget facts at will and you judge others unfairly against your own narrow-minded yardstick of values. The poorer one is, the more noble, is that it? Sometimes the poorer the lazier, Brendan. And sometimes the lazier the more dishonest."

She sniffed and took a step forward, poking a finger in the center of his chest. "You also seem to forget the months Joshua and I had to pretend to be engaged, so we could spy on Franklin Gowery and his Pinkerton cohorts. And you forget the night they would have put *you* in shackles. We risked our own freedom to spirit you out of town and save your life. And you forget the prison of a life Franklin was willing to force *me* into. Do you remember that period of time when all you did was stand by and watch, all but cheering him on? But that was just fine because, after all, I'm nothing but a filthy-rich heiress."

Brendan stepped forward and reached out to her, but she knocked his hand aside, and with more strength than she knew she possessed, shoved him on his black-clad butt in the dirt. She didn't even wait to see him land, just whirled and ran to the house. Then she tore open the side door, rushed inside and slammed and locked it. She pulled out the key for good measure, grasping it in a death grip.

She'd never let him in again.

Never.

Her breath stuttered in her chest and she wiped at her face. And stared at her wet hand. Tears! He'd made her cry. Again.

Damn him.

Chapter Four

Helena walked toward the barn, still undecided whether or not to keep her weekly luncheon appointment with Lucien Avery. She was dressed and ready.

So why was she dithering?

She never dithered!

She'd thought this out. Made up her mind about how it would look now that everyone thought Brendan had returned—supposedly to their marriage. She couldn't stop her traditional Friday luncheons with Lucien. It would be tantamount to an admission of guilt that her meals with him were about more than companionship and conversation. They talked about the books they'd read, their lives before coming to Tierra del Verde. Not much about the ranching business, though. He didn't like talking about that with her the way Alex did. But not doing so was restful, and an escape from the pressure of having responsibility for a spread as large as Shamrock resting on her shoulders. They were friends, she and Lucien. Only friends, no matter what others thought.

Helena stalked into the barn, annoyed with herself,

and stopped short as the cool darkness enveloped her. Before her eyes adjusted to the dimness, the sound of Brendan's voice floated her way.

He was chatting away to Harry, his black-as-pitch gelding, as if he didn't have a care. Harry matched Brendan's personality to a T. They were both generally easygoing until something ignited their tempers. It didn't happen often with either of them, but it wasn't pretty when it did.

The feelings engendered by hearing that voice answered the question she'd been contemplating on her way there. He was the reason she couldn't make up her mind about today. Brendan was jealous of Lucien, even if he'd deny it till death. He was wrong and she intended to prove it.

But she was in no mood to do so now, and there was no reason to set a match to dry tinder. She had time before she had to leave. He'd soon ride out to look for evidence of the presence of the raiders on her land. He did it every day. That was something they did need to talk about, but he'd been avoiding her. Truthfully, she'd been avoiding him as well. Now, though, she was annoyed enough at him to demand answers to her reasonable questions. Shamrock was hers and if Bren had found any clues pointing to the culprits and their hideout, she had a right to know.

The dim recesses of the barn came into sharper focus, so she walked toward Harry's stall. The black's head swung her way and he trumpeted a greeting. Harry's antics always made her smile.

Brendan turned, and she saw the exact moment he realized it was her. He stiffened up, his back going poker straight. "And what is it I can be doing for the boss lady on this fine mornin'?"

She tried not to rise to the little sarcastic spin he put on "boss," but some things ate at a person. "You're right." She planted her hands on her hips and nodded decisively. "I am the boss. I didn't ask to be, but it's what you made of me. So in that case, you can tell the *boss lady* what you've learned about the raiders."

Brendan seemed determined to play peacemaker that morning, after all. "Other than that they're vicious bastards? Not a thing."

"You have no idea who they are? Who it might be, given that you said the Indian agents have vouched for the whereabouts of all the Comanche warriors? To me that says these aren't Indian attacks at all."

Brendan shook his head and turned back to fastening Harry's bridle, then reached for the saddle blanket. "Frustrating as it is, there's no evidence to prove who the raiders are."

Helena stiffened. He was lying. She didn't know how she knew, but she was sure he knew more than he was willing to say.

"You're lying. You wanted nothing to do with me or Shamrock, yet now you're here and keeping secrets."

He tossed the saddle on Harry's back, then reached under the horse to buckle the cinch. "Don't know what you're talkin' about," he said finally, after he'd tightened the saddle down.

"You're not annoyed that you've spent two weeks in the saddle, combing the hills, only to come up empty-handed? You should be chewing nails. Instead you're in here chatting with your horse and ready to go on the hunt all over again."

He gave a sharp nod. "That I am."

"Either being a ranger taught you an inordinate amount of patience or you're finding plenty out there and refusing to tell me. Why continue all this scouting if it's a waste of time?"

"Didn't say it was a waste. Perhaps I'm waiting to see what direction they come in from."

"Then you picked up their trail. How else could you wait in a specific place for them to show themselves?"

Brendan blew out an impatient breath. "Or perhaps I have all corners of the spread bein' watched. Did you think of that?"

Feeling foolish and ready to forget the whole thing, Helena started to turn away. Then she stopped. "In that case, who are you, to station men on my ranch without clearing it with me? I didn't know you had my men watching our borders, because you've refused to do me the courtesy of telling me your plans for strengthening Shamrock's defenses. *My* ranch's defenses."

His green eyes sizzled, but he said mildly, "I taught you to shoot, didn't I?"

She clenched her fists, infuriated by his calmness. "You taught me to shoot, yes. But that's the last I've seen of you." Her voice rose as she continued, "From now on, clear every order with me. You'd never ride onto the Rocking R and order Alex's men around without so much as a by-your-leave to him."

Brendan smirked. "Granted, but then again, I can talk to Alex without a shoutin' match eruptin' within seconds of our first word. I told Mallory. He agreed to the plan. If he didn't tell you...well, that's not my problem, is it?"

No, Mallory certainly hadn't told her, and they'd

have words about it, but for now… "Brendan, either you learn to respect my position here and do it quickly, or you can sleep in that rocky no-man's-land canyon and not my comfortable bunkhouse. Is that clear?"

He grinned.

"I asked you a question. I'm waiting for an answer. And what are you grinning about, you fool?" she snapped.

He took a step toward her, then another. She saw his intent in his hot gaze. He meant to kiss her. He'd always crossed from anger to arousal so easily, ending quarrels before their conclusion—one of them winning by default. But they hadn't argued after they'd arrived in Tierra del Verde until that one day three years ago. That day he'd just shut down, signed the papers, then walked away—left her. And he'd stayed away.

Now, before she could decide what she wanted, lightning quick, his mouth was on hers. She tried to resist the leather-and-lime smell of him. But the battle was lost before it began. His kisses were meant to gentle her, and they always had before. They did now. And then the pleasure poured through her, along with that irresistible aroma of him. The firmness of his rangy muscles pressed against her length and the roughness of his callused fingers as he cupped her jaw made her want to feel his hands everywhere. She felt her own muscles go pliant, but then a nip on her lower lip demanded more. He wanted entrance. He wanted her to yield to him.

No.

She couldn't.

If she let him in again, he'd destroy her. Despite her resolve, her limbs felt no more substantial than gelatin as they melted into him. She finally managed to gather

her wits and summon strength, mental and physical. She pushed him away. Backward. Hard. He fell against Harry, shock written on his handsome features. She wanted to berate him for taking liberties, but she could no more get the words out than he seemed able to make one of his classic wiseacre comments.

He shook his head and mounted Harry. Then he stared down at her, cocky grin in place. "You look so damn cute when you get riled. Like a pretty little spittin' kitten. Just couldn't resist." Then he tipped his hat and ducked through the stall door that led to the corral. He was gone before she remembered to close her gaping mouth. Which left her fuming. As usual.

Damn him.

Well, she'd show him, with all his security rules and plans. "Jimmy," she called out.

The tack room door at the far end of the aisle opened and Jimmy's towhead popped out. "Yes, ma'am?" His hair was in his eyes as always and he had a smudge of something on his chin.

She forced a smile. "I need my gig." She cleared her throat and choked down the quaver she'd heard in her words. "Could you hitch it up while I go get my hat and reticule?"

"Sure thing, boss. Sorry. Forgot it was Friday. Thought with the ranger here, you might not go. You need me to ride along?"

"Ranger Kane plans to ride with me," she lied. He'd be gone longer than she would. And if not, her absence would show him who was boss. "He'll meet me along the ranch road. I'd help you harness up Gray, but…" She gestured to her green silk dress.

Jimmy frowned. "You going to meet Mr. Avery?"

She paused a second. "Are we friends, Jimmy?" she asked.

His eyes widened. "I hope so."

"Have you come and eaten with me at the house?"

"Sure have. Maria's a fine cook. Oh. Mr. Avery is…"

"My friend," she finished. "The only difference is our ages and that the restaurant at the hotel is full of other people. Now, about the gig—"

"Oh! I'll get right on it. And no need to be thanking me all the time, neither."

She put her hand on his thin shoulder. "Yes, there is. My father taught me saying please and thank you costs nothing but a moment. And that there is never an excuse for bad manners with a friend or an employee."

"Your daddy sounds like a nice man."

Helena bit her lip and blinked away tears. "He was. And a good man. He helped a lot of people during his life."

Jimmy nodded as if he understood, but she knew he didn't. Her father had been her world. No one had ever understood the utter void left in her heart when Harry Conwell's larger-than-life personality had been erased by an assassin's bullet.

All she'd felt in the months that followed had been a bottomless well of loneliness. But then she'd stumbled across Brendan, and he'd filled the void with his all-consuming love. Then he, too, had gone from her.

Twice.

Because both times he'd found her wanting.

"Ranger Kane's real nice, too," Jimmy said, breaking into her thoughts. There was a hopeful tone in the boy's voice. "I miss him when he doesn't stay in the bunkhouse, but he is your husband, so I guess he stays with you some nights."

Helena's heart froze in her chest. She couldn't answer or comment. She managed to say, "I'll be right back," then turned toward the front of the barn, blinking away hurtful thoughts and welling tears. Those were the nights he probably slept in some soiled dove's bed.

Loneliness assailed Helena. Maybe someday, somewhere, the person she'd become would be enough for someone else.

If my memories of Brendan will ever let me move on.

Until then, she'd have to make do with friends. Like a bandage over a gaping wound. She wasn't about to let Brendan deprive her of a single one of the friends she'd made.

Brendan stood after examining the fresh hoofprint. It had the distinctive nick on the right side, marking it as one ridden in the raid on Belleza. The recent print hadn't been scrubbed away by the brisk wind.

A tremor of worry moved through him. Someone had been watching them. Watching the sentries he'd placed. The home place. The entire operation.

That someone had ridden straight into the canyon not two hours earlier. He knew, because he'd tracked the bastard.

Maybe Helena was right. Maybe he should camp out near the canyon. But the trouble with that plan was if the raiders struck from the ranch road, saving the northern canyon access for escape, he'd be thirty or forty minutes away when Helena needed him.

Restless, Brendan walked with Harry to the top of

the hill. The grass was crushed where their watcher had hidden, spying for Avery.

Fury bubbled in Brendan's veins as he mounted up and started downhill toward the home place. As he rode, he tried to weigh the pros and cons of going out to keep watch on the canyon or staying around to search for more bastards watching them.

Pretty soon he came to a realization: he couldn't push his emotions out of the mix where Helena was concerned. Then the major's voice echoed in his thick skull, reminding him to delegate. So he'd station a man to watch their watcher, and he'd do the same at the canyon.

Satisfied with his solution, Brendan rode to the heart of Shamrock and dismounted near the barn. As he tied Harry to the corral fence, Jimmy came tearing out of the shadows, bug-eyed. "Ranger Kane? What are you doing here? Did you miss the boss on the ranch road? You couldn't have gone all the way and back already."

"What in hell are you talkin' on about, son? I was up north. Been up that way all day."

"But the boss said…" Jimmy's eyes widened again. "Oh. Must'a got it wrong. Forget it. You need Harry rubbed down?"

The kid knew Brendan never let anyone else rub down Harry unless it couldn't be avoided. Wouldn't be right. Not with all they'd been through together.

Brendan stepped forward and hooked his arm around the kid's neck. "Jimmy," he said, his voice quiet and low, "what's goin' on? Where has Helena got to that you thought I'd gone along? And tell me the truth. Think how bad you'd feel if somethin' happened to her." He gave the lad a little shake. "Where. Is. She?"

"She goes to the hotel restaurant Fridays…w-with a friend."

Brendan ground his teeth, stepped back from the kid and turned to untie Harry's reins, crushing them in his fist. *Avery.* He'd heard all about Helena's Friday meals with that snake in the grass. Brendan took a calming breath. Helena had no idea of the kind of man who'd befriended her, and Brendan couldn't tell her. Suppose Avery realized she knew? She'd become a sure target. That wouldn't do.

Looking back at Jimmy, Brendan saw the lad was mighty worried. "I'll keep it to myself that you told me." He pointed, hoping to get the seriousness of the matter across to the boy. "But don't you ever let her leave Shamrock alone. If she does, you find either me, Mallory or one of the men. Damn fool woman," Brendan muttered as he turned back to Harry.

As he mounted, he wondered if she'd intended to ask for an outrider. He'd noticed how pretty she looked, but he'd not put that fact together with a jaunt to town. He'd never considered she might go there on her own. She'd already admitted she was scared. He'd have thought, given that fact, she'd at least have asked one of the hands to accompany her.

And she probably would have, he realized with a sinking feeling. But then he'd had to go and kiss her, just to rile that temper of hers up a bit more. That kiss had bitten him in the butt good and proper. It had probably set her thinking she'd do as she pleased to spite him. And it had reminded him of all he'd sacrificed for injured pride and his scruples.

"Just one more question, Jimmy. Where'd you get the idea I was supposed to be her escort?"

"She said so, else I'd never have let her go alone. Mr. Mallory'd have my hide."

Brendan gave a quick tug on the reins and dug his heels into Harry's sides, enough that the gelding knew there was reason to be in a hell of a hurry. "Damn the woman," he spat out as he tore up the ranch road. It was bad enough that she'd go off alone, but now that poor kid back there was scared spitless.

And so was her stupid, thoughtless husband.

Suppose the damned watcher had seen her leave alone? Heart pounding, Brendan leaned over Harry's neck and urged him on. He found himself praying Avery was so enamored of Helena he wouldn't think to throw suspicion off him by seeing her come to harm. Brendan had hoped all along she'd be safer not suspecting her supposed friend, but jealousy still ate at him.

Jealousy he knew he had no right to feel.

He didn't know how to act when he found them having their little tête-à-tête. He'd better be deciding right quick. She was his wife, after all, and he'd already let it be known he was home to stay. So how should he approach the situation in town, with everyone watching?

No doubt Helena would act like the fine lady she was, lest she be seen in a poor light. He didn't want to lend fodder to the gossip, either, so he'd keep his own temper under wraps no matter how much he loathed that murdering bastard Avery.

It wasn't till Brendan found her gig in front of the hotel that he decided what he'd do. He climbed down, tied Harry to the rear of the conveyance, pulled off his saddle and tossed it into the back. He rubbed Harry down a bit with his blanket before tossing it next to the saddle. All that was left was to climb up, settle back in the fine leather seat and wait.

Lucien Avery was a patient man. More than one fellow who'd crossed him had found that out the hard way. But his adversary this time was a lady of some fortune. Winning this kind of battle took care. And planning. It had been moving forward perfectly until Kane decided to take an interest in Shamrock.

Avery had waited nearly two years for Helena Kane to have her fill of her husband's desertion and fall in line with Avery's plans. By his calculation, she'd been mere weeks from being able to divorce the fool. It was a bit risky to murder a Texas Ranger, but with Kane having moved to Shamrock, it had begun to look like the only option.

Today alone, while acting the perfect gentleman with her, Avery had suffered through talk of the Varga women leaving town. Somehow he'd managed not to show how angry he was with their refusal to sell him Belleza.

The don had disinherited his son, so it was the women's to dispose of. But neither would speak of selling, or cutting Dylan Varga out of the property. They preferred to take time and consider their options. Avery would have to set his men loose on the son's place again. When the damned Varga women learned the Comanche had killed Dylan and his little wife, they'd sell both places rather than return where so much tragedy had befallen their family.

After discussing the town's send-off for the women, their luncheon conversation had moved where Helena rarely pushed it. To business, such as beef prices and breeding programs, which had Lucien's thoughts going to having her in his bed, and his own personal breeding plans. Consequently, he was hard as the table legs.

At times like this he found it impossible to understand Helena. Once she was his, she'd soon learn he didn't want his wife to speak of such unseemly subjects. She was a lady and a beauty. Those were the only reasons he hadn't made a move on Shamrock. That and her bank account.

Now that the dishes had been cleared away and tea served, he finally managed to steer her toward more personal matters. Such as her marriage and the husband who'd returned home. "Helena, tell me the rumor that Kane moved in is wrong," he exclaimed.

Her angry expression gave him hope. "Part of it is, I suppose. Brendan did move to Shamrock, but he's sleeping in the bunkhouse. He's the one who started the rumor."

"Why would he do that? Is he trying to ingratiate himself to you again? You're a wealthy prize for someone like him."

Her blue eyes lit with fire, and Avery feared her anger was directed toward him and not her husband. It would be a terrible waste to kill a potential asset like Harry Conwell's daughter. The only thing that had ever gotten Lucien harder than imagining her in his bed was thoughts of all that lovely Conwell money within his control.

"Brendan doesn't want me or my money. But it doesn't change the fact that his little rumor has destroyed my ability to sue him for divorce on the grounds of desertion. I had only a month left to wait."

Son of a bitch. Avery loosened his death grip on his

knife before she noticed. "Oh, my dear, I'm so sorry," he said in his silkiest tone. "Is there any way I can help?"

"I don't see how. He's not always sleeping in the bunkhouse, apparently, so even the men couldn't testify that ours isn't a true reconciliation. I have suspicions about where he's spending those nights."

Had she sounded sad about that, or disheartened over her ruined plans?

"Pardon me for speaking so plainly to a lady, but he's not likely to have been faithful all this time. Not a man like that. You could sue him on those grounds."

Helena's eyes narrowed just a bit as she considered him. Again he worried. Had she taken offense? Then her expression cleared and she shrugged. "I wouldn't know how to go about getting proof. And frankly, it's rather humiliating that he'd prefer those women to me."

"Of course it is. It's an indelicate thing to expect you to deal with. Perhaps I could help. I have contacts all over the state. I could set a detective on him and get proof of infidelity."

Avery cursed his inability to read her, and what was probably obvious in her gaze.

"He's admitted as much," she whispered, and he almost cheered. Then she nodded, however reluctantly, and he knew she was his. Soon she would be his in every way. Her hesitation must be over her distaste for needing to stoop to Kane's level.

"I think I should be going. Thank you for the luncheon."

He stood as she did. "Next week as usual?" he asked.

She stared for a long moment, then nodded. "Of... of course. I'll see you next Friday."

He took her arm. She looked startled for a moment at

this next step in their relationship, but allowed it, however unhappy she appeared. It couldn't be easy to admit the colossal error in judgment she'd made in choosing a husband. It would indeed be humiliating.

As he held the door for her, Lucien smiled down at her, and was shocked to see her eyes soften with longing. Then he realized she'd cast her gaze over his shoulder toward someone in the street beyond.

He turned. Kane lounged in Helena's perfectly appointed gig, wearing that infernal, insulting grin of his. The man was nothing but Irish scum raised in the Pennsylvania coal patch. A man didn't get much lower than that.

Yet Helena still loved him even after all the embarrassment he'd caused her. Avery couldn't believe it. He fisted his hands behind his back. She'd pay for her disloyalty and for leading him on. He still intended to have her, but she'd pay once he had control of her.

His only recourse now was to do away with the troublemaker. Then he'd be there to comfort Helena in her grief. After a while, he'd move in for the kill. He'd win her affections, her ranch and her fortune.

No one stood in Lucien Avery's way. A good many of the ones who had were six feet under already. The rest would soon follow.

Chapter Five

Helena shook off the momentary lift she felt, knowing Brendan had ridden all the way to town for her. She
should be furious at him, though, for lolling in her gig
as if it was his right. It wasn't! He had no rights where
she was concerned. He'd given them up.

"Excuse me, Lucien," she said, marveling at how non-
chalant she sounded. "I have something to attend to."

"I'll take care of this for you," Lucien growled, and
took hold of her arm again. This time, though, his grip
was punishing, holding her next to him as if it were
his right to force his will on her. Which it wasn't and
never had been!

Shocked and angry, she glared, stunned by her usually impeccably mannered friend. His jaw had gone
rock-hard and, however unconsciously, he was hurting
her. What on earth was he thinking?

Lucien was Brendan's exact opposite. A gentleman
through and through, he dressed flawlessly in spotless,
light-colored suits, and even his blond hair never had
a strand out of place. How could he be foolish enough
to challenge Brendan?

"Lucien," she snapped. "This isn't necessary." She heard the anger in her voice. Apparently, he didn't. His harsh grip on her arm and the fury directed at Brendan remained unchanged.

The springs of the gig creaked, telling her Bren had climbed out. There was a fight brewing. She could feel it in the air. Real panic set in.

She craned her neck to gauge Brendan's reaction, praying she was wrong about his intentions. He moved with the loose-limbed grace of a prowling mountain lion. His eyes were narrowed, focused on Lucien's hold on her arm. He was clearly furious.

She had to make Lucien let go before her knight errant of a husband realized she was in pain.

"Ya really oughtn't have your hands on another man's woman, Avery," Brendan said. So far his tone was casual, but his nonchalance was deceptive. Didn't Lucien know how good Bren was with his fists and how fast he was with that gun he wore at his hip?

"I hadn't noticed she wears your brand, Kane. People would need to see one to know she belongs to you. You've shown no interest in her for years. I don't believe she even wears your ring anymore."

But she did! And Lucien knew it. She'd never managed to take it off. Helena watched Brendan's gaze flick downward to her gloved hand, then back to her face. Was it sadness she saw? Or was she so desperate to see any sign of regret over his desertion that she'd imagined it?

It was easy for her to recognize the animosity as his emerald eyes cut to Lucien. Then his perfectly sculpted lips tipped into that same grin she'd wanted to slap off his face earlier.

She glanced back and forth between the two men. She didn't need them brawling in the center of town, acting like children arguing over a ball neither wanted, except to keep the other from having it.

Rather than let Brendan overstep his place in her life, and furious with Lucien, too, Helena wrenched herself free. Fury, she decided, moving out of his reach, could be very energizing.

"Stop it," she snapped, as Brendan drew closer. "That is quite enough!" Keeping her voice low, so only these two buffoons could hear, she demanded, "What are you doing? I'll have no stupid brawl. Neither of you seem to care that my reputation would be rolling around in the dirt with you. But I care."

She appealed to Brendan. "Lucien is my friend. When you were God alone knows where, he was here for me. He knows how much you humiliated me, so perhaps he's being a bit overprotective. And Lucien, remember that I'm still married. A street fight would damage me, not you."

"Darlin', ya wound me," Bren taunted, his hand on his heart. "Avery here'd be plenty damaged. I could break that pretty nose of his with one swing."

"Try it," the rancher challenged.

"Stop it, I said," she exclaimed, again pitching her voice low. She stared at Brendan, willing him to look at her. When he finally did, she continued. "You came into town to fetch me, so let's get on the road. Lucien, we spoke about the limits of our friendship before, and you said you understood. I'll send word about next Friday. Right now I'm not sure I'll be ready to see you by then. You've overstepped yourself."

"You're angry at me? Not him?" the rancher's cheeks wore red flags of anger.

"I'm furious at both of you, but I fight my own battles. I'm shocked you don't remember that. And forget what I agreed you could handle. I'll deal with this in my own way."

She turned and walked carefully to the gig, hiding her inward turmoil with as much outward grace as she could muster. She even let Brendan help her up onto the seat. He handled her like he would a stick of dynamite, remaining extra careful and wary.

Smart man.

About ten minutes later, as they drove toward the ranch, Brendan broke the silence. "I'm sorry, Helena."

"For what? Leaving me three years ago? Coming back and making sure to ignore me long enough so everyone saw firsthand how little you cared about me? For trying to start a brawl with Lucien? Or…or for this morning…for grabbing me and kissing—"

"Not for the kiss," he interrupted. "Never for that. I'm sorry for aggravatin' Avery. I prodded a snake and you got in the middle. He's not what he seems. He wants you. You and Shamrock, and not necessarily in that order."

"Because no one would want me for just me. Is that it? There'd have to be some extra inducement. Daddy's money. Shamrock. Something. Anything." She fought tears. Of rage? Of hurt? She didn't know. "Did you ever see *me,* Bren?" Her voice was barely a whisper as she forced out the words. "Just me?"

Brendan pulled the gig to a halt and turned toward her. "That isn't what I meant. Not at all. And of course I saw you. There was no speaking of money between us at first, remember. And no land when we first got here. I still see you. Just you." He took her hand. Nearly kissed it. And she nearly let him.

Then the memory of that awful day burst into her mind. She'd have given all she had if he'd been there, holding her hand. Pain arrowed through her. She snatched her fingers from his grip in a flash of fury. "But you don't want me. I don't need you to say it." She refused to look at him. "I've seen it and heard it loud and clear for what seems like always." She took a deep, careful breath, trying to regain her composure, hoping not to reveal how deeply he could still hurt her. "So why come after me today, acting the part of a jealous husband, when you don't want to be my husband at all?"

"I'm not jealous. I told you. The man's a snake. After dealing with Gowery, I'm shocked you don't see—"

She spun around on the seat to face him. "You don't know a thing about Lucien Avery. He's been a friend. When everyone else in town either pitied me or shied away, as if I'd driven you off with a damned pitchfork, he was my friend. Later, Alex became my friend, as well."

"Well, there you see, I don't have a single thing against Alex Reynolds. He's a fine man and a friend to both of us."

"I wonder how you'd feel if he wasn't married." She shook her head. "I don't understand you. You don't want me. Why do you care if someone else does? Besides that, Lucien is only a friend."

"Jaysus, woman," Brendan growled, and slapped the reins against Gray's back. "He'd have to be a damned eunuch not to want you. And he isn't that. I saw it in his eyes and in the way he took hold of you. I also saw your surprise. Now stay quiet so I can keep my eyes peeled for trouble."

Helena folded her arms and pressed her lips together. She couldn't argue the point. She *had* been surprised both times, especially with that second aggressive grasp. She'd also been taken aback by the strength of Lucien's anger toward Brendan. She'd told Lucien nothing about her marriage. It hadn't been discussed at all since they'd met, except when he'd invited her to eat with him, and she'd told him she intended to honor her vows. Of course, he'd surely heard gossip. This was the first time he'd brought up the topic since. She gritted her teeth. Why today?

Weary as she was, Helena was grateful to see Shamrock's big iron archway come into view. When they reached the house, Brendan pulled on Gray's reins. "We need to talk," he said.

She scrambled down and turned to face him. "Make up your mind. You told me to be quiet. I was. Now it's your turn to be quiet, because I don't want to talk to you." With that, she whirled away, hurried up the walk and into the house.

As soon as the door slammed behind her, she wanted to go back out and scream and cry and stamp her foot the way she had as a child. She wanted for just an hour to be that spoiled little person whose world was so secure she could think of nothing but her own wants and needs, with no fear of being unloved.

But she wasn't that girl. Or the woman that girl had once been. Helena wished she'd never been her. Because maybe if she hadn't gone riding that day, she'd never have set her cap for Brendan Kane.

Maybe he wouldn't be so rooted in her heart that he was still the only man she could see.

Want.

Love.

And she hated him for it.

Almost.

Brendan watched as Helena tore up the ground between him and the house. In the gig next to him, her shoulders and back had been so stiff she'd looked more like a board than the soft pliant woman he'd held and kissed that morning. The memory swirled in his mind and body. He nearly smiled, remembering the feel of her perfect curves nestled against him. The recollection alone had the power to send heat pooling in his belly and below. Jaysus, he missed her.

Why couldn't he bring himself to tell her?

The door slammed, interrupting the utter bliss of those incredible few moments, and making him wince. Helena had pissed off that snake Avery more than Bren himself had.

Just seeing the angry way Avery had gripped her arm, had snapped Brendan out of his foolhardy, unthinking reaction to her trip to town. At that moment he'd realized what a hell of a strategic error he'd made. He'd figured the rumor about his reconciliation with Helena would put *him* in danger from Avery and maybe draw the man out. But Brendan hadn't considered the whole picture. And then today he'd compounded that error by going to fetch her home.

Since he'd moved to Shamrock, he'd been surprised by the changes in her. He'd never imagined Helena might step into the line of fire between him and Avery, for example. He'd known she wouldn't want them to make a scene, but she'd not only scolded him, she'd lit into Avery, too.

The man hadn't taken it well.

Bren had seen Helena's shock when the bastard grabbed hold of her. That had been before Bren even opened his mouth, so Helena must have done something to anger the rancher, though it seemed she didn't realize she had.

Brendan raked a frustrated hand through his hair and stared at Gray's hindquarters before turning the horse toward the barn. They'd have company that night from the raiders, or his name wasn't Brendan Joseph Kane.

Most of the raids had happened early in the day. But they'd begun with Adara, hitting close to dusk. Which was a puzzle. How did the raiders make it down into that canyon safely in the dark? Then it hit Brendan, and he shoved a hand through his hair again, aggravated at himself for being so blind. *Practice.* They used it for access, coming and going to do their spying. By now the horses would have learned the trail.

Using the canyon for their exodus made more sense. He thought back to each late-day raid. They'd happened on the full moon. And tonight there'd be another. He needed to rally the troops, and maybe even send word over to Alex Reynolds for help.

Brendan needed to think even more like his opponent than usual. The bastard would be furious this afternoon. Avery would act irrationally at first, still in a fury. As soon as he reached the Bar A, he'd probably order an attack.

With his mind working hard to get a read on Avery, Brendan climbed down and tied Gray to the hitching post at the barn. By the time Avery's men were ready to move on Shamrock, the snake would've calmed down. Rethought. Having an ego as big as Texas, though, he wouldn't back down. He'd tell himself it was now or never, and he'd lay out a plan.

Avery had been planning for a while, in any case. Maybe to frighten Helena and push her his way. He'd attack under the cover of darkness, but time it late, when everyone would be sleeping. Vulnerable. Because above all, Avery was a coward.

Tonight his hired guns would get one hell of a greeting, and so would their boss. Because Brendan, Shamrock's men and some from the Rocking R were spoiling for a fight.

Two hours later, Mrs. Mallory and the children left on what looked to be an excursion to visit her sister at the Rocking R. Only the expression in Regina Mallory's eyes said this was no happy occasion.

Brendan had ordered her and her children out of harm's way, and she carried his note to Alex Reynolds, asking for help. Brendan was sure Alex's men would quietly begin to drift over through the woods between the spreads right after dark. Hopefully, that would hide Shamrock's growing strength and the Rocking R's diminishing manpower.

His next move was perhaps the hardest, save facing the danger the night was nearly sure to offer. He had to tell Helena he was almost positive they'd be hit tonight, but he couldn't tell her all he knew. When they proved Avery was the mastermind, Brendan would feel the sharp blade of her tongue. But his silence wasn't about keeping secrets. It was to protect her from her own transparent emotions. If she knew Avery was a suspect, Lucien Avery himself would know the moment they met again.

Dreading a repeat of Helena's earlier outburst, Brendan headed for the house. All he had to do was keep it impersonal. Find a way to gain her trust without emotions being involved, so she'd leave with Jimmy and Maria.

Thinking he'd talk to Maria first, Brendan went to the kitchen, behind the hacienda. Made of adobe, with a tile roof, it stood on its own, designed to keep the heat from the ovens out of the main house. A common roof formed a small covered walkway between the kitchen and dining room, closing off the bottom of the courtyard.

As he entered the rear door, Brendan took in the generous height of the room, and its abundant windows, which kept the space cooler than he'd expected.

The round little housekeeper turned to face him, and anger radiated from her dark eyes. "Leave her alone, Señor Ranger Kane. Have you not done enough damage today?"

"I wasn't trying to hurt her. I don't trust—" Jaysus, the word stuck in his throat "—her friend."

Maria put down the spoon she'd been waving and propped her hands on her plump hips. "Maybe you aren't the *estúpido* man I think."

Brendan grinned as he took off his hat and leaned against the doorjamb, trying to look casual. "So, Avery's not your favorite person, either, eh?"

"*Mi hermana,* she work in his kitchen, but not long. I protect her from when we are little girls, but she marry and go there to work. Her *esposo*, he work as Bar A farmer."

Brendan's belly tightened. "What did he do to your sister, Maria?"

"He grab her." She gestured, mimicking an aggressive hold, something he'd seen for real earlier. "He try to…force her. She much frighten. Screams. He hit. Her *esposo*, he run in. Very angry to see the *señor* hit Jacinta. Alonso push Señor Avery away from his *esposa*. The *señor,* he tell Alonso they must both leave his Bar A. Go far. He say no jobs for them, but Señor Reynolds hire them." Maria smiled. "We still visit now."

Suppose Jacinta's husband hadn't come along when he had? Brendan's stomach clenched again. Remembering how Avery had grabbed Helena in town, he felt a chill to his soul. He'd have to deal with that later. And he would. But right now he had to get Helena to leave for the night.

"Maria, there's trouble brewing. I think you and Helena would be better off at the Rocking R for at least tonight. Ready bags for the two of you, will you? Jimmy's hitching up the gig. Regina and the kids took the wagon. Helena can ride Paint Box over, with you two in the gig."

Maria wrung her hands, fear a living thing in her eyes. "No, she will stay here. Only home she ever know." The housekeeper shook her head. "But I hear things. The women at Belleza—"

Brendan winced. There was no need to go on, and they both knew it. Word had got out about the atrocities. The victims hadn't left this world easily.

"Together, we might convince her," he told Maria.

The woman nodded as Helena bustled into the kitchen.

"I'm sorry I wasn't here to help you sooner. I lost track—" Helena froze when she saw Brendan standing in the back doorway. He'd swear she even paled, and every muscle stiffened. Then she glowered. "What do you want now?"

He tried to look shamefaced, and did damn well, standing there hat in hand. "Helena, you were right this mornin'. I've been tryin' not to worry you. Keeping some things from you. We've found tracks for a few days now atop the hills overlookin' the houses and barns. The raiders are watchin' us. More tracks showed up today. They watched from five vantage points. Plannin', I'd think.

"I'm also thinkin' it might be a good idea if you, Maria and Jimmy went to the Rocking R. Mallory's wife and kids left a bit ago. I tried to get Jimmy to go along, but he's refused. He's wantin' to stay here with you, to lend another gun to the house."

Maria suddenly turned into an ally. She whirled to face Helena. "Oh, please, *señora*. I cannot leave you, either. I worry for Donato, but I want to go. They are animals."

"Go pack those bags, Maria," he said. "I need to talk to the *señora* alone." Before Helena could react to him ordering her maid around, Brendan went in for the proverbial kill. "If the house is empty, we can concentrate on protectin' the barn and horses. If you stay, I'd need at least four or five men in the house, and some on the roof. And we'd all be worryin' how you're farin' up there. I promise if we don't have that worry, we can do them a good bit of damage.

"They'll leave with their tails tucked, if they manage to escape at all. They won't think I could get this place so well defended in the short time I've been here. They'd never believe a woman could have done it before I ever got here. We're ahead of the game for sure."

Helena sank onto the step leading down into the kitchen. "So the tracks and scouts watching are why you've been expecting an attack."

"Scouts?" He shook his head. About time he admitted to all she'd said that morning. "You were right about that, too. They aren't Comanche, but white men masquerading. A damned cowardly thing to do. Suppose the army went into the reservation and hung innocent men who just want peace now?"

She nodded. His Helena was a bright woman to have figured out what only a handful of people had. "They've been watching? So what good does preparation do if they know our defenses?"

Brendan smiled. "Because we knew they were there. Illusions can fool even a skeptic. They've no idea how many men we have, because I've had them dressin' alike. Several wouldn't step foot in town, or a place like the Garter, so they were your best-kept secret already. And by the way, you did a fine job of selecting your men."

Helena looked down as a blush stole across her soft, smooth cheeks. He itched to reach out and touch that soft-as-silk skin. Feel the heat build in her.

"Lucien called the original men misfits, and said they'd take advantage. He can be a tad judgmental." She shrugged. "I've never discussed my people with him again."

Brendan had to fight to keep from yelling a big old

"yee-ha!" So Avery didn't know how many men she had on the payroll and wasn't perfect in her eyes. Bren wished that last didn't gladden his stupid, traitorous heart. "Well, Avery was wrong," he said, shamefully trying to win points as he continued to lie—to himself as well as her—about what he felt for her. Pride was a bitch of a taskmaster, he thought, and got back to the subject at hand. "Your men have all done exactly as asked. It'll hopefully keep them as safe as possible."

"But you still think they'll hit soon, even tonight? Because they'd want to hit us before you can effect too many changes. They expect so little of me?"

He'd done this to her. Made her doubt herself by withholding information she had every right to know. She'd done a fine job on Shamrock.

"They hit Belleza, and that ranch operation was headed up by an experienced man. The raiders have gotten arrogant and mighty bold, but Shamrock's crew is going to send as many of them as possible straight to hell. That's because of your men's loyalty to you, and the integrity you saw in them."

She was staring at him as if trying to see through to his soul. "Bren, are you afraid that, by coming here, you put me in their sights as the next place to attack?"

He didn't want her to think he'd knowingly taken a risk with her safety when, for the first time since joining the Rangers, he hadn't planned at all. He'd left Belleza and headed straight for Shamrock, acting from an instinct born of pure emotion. How to explain and not give away his feelings for her? Brendan swallowed. "I saw those women. What they'd endured." He shook his head, hoping to dislodge the memories of that night. They still rattled him, as did the dreams he had, placing Helena there that day. "I didn't think. I just acted. And I'm sorry if I brought this to your door."

Helena stared, her blue eyes troubled. Then she gave a decisive nod and stood. "I'll go help Maria."

She'd given in so easily it made him sort of melancholy to see her so afraid. His Helena was stubborn and willful. She stood her ground. For the first time all afternoon, though, he could breathe. She'd be safe through the coming night.

Whooping and hollering echoed across Shamrock about midnight. The raiders, still clinging to the pretense of being a renegade group of Indian warriors, thundered in along the ranch road. Nearing the house, they faced their first surprise. Newly fenced pastures lined both sides of the road like a bottleneck, funneling them together into an easier target.

The time for thinking and planning was done. Brendan fired a shotgun into the air to signal the men farther back to move forward, and help shut down the canyon access. The defenders scrambled to new positions, planning to drive the raiders away from the house and into a circle of gunfire near the barn. A few others pushed two wagons across the road and rolled them on their sides, boxing the raiders in.

Forced to continue forward, the raiders thundered around the curve into the clearing near the barn, guns blazing. The supposed Ghost Warriors bled like mere mortals.

The only surprise Brendan had was the number of men bearing down on his position. There were more than anyone had estimated. But then again, Bren was damn certain Avery hadn't thought Shamrock would be quite so buttoned up and well-defended, either. With any luck, this night might see an end to the rancher's reign of terror. They needed only one or two attackers left alive to implicate him.

One of the raiders, hooting at the top of his lungs, spurred his horse over a pile of hay bales set up as a barricade. The gunslinger went down hard as his horse stumbled. But turned and fired at the same time.

If Bren remembered right, that was Dylan Varga's position. Helena's neighbor was as desperate as he was to stop these men and ferret out Avery. They'd killed his father, Don Alejandro, and had raided Adara, the spread Dylan's wife had inherited before their marriage.

When another raider jumped the same spot, he, too, went down, but Dylan was supposed to be keeping them from breaking through the line.

"Dylan? You all right?" Brendan shouted. There was no answer, so he signaled to the men nearby that he would investigate. Crouching low, he ran from position to position, praying he wouldn't have to tell Rhia Varga that she'd lost her husband. Whatever had happened, that hole in their defenses needed plugging.

"I'm hit, dammit," Varga spat out when Brendan got to him, after a few minutes of dodging flying lead.

"Bad?" Brendan asked, as he fired and sent one raider into the next world.

Varga peeled back the handkerchief he'd pressed over the hole in his side. "Hurts like a son of a bitch, but I don't think it hit anything important. The bleeding has slowed, but only if I don't move much."

"Then sit there and shoot only what you can hit from that position. And you can reload both our Winchesters for me. I'll take over fighting off these bastards from here."

And he realized a moment later he really had no choice. The raiders seemed to concentrate on trying to break through at his new position, though it wasn't the only barricade in their way. It soon became apparent that, though the attackers were boxed in and fighting for their miserable lives, they were more intent on ending his. One of them managed to get around behind them, and Dylan suddenly flipped over the Winchester he'd been about to hand Bren, and fired.

Brendan shook his head and grinned at Helena's neighbor. It never hurt to lighten the mood. "Looks like I got my wish, boyo. I put myself in Avery's sights." Another bullet buried itself in the dirt about a foot from Brendan's leg.

"That was your plan, Ranger Kane?" Dylan asked, smiling as he passed the loaded rifle to Brendan and took back the empty one. "Not smart. I should know. I did the same thing when I married Rhia. Maybe I even did it for the don." There was no mistaking the guilt in Dylan's voice.

"Just another pawn Avery was set on capturin'," Brendan told him as he grabbed the reloaded Winchester and got back to work, making sure their neighbor made it home to his pretty wife.

Brendan took aim on another raider, blowing the man out of the saddle. Unfortunately, others got lucky when Brendan fired, creasing him a good one at the shoulder and another time across the ribs. "Jaysus," he gasped, and sank next to Varga with his back to the thick wall of hay bales, gritting his teeth against the burning pain.

"You may have the right of it. I'll rethink this when I have time."

He winced as they both felt three bullets slam into the old bales at their backs. "No rest for the wicked, Dylan, my boy. What say ya keep loadin' and I'll send these bastards to hell, where they sure as the devil belong?"

"Much better plan. We need to weaken his power even if we can't put an end to him tonight."

Brendan nodded and, clenching his teeth, scrambled to his knees, switched to his nondominant eye and arm, and took aim at the raider closest to him. He managed to knock the bastard off his feet and on his ass with one to the shoulder. If the gunfighter stayed down, he might have lived a bit longer, but instead he took cover behind his horse and kept firing. Endangering an animal who lived only to serve pissed Brendan off good and proper.

"Bastard," he growled, then picked him off, sending him to sleep in flames for eternity.

As if grateful, the horse wandered close, and in the bright moonlight Brendan could see the fancy tooled-leather and silver rosettes of what was clearly a white man's saddle. Too fine a quality to have been stolen from the army. They'd been right. These were white men, not Comanche.

Before he could ponder that further, another shooter charged their position and Brendan dispatched him. Then two more came at him simultaneously, advancing toward them, making it impossible to fire back with any accuracy. Both Dylan and Brendan cursed at the same time.

As if in answer to their blasphemous prayer, Brendan caught sight of a muzzle flash brightening a side window of the main house. One of the gunmen spun in a violent circle and hit the ground, clearly still alive, but out of the fight. Then the other went down.

Brendan stared toward the house as another muzzle flash was followed by another raider falling. It made no sense. He hadn't stationed anyone inside the house, as Helena was safe at the Rocking R. Brendan's heart stuttered and every bit of starch drained out of his spine.

Helena.

Jaysus, she wouldn't. But she *would.* She'd come back to the only home Maria had said Helena had ever known, to help defend it.

Dammit! Could the woman not just once fall in line with what made perfect sense?

Someone peppered the window where the shots had originated, and the answering sound of glass exploding nearly killed him right where he knelt.

"Dylan, my boy, I'm afraid that was Helena up at the house who just saved our bacon. I have to get to her, even if it lets some of the raiders escape. You about ready to abandon this position?"

Dylan nodded. Hiding his pain, he struggled to rise, then sank back down. "More than. The bleeding about stopped, but I don't think I can make it to the barn without help."

"I figured," Brendan said, as he made a grab for the reins of the raider's wandering horse. "Hold him. This is going to hurt like a son of a bitch, so I'm apologizin' ahead of time…" He pulled Dylan to his feet, then bent to toss him over his shoulder. The man moaned and went limp. Brendan grabbed the horse's bridle from Dylan's lax hand and used the poor animal for cover as he made a run for the barn. He hated to use a horse that way, but this was about Helena.

He had to get to his wife.

Chapter Six

Struggling for breath, Helena opened her eyes. Only wrenching pain greeted her. She gritted her teeth. It felt as if someone had punched her, but this was worse. Much worse. She was in agony, pure and simple.

Her mind wandered in a strange, pain-filled fog while she struggled to focus. She narrowed her eyes, trying to think past the haze and the agony burning in her chest. She stared at the shadows cast by the moonlight on the ceiling, then looked to her right and saw the hem of her counterpane in the deeply muted light.

The fog started to clear.

She was in her bedroom, on her back, looking up at the ceiling.

At *her* ceiling.

In *her* home.

She had a home now. But why would she be on the floor? In pain? In such terrible pain?

Then a heated volley of gunfire echoed outside and sparked a memory. She moved her head and saw the shredded curtains, the moonlight glimmering on the shattered window glass.

It all flooded back. Brendan's worry about a raid. Her clandestine return, since she was unable to leave defending the ranch to those who had no stake in the fight.

The attack.

Bren and Dylan pinned down and vulnerable as the raiders made an almost singular assault on their position. Her taking aim and firing at men threatening them.

The window exploding. Then nothing...

Fighting the searing agony, Helena struggled to sit up, and looked down at herself. Blood soaked her blouse, the stain still blooming, like a macabre image of a flower.

Shot.

She'd been shot. The pain burned clear through her, stealing her breath. Her lucidity.

The Winchester lay beside her, its long barrel warming her leg through her skirts, reminding her of its presence. She reached for it, fingers scrabbling across the carpet until she found the butt. She felt a bit safer with the strong oak stock in her hand and that helped her fight harder to clear her thoughts.

As did the continued crack and boom of gunfire outside the destroyed window. The raid continued. Which meant she needed to rejoin the fray. Brendan was out there fighting for Shamrock.

Heart pounding, she managed to use the Winchester to brace herself so she could get her legs under her to kneel. But she couldn't breathe. The air clogged in her throat at the intensity of the pain. Perspiration beaded on her forehead and made her palms grow slick, and the rifle wobbled. Feeling weak, she leaned her shoulder against the wall between her bedroom windows and groaned.

She tried to take shallow breaths as the battle raged outside, but then her head began to spin and the pain swamped her. She was too hurt to help anyone, perhaps even herself. The effort to get to the window had been a foolish waste of her waning strength.

Struggling against a wave of dizziness, Helena had no choice; she dropped the rifle and slid down the wall. As she did, she grabbed for the cotton scarf on the table next to her, bunched it up and pressed it to her wound, hoping to stanch the flow of blood. Striving to hold on in the hope that someone would find her soon.

Trying to stay conscious, she thought back to those shots she'd fired. She'd assumed the darkness would hide the smoke from the Winchester, but she'd been wrong—so wrong. The flash from the barrel must have given away her position to the attackers. She'd made herself the perfect target when she'd stood to fire her next volley of shots. After that she remembered nothing till regaining consciousness on the floor.

She had ignored her own safety as she'd taken those shots. She had fired to save Bren's life. It had had nothing to do with saving Shamrock. She'd acted without a thought to anything—past, present and certainly not future.

But suddenly the future was the only thing she could think about. And with that came regret. She'd saved Bren, but she'd never told him the truth. He thought all her anger had to do with hurt and damaged pride, when it was about so much more. It encompassed loss and pain and aching emptiness.

Losing her battle to stay lucid, she felt the dizziness taking her under again. When she opened her eyes next, the gunfire seemed farther away. Perhaps for once the raiders had faced a force they couldn't crush.

Battling pain and gauging her weakness, she knew there was a good chance she'd bleed to death if she didn't get help soon. She'd faced the possibility that this could happen and had left the safety of the Rocking R and returned, anyway. She'd done so with a pounding heart and shaking hands, not courage. She couldn't have lived with the guilt if she'd hidden away and Bren or one of the others had died. After all, the men had no stake in Shamrock, and Bren had never wanted one.

Her breathing grew more and more difficult. She tried to move, and cried out in pain. Her head spun worse, making her nauseous. Her face went numb and profound weakness rolled over her. Pressing on the wound grew impossible, but she realized she could hardly feel the pain anymore. She turned her head toward the doorway and her head whirled faster.

Was this death, then? Did the good Lord take away the pain, sweetening the last moments of life? She had to hang on. Fight the yawning darkness calling to her. Gritting her teeth, she took another breath, ready for the pain to return. And it did. But she continued to force herself to breathe. She tried to conjure up an image of Bren's face. Picturing him made tears blur her darkening vision. Only seeing him in the flesh one last time could lessen her infinite sorrow.

She tried to take comfort in the knowledge that Doc would make sure she was buried next to her precious Kathleen. Georgia Clemens and Regina Mallory had found the perfect spot in the low-lying meadow behind the house, under the enfolding limbs of that beautiful oak. But that would mean Bren would learn from strangers why Helena's love had seemed to turn to hate by the time he'd returned.

He'd had a right to hear it from her. Maybe if she'd moved past her own guilt she could have summoned up the courage to tell him. Maybe then she could have begun to heal. To move forward.

She gritted her teeth against the pain. She had to hang on. She forced herself to take another aching breath, and another, blessing the agony that seemed to buttress her grip on consciousness.

Bren would find her soon. He would. She was growing so tired and weak. She closed her eyes, had to rest. Just for a few moments. This wasn't the first time this room had seen her badly injured. Or witnessed a death.

Thoughts of that awful day and the memory of Kathleen's sweet, tiny face flowed on the river of pain over Helena's drowning mind. And she heard Regina Mallory's protesting voice as if it were today....

"I don't know. Helena's been through so much already. The poor little one is barely breathing," she whispered.

"All the more reason." The voice of Georgia, Doc's wife, was gentle and full of understanding. "Take my word for it. I've had it both ways."

"Here you go, Helena dear." Doc held out the nearly weightless bundle that was her baby girl, then placed it in her arms. "She doesn't have long, but if anyone should get to hold her till she goes, it's you."

Helena gazed into the flawless little face of an angel in the making. The baby's tiny lungs struggled to draw in each desperate breath. Looking up into the doctor's solemn face, Helena said, "Is there no chance? She's so perfect." She caressed her daughter's soft cheek.

"I'm sorry. I've never seen a baby this small breathe on its own for long. You were only seven months along at most, dear."

Helena held her child a bit tighter and blinked away tears. She refused to look at any of the others again. She had to cram a lifetime of love into so short a period.

"I baptized her already," Regina said, trying to give comfort.

"Bren would want her baptized. Kathleen..." Helena whispered to the baby. She'd picked out a girl's name that meant "pure." Now it looked as if her Kathleen would be forever pure.

Helena tried to memorize the features her love for Brendan had created. She wondered if Kathleen would have had his green or her blue eyes, and her heart cried out for him. But he'd left her and didn't know about their child. Or about this final loss of their love. Helena had wanted Kathleen desperately. This baby was to get all the love Bren hadn't wanted, and to give her something of Bren she would never lose. But like everyone she'd ever loved and everything she'd ever wanted, she couldn't hold on to her baby. Her sweet pure Kathleen slipped further away with each labored breath.

"I'm your mama," Helena whispered, once again caressing her daughter's downy cheek. "And I love you so much, sweetheart. I'll love you until the day I join you," she told the infant. "I'm so sorry you were robbed of so much life can offer. But there's heartache, too, and you'll skip all that and get to heaven right away. I'm not sure I can go with you. That's up to God. Don't be afraid. My mama went there with my baby brother.

And both your grandmothers and my daddy are there waiting, too. You can give them all a hug for me." Her voice cracked and she couldn't go on, even to talk to her baby for the first and last time.

She realized then that her tears were blinding her, keeping her from seeing Kathleen clearly. Helena blinked hard, but more tears followed. Then she realized the gasping breaths had stopped. Sometime in that last minute they'd shared, Kathleen had gone ahead of her. And all Helena wanted at that moment was to follow....

Pounding feet startled Helena out of the dream, which came to her less often now. Awareness and pain flooded in. She was on the floor. Shot. She wondered if she'd go to meet Kathleen now. Shamrock, the only thing she lived for, might be gone, too.

Then she realized only the heavy footfalls echoed in the room. The gunfire had stopped and silence reigned outside. She must have fallen asleep or unconscious. Whatever had happened, she'd dreamed of that beautiful awful day, maybe because it had happened in this very room. How much time had she lost, and who hurried toward her with those heavy footsteps now—friend or foe?

She wasn't sure she cared, but then Bren filled the doorway. He scanned the room at window height, then his gaze dropped to the floor. He gasped. "Oh, Jaysus, no." The next moment he skidded onto his knees at her side and gathered her against his strong chest. She groaned at the renewed agony, but knew she wanted to live. For him. But she didn't have any more control over life and death now than she'd had that other day.

The moonlight cut a swath across the room. It was

like being granted a miracle—a last wish. He lowered her to his lap, then pushed her lax hand off the wound and pressed. Her eyes filled with tears to see Bren's features so tortured. So desperate.

"Why, Helena? Why, when I had you tucked away safe and sound?"

She reached up, touched his worried face, her fingers smearing his cheek with her blood. "Isn't the men's spread. And you didn't want…it…or me."

She expected him to say it had been his job to try to stop the raiders, but he didn't say that at all. "No. 'Tisn't true. I *did.* I wanted both you *and* the ranch. Stupid pride and scruples kept makin' me deny it."

It hurt to hear pain in his voice, but it was confusing, as well. "But you left." She fought for the next breath. "Stayed away…so long."

"Because I knew you'd been right that day. If I saw you, I'd never be leavin' again. Why do ya think I came straight here after Belleza?"

She settled for half a breath this time. "Catch them?"

"No. To keep you safe, lovey. That's what catchin' them is about."

"Oh. But…" She frowned and shook her head. At least she thought she did. "So tired," she whispered. "I hurt, Bren." Her eyelids grew heavy and she couldn't seem to keep them open. Being in his arms comforted her. Made her feel safe. Any feelings of betrayal and anger melted away as if they'd never existed. She was dying.

She wanted to leave him with kind words. Ones to remember with fondness, not guilt. "It'll be okay. Shamrock…is yours. Always was…for you."

The moon seemed to go into hiding then, or her vision darkened. She'd run out of time. "Tell…you why so angry. So guilty. Shouldn't have…gone that day—" She tried to suck in another breath. Failed. Reached for a bit more strength. None. She had no more to give. She closed her eyes.

"Don't you go," Brendan ordered sharply.

Poor Bren. Didn't he understand what a waste of effort it was? Tears leaked from the sides of her eyes and ran into her hair, as his tears landed on her cheek.

"Don't you dare leave me. Do ya hear?"

Another order. Just like him. She tried to smile, but it was so sad. He didn't understand it was too late.

Too late to fix her.

Too late to fix them.

Her time had run out.

"Helena?" Brendan shouted. "No. Please, lovey." He looked at the sky beyond the shattered window. "You can't have her. Do you hear me? You can't have her. Please. Not like this. Please." Pressing down tighter on the wound, he tried to duck his head and feel her breath on his face. Holding her a bit tighter, he wiped his tears in her silky hair, then sat back.

Letting the pressure off the wound, he moved his hand lower, frantically seeking signs of life. And he found it in the faint beating of her heart. Relief flooded his soul and a tiny spark of hope ignited in his chest.

"Kane?" Sean Mallory said from behind him. "How bad is she hurt?"

Brendan hadn't even heard Helena's foreman approach. Had it been an enemy, he'd have failed at protecting her. Again.

Looking over his shoulder, he managed to say, "Bad.

She's still breathing, but barely." He looked back at his sweet, infuriating Helena. She was in his arms at last, but it shouldn't have been this way. She looked so fragile and broken, with his one arm cradling her back and his other hand holding pressure on a serious-looking bullet wound. He gathered himself enough to go on. "She's unconscious. Send for Doc and my family."

"Done and done. I kept a man hiding near the ranch road with orders to go for him and the sheriff. I knew there'd likely be a need of both, but if the raiders didn't strike there'd be no need to send for them." The foreman huffed out a breath before going into action and lighting the lamps on either side of the bed.

Brendan continued to keep pressure on Helena's wound, but he cursed when the light revealed the terrifying amount of blood on the carpet, soaking her dress, his arm and his pant leg. He realized then that the bullet had passed through her. He wasn't sure if that was good or not. There'd be no need to painfully dig out the bullet, but this way there were two wounds.

"Grab me those towels on the washstand," he said, pointing toward the piece of furniture.

Mallory hurried to hand him the towels, folded to form a thick pad. Brendan quickly pressed one to the exit wound and changed the soaked cloth on the entrance wound.

He felt Mallory's hand on his shoulder. "Looks like you've managed to slow the bleeding. She's tough. Don't lose hope," the older man said. "We should shift her to the bed for when Doc gets here."

Brendan nodded. Moving together, they lifted her, while holding the towels tight against both wounds so she wouldn't lose any of the ground she'd gained. Mindful of keeping her as steady as possible, they transferred her as smoothly as if they had been working in tandem for years.

But Helena lay so still.

Then, for the first time in three years, Brendan got on his knees and really prayed. This time he begged for help instead of screaming worthless threats at the Lord above.

Mallory waited before clearing his throat. "Varga'll need some doctoring, too. I can handle any of the others who need patching up."

Brendan opened his eyes, looked up and nodded, his hands continuing to keep pressure on the wounds. "Put Dylan across the hall, then. That way the doc'll be under the same roof with both his patients."

"Wish the wife was here. We could sure use her help."

Brendan winced. "No. Your kids need Regina, and she was better off at the Rockin' R. So was Helena." He swallowed. "But she came back, anyway."

Mallory frowned, then sighed, shaking his head. "She is a stubborn one. No sense crying over spilled milk, old son. Best thing you can do is deal with what is."

Brendan looked back at Helena, so pale and still. Easy for Mallory to say, he thought, considering all he had to make up for. If he got the chance, he'd spend the rest of his life doing exactly that. If not? He'd go on as he had been, uncaring if a dangerous assignment ended his lonely, miserable life.

Mallory walked to the door. "I'll see to getting Varga moved in, and bandages for Doc. I know where she keeps them. I'll be in the kitchen boiling water for him."

Brendan looked up as the foreman added, "You'll see. She'll be good as new in a few weeks and driving you crazy again. Like I said, she's stronger than you may think."

Brendan nodded as Mallory strode out, then gave Helena his undivided attention again. Of course she was stronger than her sweet face and delicate body indicated. Look at the legacy she'd built from a broken-down, trouble-laden ranch. She'd done it with tough, wise decisions that had guided Shamrock to be all it had become.

And she was more of a hands-on owner than he'd ever assumed. More than once he'd come upon her doing work he'd never have thought she'd stoop to. There was that day Jimmy had been too under the weather to handle his duties. Brendan had walked into the barn and found Helena mucking out stalls. Then there was the time he'd found her up to her hips in a muddy bog, orchestrating the rescue of Joker. And now that Brendan had shown her how, she shot as straight as any man on the spread. But none of that meant she wasn't all woman, with a woman's allure.

He'd wanted her more and more every day—a condition not helped by the jeans she wore while working on the ranch, and the lovely garments she wore in the evening after she'd bathed and dressed for dinner.

And he knew she had a woman's tender feelings. He'd seen her hand-feed two heifers that had lost their mothers. She cared for those future mothers of the herd as if they were beloved pets, the same way she'd reportedly nursed Paint Box back to health.

Brendan had also seen her cry.

His stomach twisted. He'd seen it because he'd caused it.

He had so damned much to make up for.

So damned much.

Doc Clemens arrived more quickly than Brendan had expected. The jangle of harness and rumble of swiftly moving wheels stopped right in front of the house. Doc rushed along the hall moments later and tossed his bag and a pile of bandages on the dresser.

"You," he said to Brendan. "Move."

Brendan complied, but not fast enough for the gruff doctor. Clemens hurried around the bed and, though rail thin, shoved Bren with considerably more strength than he'd expected. Doc got right to work and quickly checked the wound. "Good. You're good for something. You've slowed the bleeding." He reapplied pressure, as Brendan had been doing.

The older man's wife, Georgia, rushed into the room and began arranging his surgical instruments and the bandages Mallory had brought in. It appeared she doubled as his nurse. "Georgia," Doc ordered, "cut her out of these clothes."

Doc glanced at the marble-topped dresser when Mallory came in with the boiling water. "Good," he said, then looked back to Brendan. "What are you still doing here? Get *out*. I don't need a hysterical husband in the way."

"I'm not," Brendan said, in a voice so raw and flat he barely recognized it.

"What? A husband? Or hysterical?" Doc snapped. "Haven't been the first for a good long time." He soaked a piece of cloth with alcohol and swabbed the wounds.

"And now you look like you're about to become the second. Out!"

Abby entered as Mallory left. The foreman murmured something to her as they passed each other. Brendan watched her go pale as she looked at Helena, then him. "Saints preserve us. It's worse than I feared," she murmured.

Brendan grabbed hold of her, squeezing his eyes shut as he hugged his sister. He let her go after a protracted moment, his eyes seeking hers. Calmer now, she put her hand on his shoulder.

"Go on with you now, Bren," she said, her tone soothing. "You've done all you can." She pushed him toward the door. "We'll take good care of her." She glanced to the bed.

He followed her gaze. "I had her tucked away safe at the Rocking R. She snuck back. Always had a mind of her own," he said, lost in the memory of her in the church, holding Father Rafferty's pistol. His throat ached with repressed tears. He wanted to go out and wail at the setting moon.

Abby nodded. "That she has. The sheriff and Mallory need to talk to you. They're waiting in the kitchen. I'll keep you informed of how she's doing. Go. It's out of your hands now."

Brendan shot Doc Clemens a dark look. "That doesn't mean I have to like it." He glanced at Helena again, then grabbed Abby by the upper arms like a drowning man would a life preserver. "She's more fragile than some think, Ab."

His sister put her hand on his forearm. "We all know that, Bren."

Nodding, he started to step into the hall, but then

turned back. Defying them all, he rushed to the bed and bent to kiss Helena's forehead. "Please stay with me," he whispered, and kissed her lips.

He straightened then and saw that Doc was looking at him. "I can't lose her," he told the impatient physician.

"I can't deal with you right now. Out!"

Brendan could only stare at the doctor, who clearly blamed him. Why not? He blamed himself. He couldn't seem to focus on anything but losing her. But a sudden vision of standing at an open grave, *her* grave, froze him in place.

"Go, Bren," Abby said again.

He nodded and fled, before the tears burning at the back of his throat showed themselves. Once in the hall, he leaned on the wall next to the door and dropped his head back, closing his eyes. After a few minutes of deep breathing, when he thought he had himself in hand, he went across the hall to look in on Dylan Varga. The neighbor asked that someone go for his wife. Brendan promised to see to it, then left him in the watchful care of one of Shamrock's men.

Walking through the courtyard and down the short set of stairs into the kitchen, he fought to keep his mind on business. He found Quinn and Mallory waiting where Abby had said they'd be. There was a pot of coffee on the stove, but Mallory walked over to him and put a glass in his hand. "You look like you could use a good shot of bourbon. How is she?"

Brendan nodded his thanks and moved across the big room to join the sheriff at the long trestle table near the side window. For a few moments he couldn't speak.

A heavy predawn fog lay like a blanket over the valley and meadow beyond. That was the view Helena looked at as she greeted each day and ended each evening. He turned away from the misty scene and sat at the table.

"Doc's with her. My sister promised to let me know how she's doing. So, how bad are our losses?" he asked Mallory. "Helena'll be inconsolable if she lost anyone."

The foreman nodded. "No dead on our side," he said, after that long look. "But we've twenty or so raiders out there who won't see the sun rise."

"They're yours to deal with, Quinn," Brendan said. "The town can bury them, or leave them on the range for the buzzards, for all I care. But I won't have them buried on Shamrock."

"Most of your men share your sentiment," Quinn replied. "They wouldn't be happy having to dig decent graves for the likes of them. I have them loading the bodies into a wagon."

"Some of the raiders got away," Mallory said.

"That was a given, considerin' their numbers."

"There were so many more than anyone thought. The strange thing is, Brendan, we didn't kill all those who're dead. When they broke through our lines, the raiders killed their own wounded." Mallory shook his head. "Maybe so they couldn't be tracked to the one paying them."

"They might have worried the wounded would talk. Coldhearted bastards," the sheriff said. "But we've seen that all along, haven't we?"

"Could be they're more afraid of their boss than of losing friends," the foreman ventured. "They did run for the hills with our guns blazing at their backs, yet they took the time to kill their wounded. That has to be so their leader stays anonymous."

"Says something about whoever is behind this, doesn't it?" Quinn asked, clearly concerned. Until Brendan's arrival, he'd been one lone lawman against what they now knew was a damned army.

Brendan took a pull from his glass. "It sure as hell proves what we suspected."

Mallory crossed his arms and sat back, tipping his chair to lean his shoulders against the wall. "Well, none of those left behind are Comanche. Or from any other tribe, for that matter. They're all white as a lily come Easter morn."

"I talked to your cowhands when I took my horse down to the stable," Quinn said, and got up to refill his coffee cup. "Not a man recognized a single one of those bastards. So we still can't prove who's behind this."

"Dammit," Brendan growled, and slapped his fingers against the edge of the table.

"But we do have proof it isn't some faction of the Comanche on the warpath. I imagine you want to stay put, so I'll wire the Indian agent for you when we get back to town," Quinn said.

Brendan blinked and nodded sharply. "Thanks."

Knowing Helena was lying upstairs, so hurt, possibly dying, haunted him. He couldn't leave the ranch. It was hard to think beyond the knowledge that he could lose her. He stared ahead at the blank wall. "Even if we'd killed them all and found Avery among the dead, it cost too damned much."

"There's not one among us who'd say it didn't," Mallory agreed, his tone conciliatory. "Don't lose hope. Helena will recover. You've prevented an Indian war, slowed Avery down and bought some time for the other ranchers. Maybe you and Quinn can gather the proof you need before Avery rebuilds and attacks again."

The foreman put a hand on Brendan's forearm and went on, "About Helena. She came back here last night of her own accord. She isn't stupid. She knew the risks."

"And she fired that Winchester to save my ass."

"I think she saw what the rest of us did. Avery was livid at you yesterday, right?"

Brendan nodded.

"Well, during the gunplay, after you went to Varga's rescue, the raiders mostly focused on you. That has Avery written all over it. You're in his way. He wants to marry Helena and absorb Shamrock. We all know it, even if she refuses to see him as more than a friend."

Brendan had to smile at that. "She's stubborn, is our Helena."

Mallory shot him a grin. "That she is."

Brendan's mind wandered to the future. His future. Helena's future. If she came out of this, he intended to move heaven and earth to reconcile with her.

The problem with that was that if her leaving town with him yesterday had spawned a raid, in the hope of getting rid of him, then their reconciliation would surely have Avery doubling his efforts.

Well, Brendan was a Texas Ranger, wasn't he? Supposedly the best of the best. He'd figure out some way to get his man. Ignoring the byplay between the others, he narrowed his eyes, considering. What was better than one Texas Ranger in a fight?

More of them.

He looked up. "I think I know how to stop the bastard. He suddenly has vacancies on his payroll. Quinn,

I've another wire I need you to send. I think it's time we play by Avery's rules."

"He has rules?" the sheriff sneered.

Brendan flashed what he knew was a nasty grin. But he was feeling pretty damned nasty. They all were. "Oh, he has rules. Dirty ones, boyo. And it's time we fought just like him."

Chapter Seven

Muffled voices intruded into a dream come true. Helena pushed the sounds away and reveled in the feel of Brendan holding her, looking frantic and adoring. Of course, it was only a dream.

On some level aware she'd been dreaming, she was only too happy that the nightmare of the whooping, dreaded Ghost Warriors' attack on Shamrock had disappeared. But she didn't want the feeling of Brendan holding her to fade the same way.

She hovered for moments between her dream and full consciousness. Then she recognized Abby's as one of the voices, and the dream faded like the morning mist that often hovered over the meadow before the sun burned it away. Opening her eyes, Helena struggled to sit up, but pain, sharp and deep, startled a shocked yelp from her, and she fell back to the pillow.

She looked around and disappointment flowed over her. Brendan's hadn't been one of the voices, and only Doc and Abby were in the room. Helena had been dreaming; Brendan wasn't there. The pain sliced clean and deep. She moaned.

The two moved toward her in the muted light that filtered into the room from the window behind them. She watched, curious and annoyed that they'd interrupted her happy if incoherent dream.

Then she looked past them to the window. It was shattered. A tiny flicker of hope warmed her. The raid hadn't been a nightmare. She was hurt, so maybe Brendan holding her and whispering sweet words hadn't been a dream.

The doctor leaned over her. He was in his shirtsleeves, his usual frock coat and wide necktie discarded. Even his gray hair was mussed. "Welcome back, young lady." He straightened the pillow beneath her shoulders and the pain eased. "No more trying to sit up. You're to stay as still as possible." He moved the covers aside, then peered behind the layers of bandage. "Good. Good. It looks as if that stunt didn't start the bleeding again. Trying to sit up and undo my good work like that— what were you thinking? No moving around! I'll let you know when you can."

She grimaced. "Don't worry. I plan to move as little as possible."

"You gave us all quite a scare." Abby's pretty face filled her vision from the opposite side of the bed. She bent over and kissed Helena on the cheek. "Thank God Brendan found you in time. I can't wait to tell him you're awake."

Helena's heart lightened even more. "He's still here?" When his sister nodded, the flicker became a firestorm of hope engulfing Helena's whole being. So she really hadn't been dreaming. Maybe he had meant all the things she thought she remembered him saying.

Maybe there was a chance for them, even after they'd both made so many mistakes.

Mistakes. She sighed. That word brought back the nightmare portion of her memories. She shook her head slowly. "A raid on Shamrock. I can hardly believe it," she whispered.

Abby took her hand. "Bren wishes he hadn't been right. How he knew I'll never understand."

"He has good instincts, I guess," Helena said, disquieted by what that implied. "I suppose he was meant to be a lawman. At least we all survived. Everyone did. Right?"

Again Abby nodded. "Doesn't hurt to have a ranger in the family, does it?"

Helena's ears perked up at that. "Is that what we are, Abby?" she asked, squeezing tight, afraid of the answer, but just as anxious to hear it.

"Helena," Abby said gravely, "you've been family to me since you saved my brother's life back in Wheatonburg. As for Bren, he's in the kitchen, pacing. We nearly had to hog-tie him to get him out of here. I'd say that means something. And himself with two bullet wounds of his own."

Helena's whole body tensed, making her wince. "He's hurt?" Another fear rose up to join her worry for his safety. Had Brendan developed a taste for adventure? Would that mean the routine of life on a ranch couldn't fulfill that need in him? A need that could lead him into danger and get him killed. She looked from Abby to Doc. "Is he going to be all right?"

"Maybe you should worry about yourself," Doc Clemens snapped. "It was a fool stunt, sneaking back here the way you did."

Helena didn't regret her decision. She met the doctor's gaze. "I did what I had to do. Now tell me what happened to Brendan. He was here with me. I remember it." She paused for a breath. "Was he shot later? I'd thought the raid was over by the time he found me."

Doc shook his head. "Your fool husband apparently took two bullet grazes trying to protect Dylan Varga and contain the raiders, so they couldn't get away. He'll be sore, but otherwise he should be fine. Damn lucky it wasn't worse and that I don't have a houseful of patients. The whole lot of you ended up facing what sounds like a damned army."

"Doc, don't be too hard on Brendan. He had his reasons. We both made mistakes. Much as I've tried to convince myself he isn't, Bren is still my husband. If he wants to come home, I'm willing to try."

The older man glanced over to Abby. "You can get that brother of yours now. But warn him I don't want her upset."

She nodded. "I'll send him up."

As Abby left, Doc placed his hand on Helena's forehead and shook his head. "You're getting a bit warm. You're still liable to have an infection to fight, now that you fought off the raiders." He sat on the dressing table stool. "You want to tell me what is worrying you?"

Helena didn't bother to deny it. "You didn't tell Brendan or Abby anything, did you?"

Doc scowled. "No. Not with him caterwauling about not wanting to leave you."

She pulled a face. "Brendan would never *caterwaul*."

"Think not?" Doc said, grimacing again. "He ought to know what his leaving cost you. Why would it matter if I'd told him?"

And there was the question that haunted her, spoken in plain words. Wondering about what-ifs had led her to her own private hell these last three years. "Did it, Doc? I used to believe that. But was I so angry and pigheaded that I went ahead and rode out with the men, when hiring another hand to do the job would have served just as well? Was I a good enough rider at the time to herd cattle, or did I fool myself into thinking I was?" She sighed. "Was I trying to get back at him by proving I didn't need him?"

Doc took her hand and gave it a sharp squeeze. "You didn't purposely go out to get yourself busted up. I won't listen to you do this to yourself. You were badly short-handed. What is the point of questioning yourself now? It happened. No amount of stewing can change that."

"But…" Helena looked away, unable to meet his gaze.

"And if you're really going to take up with him again," Doc said, "he should know."

"We're married, not having an illicit affair. I'm not 'taking up' with him."

"Call it what you want, but the result is the same. And much as I personally didn't think he had any rights in the matter after he left, he does have a right to know what happened and the risks it still poses to you. Is it that you think he'll blame you? Think of you as less worthy?"

"I told you, I blame myself as well as him. I know it doesn't make sense, but I do." And if she blamed herself, maybe he would as well. "You have to promise not to tell him. I will tell him when the time is right. Promise, Doc? Please."

The man frowned. "I don't see it as my place to tell

him. Most of my colleagues wouldn't agree, but I was raised by a woman surviving on her own. My father left when I was a boy, then reappeared when I was nearly an adult. Took my ma to court to get half what she had in the bank. It was money she'd worked hard for at her little millinery shop. Then he disappeared with the money the court said she owed him. That left her shop struggling. Same way Ranger Kane can take Shamrock. You realize that, don't you?"

She shook her head, feeling suddenly played out. "Thanks for caring, but no. Not Bren. He'd never do that. He's too honorable. Not Bren." She closed her eyes. "Maybe I'll sleep a bit more," she murmured. "Just for a little while, till he comes…"

"Good idea," she heard Doc say, from what sounded like very far away. And there was a smile in his voice. She was sure of it. Maybe he wouldn't be too hard on Bren. And when she opened her eyes, Bren would be with her.

She tumbled into sleep then, ordering her mind and heart to forgive and forget. If only the guilt would go away as easily.

Brendan glanced up as Abby came into the kitchen. He didn't like the militant look in her eyes. He knew his sister, and realized his skin was in jeopardy. What in hell had he done now?

"We need to talk," she said, her tone one he recognized. It went along with her hell-to-pay expression. He was about to get one of Abby's lectures. Not his first. Probably not his last.

Even though he was older, she'd ruled the roost as the woman of the Kane household for the ten years after their mother's death, until he'd left Wheatonburg and she'd married.

"I'll be talking to my brother now, if you gentlemen will excuse us. Brendan, shall we move to the porch?"

Knowing it was foolhardy to fight the inevitable, and hoping for news of Helena's condition, Brendan followed her through the house to a side porch. "How is she?" he asked as he settled on the bench under a window. "When can I see her?"

Abby faced him, crossed her arms and leaned against the railing. "She's conscious. Doc says she'll live, barring any serious infection. But I'm not letting you see her. Not until I know what it is you're playing at. Talk," she ordered.

"What do ya think I'm playin' at, I'd like to ask? Helena's my wife. I'll see her if I want."

"It's good to see you've finally remembered who she is to you. But don't push your luck, boyo. Right now Doc and I hold the key to her bedroom door. Understood?"

Brendan glarèd, but he nodded. He knew his sister. Too much pushing back would only get her dander up. He stayed silent so she'd get on with what she planned to say.

"Before today," his sister went on, "if I remember it as you told it, you were only here at Shamrock to catch the raiders. Then Helena turns up hurt, and here you are, falling all over yourself like a two-year-old with a broken toy. Well, she's no toy. She's a real woman, with hopes and dreams and feelings. She deserves loyalty and devotion. Consistent loyalty. Consistent devotion. Don't put yourself in her life again if you're planning to get a wild hare and go off chasing freedom and adventure."

"I told you before, being a Texas Ranger isn't about adventure or freedom. It's about makin' sure those who need protectin' are protected. And that those caught up in the law's snare deserve to be there."

"The way you didn't. And it was because of Helena's guardian. Were you punishing her for what Franklin Gowery tried to do to you?"

"N-no. No," he said, stumbling over the denial.

He guessed he'd shown his hesitation, because Abby's temper started to flare. "You blame her for what that bastard did? How, I'd like to know, considering how she feels about you? And what she *did* for you?"

"I feel the same for her," he admitted.

"Then what was that? She risked a lot back in Wheatonburg. She helped Joshua spy on Gowery to keep you safe. For the love of you, she risked losing everything her father intended her to have. Had Gowery found out, her life would have been a misery. He'd have forced her to marry someone she hated, and her father's legacy would have gone to whoever married her."

The mention of Harry Conwell and his legacy had Brendan gritting his teeth.

"What?" Abby demanded. She knew him too damned well.

"He was Gowery's friend, so he mustn't have been much different. Why else would he have appointed Gowery Helena's guardian?" Brendan retorted.

Abby toned down her annoyance. "She's told me about her father, Bren. He sounded like a wonderful man, despite that he was blind to the needs of a girl growing into a young woman. He certainly wasn't the first widowed father not to understand what a daughter needs. Our own da comes to mind. And from what I hear, her da began to doubt his choice of a guardian, but he'd put off changing his will too long."

"So he was a good da. So what?"

"Oh, Bren. I've tried to stay out of this, but...what is it all really about? You've not acted like yourself since you rejected her back in Pennsylvania. But once she was your wife, forced though the marriage was, you lived together, and by all accounts, happily. Then you deserted her. Da's ready to come West to take a switch to you. And don't fall back on the 'forced' part. You know good and well no one has ever forced you to do a thing you didn't want to do or felt you should do."

"It's this place, dammit," he raged, the burden and pain too much to handle, with Helena up there so hurt, her life still in danger.

Abby's eyes widened and her lips thinned. "Pride? Because it didn't come from *you?* I hadn't wanted to believe it, though she told me. Was she so wrong in wanting this? All she did was try to give the man she loves the deepest dream of his heart. If the shoe had been on the other foot, would you have been wrong to reach out and grab her dream for her?"

"I don't mean Shamrock itself," he snarled, and got to his feet, pacing to the end of the porch and back, to finally throw himself on the bench again in frustration. His own sister, raised in the same kind of poverty and shame he'd been—how could she not understand?

"The money," he barked. "How can you not know it's about the money that bought this place?" When Abby's eyes showed only confusion, he added, "Jaysus, Ab. Where do you suppose it all came from? Only one place I can think of."

His sister's eyes widened, then color rose to her cheeks. "You idiot. You fool. You mean you've let prejudice and pride rise to a place more important than love and happiness? And for all this time? You made her and yourself miserable because you've assumed things about her father?"

Brendan shook his head. How could she not know? Not understand? "Oh, her sainted father. How would he have treated the family of one of his mine workers who'd just lost his leg in his damned mine? Would he have looked at the man's sons and demanded one of them go into the mines the very next day? I was a damned fine carpenter. I hated closed-in spaces so much that I slept outdoors unless rain, snow or bitter cold chased me inside."

"I know. I remember. And it's sorry I am to have been an added burden. You know Josh and I, and Daniel, too, love you for all you did to keep that miserable roof over our heads till Josh came back."

"Dammit, Ab. It isn't about that part of it. You're right, and I did what I had to do for all of you. Da couldn't be moved, and we had the debt to Wheaton to pay off. It's about Conwell and men like him. How many men and their families did he climb over to build—what was it you called it?—his legacy?"

Now Abby's green eyes blazed. "So, Josh isn't worthy to be called 'friend' any longer? Or worthy to be my husband? My house, my marriage itself, are betrayals of Da and you, and even Daniel?"

Brendan felt twin flags of color flame on his cheeks now. He looked down. "No. I told you Joshua isn't—"

"Rich? I beg to differ. He's rich as Croesus, and if you remember, it was his father who nearly destroyed not only you, but me…all of us. Oh, and Josh as well, but he's rich, so he doesn't *feel?* Do you think Josh deserved to know nothing of his own son for nine years? And he must have deserved to lose me—the woman he loved for all that time—as well."

Brendan raked a hand through his hair. It all sounded not just foolish but wrongheaded in every way. He leaned forward and propped his elbows on his knees, his hands hanging in defeat.

"You're a fool," Abby spat.

"Aye. Put that way, I suppose I am."

"Have you never talked to Helena about her da?"

"It was a sore subject, so I stayed away from it."

"I suppose you stayed off the subject with Josh as well. Bren, Harry Conwell didn't own companies just so he could have employees to lord it over. He used his money to invest in new ones, or others that needed capital to expand. For the most part he financed the growth of jobs in good, fair companies. Someone has to be wealthy, boyo. If not, there'd be no industries, no jobs. We'd all starve. Every man who owns a business isn't Harlan Wheaton, Franklin Gowery or men of their ilk."

Brendan really had been a fool. Make that blind fool. His da had taught him from the cradle that it was the individual who mattered, not the money a person owned or position he or she held.

Abby's defense of Harry Conwell should haunt Brendan. But it was Helena's words that haunted him most now. *"That man meant the world to me!"* she'd shouted. *"He was all I had after my mother died… All I had to do to get my hands on that lovely money was see him gunned down in the street, then be left alone in the world with Franklin Gowery as a guardian."*

Jaysus! Brendan felt like an ass. "I'll make her happy. I'll put it all behind me," he swore.

Abby arched an imperious eyebrow. "Can you forget being forced into the same dangerous mines that took Da's leg? The years you comforted Daniel when the boys teased him, because everyone knew he was born on the wrong side of the blanket? Can you leave behind the anger you feel for all those reasons? Because she deserves nothing less."

Brendan nodded and resolved to give his Helena no less. He knew she deserved that and more. He'd known it for some time. That knowledge was all mixed up in feeling inadequate because of the poverty of his upbringing. He wished he knew if she still felt more for him than the loyalty of a wife for her husband, and the desire that had always burned bright between them.

He wished he was sure that inside—deep inside, where life had hardened a corner of his heart and left another corner unsure of his own worth—he could learn to think around those feelings with the love he felt for her.

Only time and determination would show how well he succeeded.

"Are you still wanting to see her?" Abby asked sternly. Her sharp question snapped him out of his reverie.

"Aye. It's what I want most in the world."

"Then let's get you up there. She asked after you straight away."

So just as thoughts of Helena had been at the forefront of Brendan's mind these last hours, somehow through the pain, she'd been thinking of him, as well.

Chapter Eight

Again, Helena woke to the sound of hushed words being whispered in the room, then footsteps coming and going as Abby arrived and asked Doc to leave with her. Helena smiled. Some of those hushed words had the lilt of an Irish accent. "Bren?" she whispered, keeping her heavy lids closed. Brendan was near. She felt him.

"It's me. Would you do me the honor of openin' those pretty blues? I've missed seeing them these last hours." He spoke softly, like a caress. She opened her eyes to find him sitting close by her side, his face even closer.

"You're here." She lifted her hand to touch his face.

A slight smile tipped his lips and lit his green eyes with an inner sparkle as the backs of his fingers stroked her cheek. "And where else would I be, I'd like to know?"

She was tempted to smile back at him and ignore the worry in her heart. But if she'd learned one thing in this marriage, it was that by not talking problems out they would eventually sneak in on cat's feet, and heartbreak would follow. Luckily, there was no rule saying she had to let him know how much she wished their lives could be different. She found herself still reluctant to say the words that might bring them together.

She looked away. "You could have gone off chasing the raiders. Or be arresting them right now." She sighed, remembering the lonely years she'd endured since he'd left. It was something she could have been spared, had she just listened to what he'd said about living within the means he could provide. "You could be anywhere but here."

Silence greeted her words. She pressed her lips together as the thick quiet stretched out and grew uncomfortable. Then Brendan's fingertips settled beneath her chin and redirected her face toward his. He looked as regretful as she felt.

He smiled, though the crooked grin he wore didn't match the solemn expression in his eyes, which had lost their sparkle. She was sorry for it, but some things needed saying.

"You mean, the way it's been with us for the last three years?" he asked, then continued, clearly knowing the answer. "Truth is, there isn't anywhere I'd rather be than right here. Never has been. Never will be. I spent the last three years being an ass of the first water. And it started when I refused to listen to what you wanted. Can ya ever forgive me?"

She frowned, still not sure they understood each other, even in their apologies. "If you can forgive me for being so headstrong. I was so sure I was right, and that you'd understand when you saw Shamrock. But you never saw it for what it was supposed to be. You just rode away without a backward glance."

"Oh, there were hundreds of glances backward, lovey. As for the other, there's nothing to forgive. And

I'm a stubborn one myself. I see it all clearly now. Can we start over from where we were that morning, do you think?"

She didn't know how to explain that if he hadn't walked away, if he'd given her a choice between Shamrock and him that day, she'd have chosen him. But it was too late for that. If the ranch still stood between them, she didn't think she could leave. Her heart was tied to one small but precious piece of the meadowland.

"Where were we that morning, Bren?" she asked carefully. "Do you still feel about Shamrock the way you did then? Does it still stand between us?"

Smoothly, without creating so much as a ripple or dip in the mattress, he slid onto the bed and cradled her in his embrace, tucking her head under his chin. The scent of him hadn't changed. He still bathed with the same clean-smelling soap. Still used the same limey aftershave.

"I meant what I said," he purred into her ear. "I was a prize idiot. This is your home, and according to Maria, the first you've had. I couldn't take you away from that. I wouldn't. You deserve a lovely place to lay your head and to stable your ridiculously named horses."

She smiled at that, then sobered. "But that's what I wanted for you. A place to call your own. A place to build your own dreams. A place where you were boss and beholden to no one. You supported your whole family, doing work you hated, with bosses who liked to lord their power over you and the other miners. You seemed to carry a ton of coal on your shoulders each and every day. I wanted to free you of that and its memories. But all I did was drive you away."

"I suppose we've settled that. So we both want the

best for each other. Shall we begin again, but at Shamrock this time?"

She tilted her head back, needing to gauge his answer not just by his voice, but by what she saw written in his expression. "What about you being a ranger?"

He gave her a direct look. "I have to stop these raids. I need to be able to face myself in a mirror, and I couldn't if I didn't stick with this. The town, the ranchers and Ryan Quinn—they need me. I shouldn't have to travel except to Mountain Home or maybe San Antonio. And then only for a day or so."

Feeling a tiny bit timid, she said, "I can handle a day or so. I did that when we got to town. It's just that I was so worried. Abby stopped getting letters. It was as if you'd disappeared."

"I can take care of myself. But I'll not be happy to let you out of my sight for some time to come. And before you say it, you're gonna have to be puttin' up with a great deal of natterin' from me. I won't easily get over finding you bleedin' on the floor. No more valiant deeds. My heart couldn't take it."

She frowned and poked one of his hard biceps. "I wasn't valiant. I was scared spitless."

"And still you fired, when Dylan and I were about to be overrun. You saved us and took a bullet for your trouble."

"You were hurt, too," she countered. "While being pretty valiant yourself. Even wounded, you got Dylan to safety. Then came for me."

His mouth formed a stubborn line. "And who was it that squealed? Probably that over-zealous old woman of a doctor. Imagine tossing a woman's husband out of her sickroom. Was he afraid I'd see part of you I haven't before?"

She had to smile at that. Brendan was not a man who'd ever turned down the lamps or waited to get to a bed when he'd wanted her. Nor had he waited for marriage. He'd made a blanket in a secluded spot magical.

"It was Abby who told me you were hurt."

"Betrayed by my own sister."

Helena grinned. "She said Doc was afraid you'd pass out."

"I admit to bein' a mite anxious. More than a mite." He captured Helena's chin and tipped her head up so their gazes met. Locked. "Never scare me like that again, hear?"

"Don't worry, getting shot is no fun. Is it?"

Bren sighed, closed his eyes and tucked her head under his chin. "No. No fun a'tall."

Seconds later his soft snore echoed in her ears. And sleep beckoned her again.

Brendan waved to Ryan Quinn as the sheriff rode past the house on his way back to town. He'd arrived as Brendan and Mallory were deciding where to station Shamrock's men, and what needed handling in the scope of ranching. Quinn had picked up the return wire from Major Jones. He'd agreed to send the three rangers Brendan had requested. They would wire Brendan in code, and then the four would meet once they got to the area. With ears inside the Bar A, maybe they could stop Avery, and bring him to justice with no more innocent blood spilled.

Brendan walked to the end of the porch, his gaze falling on the corrals, bunkhouse and cabins. It was a mighty nice place to look forward to spending the rest of his life in. But with it came some burdens that weighed on him.

How much to tell Helena about the raids and his suspicions had become an even bigger worry now. Lies and half-truths were no way to begin their marriage anew. He wanted to tell her everything, but she had a direct way of gazing at folks. And if someone was looking— and he knew Avery would be, once he learned they'd reconciled—her opinion would be right there, written on her face for the bastard to see.

When Doc left yesterday, he'd said he wanted Helena kept as calm and worry-free as possible, so he'd made talking about the raids forbidden territory.

The sound of hoofbeats and the jingle of harness drew Brendan's attention back toward the road. "Well, speak of the devil himself," he muttered, and sauntered down the walk to swing the picket gate open. "Mornin', Doc. Come to check on your patients?"

"How is Helena today?"

"I haven't seen her for over an hour. She was still a bit warm when I left, but chatterin' with Ab, who keeps saying the fever's to be expected. But it's Helena and—"

"A worry," Doc interjected, his tone gruff and annoyed. "I know you're anxious, but try not to let her see you fret about it. We don't need her getting upset."

"First I don't worry enough, then too much. If I ever do anything right, let me know," Brendan replied. He'd tried being amiable, but Doc got his back up.

The doctor took a deep breath. "Look, son, you left that young woman alone in a forbidding land. Shamrock was a badly managed, practically abandoned ranch when she bought it. Her stock was scattered all over the place and beyond. By fall she and those first men in the outfit had gathered a sizable herd. One bigger than expected. She got caught in a stampede, trying to do your job. She picked out a spot for a cemetery, but we—me and Georgia—managed to patch her up."

Brendan could only stare, slightly sick to his stomach. "No one ever said."

"Because the only others who knew were the Mallorys and her first hands. Helena swore us all to secrecy. That was how she wanted it, and none of us cared to go against her wishes. She and Abby didn't get close till after Helena was up and around and ready to face the folks in town again.

"But if she's decided to take you back, it's her choice, her life. For her sake, suppose we start over and put my remarks behind us?" Doc climbed down and offered his hand.

Brendan shook it firmly, knowing he deserved the doctor's scorn and then some. Running through his mind, piercing his heart, was this new knowledge of another wrong he'd done Helena. She'd been hurt. And alone. Because of him.

Doc Clemens snatched up his bag and a small cotton sack. "She'll be fine," he added. But a note of worry had crept into his tone.

For a man saying she'd be fine, he was a mite too twitchy for Brendan's liking. "Are you worried about the fever? You said to expect it. So did Ab."

"It truly is to be expected, but it never sits well with me. I brought along something to treat it. I've seen this work wonders."

Brendan narrowed his eyes. "What is it? And why do you think I won't like you usin' it?"

Doc sighed, then shook his head with a small smile. "Do all rangers read minds or just you? It's an Indian remedy—an infusion made of black willow bark. Most folks don't have open minds about Indian potions. You know how it is—they're still touchy on the subject of a people they see as savages. To them, using one of their remedies is akin to calling in a Comanche medicine man."

Shrugging his shoulders, Brendan said, "My own mother used plants as cures. And I've heard about using willow." He stepped aside, gesturing toward the door. "If you say it'll help, go at it."

Doc stopped and sent him a long look. "Maybe there's more to you than I thought." He gave a sharp nod and hurried ahead.

Brendan followed, thinking things were looking up. But when he reached the doorway of Helena's room, he froze. His wife lay in bed, tossing her head fitfully, with a look of pain on her face. Her eyes were closed tight and her lips cracked.

Abby was busy sponging her off, murmuring soothing words, but looking as frantic as he now felt. Though it was an unusually cool day for late May, she had the windows sky-high, letting in the breeze.

How could Helena have gotten so bad so quickly? He'd not been gone that long. Beyond his spinning thoughts, Brendan heard Abby say, "Oh, Doc, thank God you've come. She's burning up and I've run out of tricks."

"Let's fetch some boiling water, Abby. I'll wash up in the kitchen," Doc said, and turned, running smack into Brendan in the doorway. "Make yourself useful, dammit. Sponge her down while we're getting the willow brewed."

So much for a new start. Brendan nodded and moved to where Abby stood at the washstand. She handed him the cloth she'd just wrung out. "Just wipe her down. I've put some witch hazel in the water."

"I know what to do. I did it enough with Daniel way back when. But he never looked this bad. I can't lose her, Ab. Not now, when happiness is so close."

She nodded and blinked away tears rising in her eyes. "She'll be fine."

"So everyone keeps tellin' me, but ya all look as worried as I feel."

She gave his arm a squeeze and left with the doctor.

Brendan sat next to Helena and began wiping her face with the tepid cloth. "What are you doin' to me, lovey?" he asked her, not expecting an answer.

But she opened her eyes. They were rheumy and glazed with fever, her expression confused. She grabbed his arm as he swiped the cloth over her neck and upper chest. "Are you really here? Not a dream?"

He forced a grin he didn't feel. "Ya keep askin' that. I'm here and I'm not goin' anywhere. I was takin' care of a few things with Mallory."

She frowned, her eyebrows forming a deep V. "Is something wrong?"

"A few things I need to get to, is all." Things like posting new lookouts. He'd put nothing past Avery, not even a second hit.

"I'm so hot. Burning up," she whispered, her throat sounding dry as dust.

"Doc brought along medicine. You'll see. It'll help. Supposin' I get you a bit of water in the meanwhile?

You'll be doin' better in no time a'tall," he told her, trying to pitch his voice to soothe her. He got up, put some water in a glass and dipped the cloth in the bowl on the washstand. When he turned back to sponge off her forehead and cheeks, she'd fallen asleep.

He told himself that was good. She needed to rest. And if she was sleeping, she wasn't hurting. But worry was an evil little bugger. It turned good to bad, relief to fear. He kept talking to her as he tried to drive the fever down, until Doc and Abby came back.

Like a baby bird, eyes closed, Helena would open her mouth when Brendan, Ab or Maria dribbled the willow infusion past her cracked lips. Then she'd swallow as ordered.

The next two days passed in a blur, with the only difference being the women taking turns helping him nurse her. Doc's wife, Mallory's wife and Abby took turns during daylight hours. Brendan slept in snatches, as did Maria, so they'd be available to take turns tending her during the night.

The housekeeper came to get him when Helena's fever finally broke, in the wee hours of Wednesday morning. When Brendan rushed into the room, he found Helena sitting on the side of the bed. "Why did Maria wake you?" she groaned. "I'm a sweaty mess."

"I've never seen anything more lovely," he told her as he went down on his knees in front of her and reached up to caress her cheek. "Are you after driving me mad, woman? Stay healthy this time, ya hear me? You'll have a total loon for a husband otherwise."

She smiled. It was a relief and a gift, her accepting the title of husband for him. "I promise. I feel weak as a kitten, Bren, but I'd kill for a bath and something to eat."

He arched an eyebrow. "Would ya now. Then I better be providin' a bit of a cleanup, hadn't I? You can be fierce when someone gets in your way."

Her eyes clouded with something he couldn't put a name to. "Did I kill them? Those men I shot?" she asked, looking at her knotted hands.

Dammit. He'd not meant to remind her of the raid, with her still in her sickbed. "No, you didn't," he told her. "Ya just gave me a chance to get myself and Dylan out of harm's way, which we're grateful for." He didn't add that because she'd shot them, the three outlaws were dead, though ultimately at the hands of their compatriots. As they'd been murderous bastards, he couldn't say he cared.

Trying to change the subject, he said, "Supposin' Maria helps you sponge off and gets you into a clean nightgown, while I change the bedding and fetch you somethin' to eat?"

She snickered. "You're going to get me something to eat?" She poked his belly. "Did the rangers teach you to cook?"

He could feel his face heat like an untried boy. He'd nearly set their cabin on fire when they'd first arrived in Tierra del Verde. He'd been trying to show her how easy it was to cook on the potbelly stove. At least, Abby had always made it look easy.

Brendan rolled his eyes now, making Helena laugh a bit. To hear that tinkling sound, he'd play the fool any day. "Fine. I'll bow to Maria's expertise in the kitchen and be helpful by makin' the bed."

"Oh," Helena said, sounding disappointed that he hadn't completely switched tasks with Maria. He stood, to cover his nervousness. If he had to help her wash up, now that she was all bright-eyed and looking healthier, he didn't know how he'd keep his hands off her.

And so he made the bed and then made himself scarce, heating water and carrying it upstairs to Maria, so she could help Helena wash up. He went back down to brew a spot of real tea for her while she bathed. When Maria called to him, he hurried in, cup of tea in hand, expecting to deposit Helena back in bed. Instead he found her sitting in the bed looking pleased and comfortable, propped up on several pillows. "Well, aren't you lookin' more like the beautiful Mrs. Kane?"

"Liar. I feel exhausted again," she said, and sighed.

He grinned. "Should I have said you look like you were dragged backward through the keyhole? Twice?"

She pulled a face. "Did you have to be so honest?"

"Apparently, as you were supposed to wait in the chair where I left you. No wonder you've tired yourself out."

"I hate putting anyone to trouble for me."

"It's my job to take care of you, just as it's Maria's."

"But I pay Maria. And…Doc says we can't…" Her blush finished her thought just fine, despite her hesitation.

"That's enough of that. Makin' love isn't about payment. It never was. Not between us. And it can wait for Doc's go-ahead. I can wait."

"You don't want me?"

She sounded so unsure of herself. Of them. "Darlin', why do ya think I bowed out of helpin' you wash up? A man can take only so much when he's finally back with his woman. Especially after a three-year dry spell."

Her tired eyes widened. "You didn't…?"

He lifted her hand to his lips, placing one kiss on her

palm and closing her fingers around it, then kissing the back. He met her gaze. "I took my vows as seriously as I know you did. Why was it we kept tryin' to hurt each other, even to the point of lyin' to accomplish it, when neither of us are liars?"

"Hurt can be deeper than scruples, I suppose," she said, then put her head back and closed her eyes. "Oh, I'm so tired. I guess Doc is right about waiting, huh?"

Brendan started to agree, when her breathing changed. She'd tumbled into sleep. He brushed a stray lock off her cheek, then leaned forward and kissed her. "Sleep, lovey. I'll be here waitin' for you, just as you've been waitin' for me all these stupid wasted years. I promise."

Chapter Nine

"Do I smell maple syrup?" Helena called out to her sister-in-law as the scent floated into the room ahead of her. Helena's stomach growled as Abby arrived, tray in hand.

"I'd say you're a mite hungry if that growling tummy is anything to go by," she replied with a chuckle. "Brendan told Maria you'd asked for flapjacks, but she'd already cooked up Indian pudding. She promises those flapjacks tomorrow. I added a bit of maple syrup to this instead of molasses. That's the only way Bren would eat porridge of any kind as a boy. Ma used to tap the maple trees in the woods near Wheatonburg to make her own. She spoiled him."

"The same way you're spoiling me. And Brendan is, too."

Helena straightened her coverlet so the bed tray Brendan had crafted for her convalescence would sit evenly over her legs. Abby patted her shoulder. "You deserve it. You needed the rest. And you have to let Bren work out some of these guilty feelings eating at him."

Abby sat on the bed. "He feels terrible that none of us were here for you the last time you were hurt. So do I."

Helena's breath stalled in her lungs. "Last time?" she managed to ask.

"Doc told Brendan you were hurt in a stampede in Shamrock's early days, and that it was serious. Josh and I were in town. Why wouldn't you have sent for us? We're your family."

For a second or two Helena gritted her teeth. She didn't think she'd be able to unlock her jaw to speak. She'd kill Doc as soon as he let her out of this bed. "That old gossip," she finally managed to say. "Doc had no right. Is that all he told Bren?" She held her breath, praying he hadn't said too much.

Abby, looking pensive, said, "Only that. Why?"

Helena was a bad liar. She'd succeeded in Wheatonburg because she'd been desperate and trying to save Brendan's life. She'd acted a bit unstable, but they'd been looking for wild actions and not subtle expressions from her. Now Helena looked away from Abby's clever gaze and picked at a piece of fuzz on the counterpane. Her chest tightened and the air dammed in her throat. "I don't want Bren feeling guiltier than he already does," she said. That *was* part of it. "I was shot saving him, and he knows it. When did Doc tell him?"

Abby frowned. "The day your fever spiked. Why?"

"Because I never wanted Bren to come back to me out of guilt."

"I know my brother. He's crazy for you. You got hurt and he realized nothing was more important than being with you. He cares."

Helena's breathing eased a bit. Caring was good. It had to be enough. Hopefully, he wouldn't question her too closely about the stampede. Even two and a half years later, she wasn't strong enough to deal with the loss. Her guilt over it, coupled with residual anger at Bren, was enough to cope with right then.

Lying here with nothing to occupy her, she'd already had too much time to think. Clamping down on thoughts of that horrible day was hard enough on a regular busy day around the ranch. Dwelling on it only made the loss harder to handle.

For going on two years she'd given herself five minutes every morning and five at dusk to remember, and pray for peace of mind. Then she'd put it away. And that had worked for her.

Now life promised to become a dream come true. Or as close to one as she could hope for.

Bren had promised to leave the rangers after he stopped the raids. The longer he stayed at Shamrock, working the ranch, learning at Mallory's side, the easier it was to believe he'd be happy here.

He'd even agreed to look at the ranch's books as soon as she was up to it, which showed even more progress. The numbers in the books represented money. Her money. And that had always been the sticking point between them.

Abby put a hand on her shoulder, drawing Helena's attention. "You never said why you didn't let us know you'd been hurt."

"Because then you'd be obligated to tell Brendan. As I said, I didn't want him back because he felt guilty."

Abby snorted. "Let him feel guilty. He should have been here with you."

Helena bit her lip. "I understand why he wasn't. I hurt his pride."

Abby opened her mouth to say something, but then shook her head and seemed to change her mind. "I only meant a little guilt is good for the soul sometimes. And he came back well in advance of your injuries this time, because he was worried about you."

"Are you tellin' tales about me, Abaigeal Kane Wheaton," Brendan growled from the doorway. "And what is that I smell?" He scooted to the bed, picked up the spoon and dipped it into the untouched bowl of Indian pudding.

Abby planted her hands on her hips and turned to face him. "Brendan Joseph Kane," she said, in that curious whole-name address he and Abby used when annoyed with each other. "If you eat her breakfast, she isn't going to get her strength back."

"Granted." He scooped up a big spoonful and moved it toward Helena's mouth. "It'll stick to your ribs, lovey. And it's a treat. Eat up, now."

Helena opened her mouth, then snatched the spoon. "I think I can manage to feed myself." Before he could object, she dug in, feeling ridiculously envious of Abby and Brendan's close relationship.

She watched them chat and tease each other as she ate. Every year of her childhood her Christmas wish had been for a new mother and a brother or sister. She had wanted someone to play with. Someone to keep her company on the long trips and in lonely hotel rooms. Her life would have been so different if she hadn't always been alone except for a tutor and her father. Maybe if she had learned she couldn't have everything she wanted, she wouldn't have been so determined to marry Brendan that frightening night they'd fled Pennsylvania ahead of the Pinkertons. She'd been hell-bent certain Brendan would eventually see it her way because he loved her. Hadn't her father always given in because he'd loved her, too?

As Brendan took the empty bowl and tray away, Daniel crept into the room. "Hi, Aunt Helena," the boy whispered, his expression grave and unsure.

Helena felt her heart gladden. "Daniel. Oh, I've missed you."

"I finally got to come see you today. Da stayed at the store so I could come out with Ma. I've been real worried about you. And Uncle Brendan, too. Those Ghost Warriors are just plain scary."

"Come here, Danny. I could use a hug from my favorite nephew."

He rolled his eyes. "I'm your only nephew," he said, and settled on his knees next to the bed. Helena brushed her hand through his hair as he gave her a sweet kiss on her cheek, then scooted back onto the chair at her side.

She held out her hand to him, giving his a squeeze, and said, "I promise these Ghost Warriors aren't anything but very bad real men bent on scaring us all. They were bullies and your uncle Brendan knew how to deal with them. We're all fine. Hopefully, no one will ever hear from them again after the thrashing the men gave them that night."

Daniel's blue eyes sparkled with delight now that he'd been reassured. "And you, Aunt Helena. You killed three of them. Pow. Pow. Pow."

Helena frowned, hating to disappoint her nephew. "No, honey. I just wounded those men. They aren't dead. Aren't they in Tierra del Verde's jail?"

She looked at Brendan, who winced and moved around the bed to sit next to her. After taking her hand, he said, "No, lovey. They aren't in jail." His hand squeezed hers.

"Bren, just tell me," she insisted.

"Once the raiders saw the opportunity to escape, they killed their own wounded."

Unsure how she felt at that moment, she stared out the window. If she hadn't wounded those men, they wouldn't have been killed. She looked down at her and Bren's linked hands. What else could she have done? The men she'd shot had been charging him and Dylan. The raiders would have killed them. They'd left her no choice.

"I hated to lie to ya," Brendan said after a few moments of silence, "but you were so badly hurt, then sick with fever. Doc didn't want us to talk to you about the raid. He wanted to lessen the chance you'd have nightmares and open up your wound, thrashin' around the way you did that first night."

She looked up. Worry creased Bren's forehead and tension bracketed his mouth. He sounded as if he felt he needed to walk on eggs around her. And that wasn't fair, to either of them. She wouldn't let those killers heap guilt on her, nor would she let their actions burden Brendan from their shameful graves on Boot Hill.

Stiffening her spine, Helena sat a little straighter, as her father had taught her to do. "Stand up straight and face life head-on," he'd always said. "Speak from a position of power and right, even if you haven't one iota of strength left in you."

"I built Shamrock," she said, holding Brendan's gaze by sheer will. Harry Conwell would have expected nothing less of her. "I came back to defend her. Her men. And you. Mostly you. They would have killed you—

killed all of us. I'm fine with what I had to do. They left none of us with a choice. And they paid for it with their lives."

Brendan nodded, his eyes shining with pride. "You're a strong woman, Helena Kane. I doubted that strength. I thought you'd turn tail and run back East if I left you to your own devices. I didn't see how a pampered society princess could give up mansions and fine hotels for a life in Texas running a cattle operation. I was wrong and I won't make that mistake again."

Hearing the conviction in Bren's voice made her pulse quicken. She continued to hold his gaze. "I won't pretend I didn't think about retreating East a few times. But coming West was a dream I'd had since I was fifteen, when I found a dime novel my tutor left lying around. I read it over and over that year. But life has a way of making dreams seem foolish. I'd nearly forgotten all those wonderful wishes until we met. Hearing you talk about your plans to head West made my dream feel less childish. I knew I could belong here—"

"But Ma…!" Daniel's plaintive tones floating up the hall interrupted them.

"Hush. We're giving your uncle and aunt a few minutes alone. We'll be here the rest of the day. You'll see plenty of both of them," Abby answered.

Brendan snickered. "So much for my sister's graceful exit." Then his gaze grew serious. "Back when we met, you never said a thing about a dime novel or wanting to escape Gowery. You only said the West sounded wonderful."

"My time with you meant too much. You were more than a friend. More than a lover. You were sanity at a time when I was little more than a prisoner and a commodity. I didn't want you to think I was only using you to escape. Without you none of those dreams would have mattered.

"Then you realized how much money I'd inherited, who I was, and you said you had nothing to offer me. You wouldn't see me. Talk to me. Before I could find a way to get you to listen to me, Franklin dragged me back to New York and started trying to peddle me to the highest bidder."

"Jaysus. Sometime I'd love to get my hands on him." Brendan paced across the room. "I'd like to kick *myself* in the tail, too."

She couldn't laugh over the past, though she was sure Brendan had meant for her to at least chuckle. Secrets. They were dangerous. Look how innocently the truth about the deaths of the raiders she'd shot had come to light just now.

Before he found some other way to try distracting her, it was time to bring one of her secrets to light. Time to test this fragile union before she put too much stock in promises made out of fear and regret.

She held out her good hand, and he moved toward her and took it, sinking down next to her. Her tone serious, she related, "I was furious. My life lay in tatters around me and Franklin was trying to make me encourage certain men—men I hated because they weren't you. I wanted only you." She blinked back tears, unable to look at Brendan, though she could feel the sudden stiffness in his body.

She forced herself to go on. "Then one of the men I'd met before my father was killed began to court me seriously. I lashed out at him, and all my hurt and anger came pouring out. I told him about us—*all* about us. I thought it would discourage him. But he went to Franklin, thinking you'd taken advantage of me."

Brendan did something she hadn't expected, hadn't dared hope for. He exhaled, brushed his thumb over the back of her hand, then bent to kiss it before tipping his head up so they were eye to eye. She was shocked to her toes to see he wore a small, understanding smile. "I knew it had to be something like that," he said. "It's all in the past."

Would he never do as she expected? He wasn't angry at all. Perplexed, she stared at him. "Why aren't you angry? I lashed out in spite and nearly got you hanged."

Brendan pressed his lips together and shook his head. "You'd a right to your anger. It was my fault, wasn't it? I took your innocence, then discarded you like the pigheaded idiot I am."

She smiled at his teasing ways. "Pigheaded is right," she teased right back, but then got serious again. "You thought you didn't have anything to offer me. You were trying to be noble. But, Bren, what you gave me was happiness and laughter. And a curious kind of freedom, even though I was still under Franklin Gowery's thumb. You wanted me for me, and not for my father's money. Then I bought Shamrock and hurt your pride."

He nodded, but his expression grew more serious, too. "I've told myself both those lies for years."

She blinked. "Lies?"

He raked his fingers through his hair, clearly agitated and worried. "Maybe this should wait. Doc doesn't want you upset. Neither do I."

"*Not* talking to each other hasn't worked, has it?" She reached for his hand and gave it a reassuring squeeze. "Seeing you this worried is going to upset me more than getting whatever it is out in the open. What do you mean, lies?"

He sighed. "Fine. All along I told myself I broke off our unofficial engagement for your good because I had so little to offer you. After you were shot and Abby saw how upset I was, my little sister held a clear mirror up and made me look in it. What I saw was how blind and hypocritical I've been. It wasn't all pride, lovey. I'm afraid mostly it was hatred."

She blinked back tears.

"Not of you," he went on quickly. "Men like Joshua's father and Franklin Gowery enslave people. They use money to do it. When I found out how wealthy you were I—I…"

Perhaps it was her turn to surprise him. She slid her hand under his and interwove their fingers, holding on as tightly as her wound allowed. "I know, Bren. Your hatred bled over to me. I saw it in your eyes that day I told you how much money I'd have once I had access to it. Suddenly you wouldn't listen to anything I said."

"We're a couple of prize idiots." He leaned in closer. "I knew your secret and you knew mine." A smile tipped his full lips, then he moved nearer, his gaze soft and slumberous. Against her lips he whispered, "Two prize idiots fated to be together." Then he let his eyes close and their lips seemed to melt together. The oneness with him and the tenderness of his kiss brought tears springing to Helena's eyes. His hand moved to her breast and hope for a real future erupted in her heart and made it pound.

He continued his gentle caress until his fingers bumped into her bandage. Then he cursed softly and sat back with a deep sigh. "Enough of that. Clemens has spies everywhere," he growled, his voice low, his expression strained. But he forced a grin, and even though he sounded frustrated and disgruntled, he was clearly determined to behave.

Helena had to laugh. "Doc means well. Really he does. And he has a good heart."

"I suppose he does. And he saved you, didn't he? The man is a king. A prince among men. And a pain in the tail all wrapped up in his stuffy frock coat, bright white shirts and silly neckties."

She patted Brendan's hand, still smiling, not wanting him to feel his teasing had failed. It had always been so easy to smile around Bren. And just as easy to cry; hard times had been such a shock and so heartbreaking after all the laughter.

When she thought of all the energy she'd used trying to hate him, she wanted to scream at that foolish woman. What had she thought to accomplish? Perhaps Brendan hadn't been the only one suffering from an excess of pride.

Chapter Ten

At dawn, two weeks after the raid, Brendan walked down the hall in his stockinged feet on his way to check on Helena. He hated not saying goodbye before leaving for his meeting, but he didn't want to wake her. Not only because Doc said she needed rest, but because he didn't want to lie about seeing the three rangers coming in today.

He sighed, his mind sliding to Lucien Avery. Brendan had checked with Alex and Joshua. Sadly, the men knew the Helena of today better than he did, though that was quickly changing. He'd wanted their opinion on whether or not she could hide her anger and the betrayal she would feel toward Avery when she learned he was the mastermind of the raids. They agreed she was too open with her feelings and her emotions would show. Which left Brendan keeping the truth from her.

He weighed that against her anger when she found out he'd kept his suspicions about Avery to himself. But her safety was paramount. She'd be in grave danger if she saw Avery and couldn't hide her feelings. Brendan decided keeping silent was worth the risk.

Mallory, Josh and Alex didn't tell their wives for the same reason, and because all three women were in the family way. Their husbands didn't want them upset.

Brendan was to meet up with the rangers about eight that morning, at a canyon a few hours' ride northeast of Tierra del Verde. It was the perfect secluded rendezvous spot.

When the floorboards creaked under his feet, Helena opened her eyes and turned her head to where he stood in the doorway. Caught, he set his boots down in the hall and entered the room. "Good morning, lovey."

"Don't good morning me! Get me out of this bed, Brendan Kane. I mean it. I simply cannot lie here another day. I refuse to be a complacent patient from here on."

He grinned. "You're becomin' a poet, Helena Kane."

"Today isn't a day for teasing me, Brendan," she warned through her pretty teeth.

"It's a sad day when my own sweet Helena all but growls at me because I said good mornin'. Are you restive?"

"I've rested enough. If I *rest* any more, I swear I'll get a pistol and shoot the next person who tells me to!"

He valiantly fought a smile. "*Restive,* lovey. As in fidgety, agitated or irked."

"I'm all those and more." She took a breath. "I'm sorry I'm being impatient with you. I just woke from a dream about being chained to this bed."

"In that case, I'll tell you what we'll do," he said, and quickly let the lie fall from his tongue. Too quickly. "I have to meet a ranger who's passing through, and give him a message from my commanding officer. I expect to be back no later than noon. Suppose I carry you outside for a few hours once I get back?"

He knew his skill at lying had kept him alive while dealing with the Lyons gang, but it wasn't a gift he was particularly proud of. That was one of the reasons he wanted to settle down, a life with Helena being the chief reason.

Good as he was at it, her blue eyes still shot sparks, like twin flames. "Suppose *you* go about your business and Maria helps me dress, and then I'll *walk* to the porch."

"Oh. It's that way, is it?" Brendan raised both eyebrows, trying to look surprised at her rebellion, when he'd expected some sort of mutiny days ago. He breathed a big sigh of relief that she was finally showing signs of being truly on the mend. Still, he daren't let on how thankful he was not wanting to encourage her to overdo.

She pushed herself to a sitting position, which by now she seemed able to do without pain. With her legs bent under the coverlet and her good arm braced atop her knees, she curled her small hand into a tight fist. "I can't stand this a minute longer. I need to get up and out of this room. I'm already weak as a kitten and it's getting worse. Please, Bren."

"Well, it just so happens the good doctor says you can get up and put on a dressing gown if you promise…" He stopped and held up his index finger for emphasis. "A solemn vow, mind you! Promise that all you'll do is take air on the porch, sittin' your cute little bottom on that comfy wicker chaise. And you'll nap for at least two hours this afternoon, either there or in bed."

"I solemnly vow," she said quickly.

Brendan eyed her with suspicion. "That was a bit too easy."

"I promise. Truly I do. For a view of something other than these four walls, and the feel of the breeze and the sun, I'll do anything."

Anything? The second that thought hit, his mind went straight below his belt, and so did all the blood in his brain. It was too provocative a statement for a man close to the end of a three-year-long dry spell. And there she was, innocent as the day she was born, clearly having no idea what she'd said.

He was an animal, sure as before him was an angel come to earth. And her not yet out of her sickbed. But he couldn't seem to summon anything but a grin. "Now why did you go and put it that way?"

She blushed, her cheeks going rosy.

His grin widened and hers went sassy, telling him she didn't mind that his thoughts had gone where they had. Unfortunately, he wasn't in a position to do a damn thing about his thoughts or hers. It was torture, plain and simple.

He gave his most long-suffering sigh. "And what are ya grinnin' for, temptress? Do ya want Doc to castrate me? And don't go sayin' he wouldn't, because he looked mighty serious when he threatened it." Brendan folded his arms. "In retaliation, no kisses goodbye. Not with you looking all pink and soft in that bed. I've plans for you *and* my private parts in the near future, so I'm willin' to wait for the go-ahead from Doc for the sake of my manly equipage.

"Now if you'll excuse me, I'll go set things up with Maria." With that said, and with the sound of her throaty chuckle following him, he walked out, grabbed his

boots and headed for the kitchen. He stopped halfway
there and sat on the living room sofa, put on his boots
and adjusted the fit of his suddenly too tight trousers.
He was mighty glad for the hat he held in front of himself while he filled Maria in on the plans for the day.

Then, feeling a bit more in control, he went back to
Helena's room, helped her get into her pretty dressing
gown and carried her out to the porch, where the housekeeper waited with her breakfast on a tray. After a quick
peck on the cheek from him, and one more promise of
good behavior from her, Brendan headed for the barn.

As Harry carried him away from Shamrock, the fool
gelding had a decidedly happy spring in his step. Of
course, the simple beast had pranced right up to the
porch regardless of Brendan's attempts to control him
when they passed the house. In spite of the flowers
Harry had trampled trying to get closer, Helena had
rewarded him for his bad behavior with a happy good-
morning pat when he'd hung his big head over the porch
rail. And she was rewarded for *her* bad behavior with
a lippy, horsey kiss on the cheek.

Brendan was damn happy himself. She'd sent him
off with a smile bright as the morn, a blown kiss and a
merry wave. She'd been none the wiser about the seriousness of his meeting or the white lie he'd told.

The closer he got to the rendezvous point the more
the whole situation weighed on him again. He hoped
and prayed this idea would be the beginning of the end
of Lucien Avery.

About eight, watchful and alert, Brendan approached
the piñon-covered hillock he'd been headed toward. It
rose sharply in the midst of the rolling Texas Hill
Country. The incline was so steep it gave the instant

impression the formation would be easier ridden around than over.

He tethered Harry deep in the piñon grove then scrambled up to the crest. If someone really looked, there was a hint that this was more than a steep hill, because a tall, majestic bald cypress, a tree that usually grew along streams and rivers, speared upward from somewhere on the other side. At the crest, the ground fell off sharply. The drop was steep and rocky, like a canyon wall. Running along the floor, as the cypress indicated, was a stream.

From the top of the hillock, Brendan was able to check for observers, to make sure the meeting would remain secret. Spotting no one, he skittered back down the slope, took up Harry's reins and led the big black to a narrow fissure he'd found last winter. It led into the best natural hiding place he'd ever come across.

He loosened his saddle and gave the gelding an affectionate rub along his white blaze, down to his velvety nose. Harry settled nicely, so Brendan sat under the bald cypress, tipped his hat over his eyes and leaned back for a bit of a rest while awaiting his friends.

About ten minutes later he heard the clip-clop of hooves echoing from the fissure, and got to his feet. Ted James came along the rocky path first.

Most folks who met Ted off the job thought he was just a quiet, shy kid, but they'd be wrong, because most folks saw what he wanted them to see. He was only twenty-three, but he had a soul as old as the Texas hills he rode for the law. His hair was long, wavy and black as pitch, his skin well tanned. He wore Levi's jeans and shirts that matched his wintery eyes, which were a fathomless gray.

Ted could be cold and deliberately hard, but he was loyal to a fault. No one knew his origins. He never spoke of family or a childhood. In fact, he rarely spoke at all unless it was part of a personality he'd assumed. But when he did say something you were smart to listen, because his intelligence was keener than almost anyone Brendan knew.

He nodded and Ted nodded back, moving his way as Severn Duvall came into view. He was Ted's opposite in looks, though their personalities were quite similar. Traveling with those two made for quiet days and nights, and way too much time to think. Unless there was a deck of cards involved, and then you were lucky to have your shirt come morning.

Striking and unforgettable as Severn was, no one had ever guessed him as a lawman, and Brendan doubted anyone ever would. He had the palest hair and eyes Brendan had come across, and he was as fast with a gun as he was with a deck of cards. He dressed like a riverboat gambler, in expensive formal clothes, his civilian reputation being that of a near legendary gambler. As a ranger, his reputation was as hard as the rock surrounding him. Though he could turn on the charm as a pretense, that's what it was—pretense.

Brendan had only four years on Severn, but something had added a decade to the look in the other man's eyes. He'd once said his first name meant "boundary." The name fit. No one crossed the invisible borders Severn carried with him, as palpable as his Colt. Brendan hoped he was around when the walls cracked and fell. It would be some show.

Nathaniel Richards came in last, wearing his customary buckskins. Nate had a full head of short, dark brown hair, blue-green eyes, and was damned good-looking, if the saloon girls who flocked around him were anything to judge by. If he had a fault it was that he liked them too much in return. He came across as amiable and fun loving, but even when distracted by his current dove, he was as deadly with a knife as he was with a pistol or rifle. He wrote to his mother back East religiously, but like Ted, he never talked about the family he'd left behind.

After shaking hands, Bren got right to the point, anxious to get back to Helena. He explained the history of the raids and their brutality. When he mentioned the number of men, women and children Avery had ordered killed, fury seemed to burn more brightly in Ted's eyes than in those of the others.

"You okay with this? If you don't want in, I'll understand. You'll be workin' for the snake till we have enough to see him hanged. I don't want anything less than murder charges leveled and proved."

Ted's even white teeth showed in a chilly smile. "Wouldn't miss it for the world. When do we start?"

"That's the first stumbling block you'll have to overcome. You'll have to get hired. We hurt him." Brendan grinned nastily. "He has at least twenty positions open all of a sudden. We're hoping he's hiring through someone in Mountain Home or Leesburg."

"Mountain Home," Nate Richards said. "I came straight from Huntsville. Got myself put in with that prisoner you wanted questioned. I thought Lynch would be more likely to open up to another inmate. He was a talkative son of a bitch, but stupid as a stone. He was never more than a cowpuncher for Avery. Apparently he failed the boss by getting fired from a neighboring ranch he was supposed to be spying on."

"Unfortunately, you ate bad grub for nothing," Brendan told him. "I knew all that already. He was at the Rocking R and insulted the foreman's wife. Idiot."

Richards let his eyes go lazy. "You doubting me? I'd still be back in a cell if Lynch hadn't given me something usable, and you know it. He found out about Avery through a guy named Tolliver over in Mountain Home. This Tolliver put him in touch with Avery."

"Tolliver, huh?" Brendan pressed his lips in a straight line and gave a sharp nod. "We'll have to make sure we collect him when this is all over. Must be something we can put him away for. You get anything else?"

"Just that Avery keeps the legal part of the Bar A and his cowhands as separate from the others as possible. Apparently he spoils these men, calls them guards. They never leave the ranch, and act as guards in the house and around the ranch. He invites them to dinner and provides entertainment in the form of doves Tolliver brings to the Bar A once a month."

Brendan nodded again. "They must be the raiders. No one has ever seen the men who died at Shamrock before, so we can't tie them to Avery. I've been wondering how he talked them into staying out of town. I thought about sneakin' over there in a few days to see if I can spot any of the raiders."

Ted James grinned. "Kane, are you trying harder than usual to buck out on us?"

Brendan turned to glare at him. "I'm not trying to get killed, but they nearly killed my wife. I want these bastards."

"How is she?" Nate asked quietly.

Brendan's memory went back to the greeting he'd gotten at dawn that morning, and he grinned. "She's mad as a wet hen at being kept down for so long."

Nate chuckled like a man who knew women inside out and backward, too. "Ah, so she's on the mend?"

Bren nodded as his mind skittered further back than that morning. Back to the raid. To seeing the muzzle flash and hearing her bedroom window shatter seconds later. To the eons it took for him to fight his way to the house. "Thank God she *is* on the mend. I want this bastard and every mother's son whose gun he's hired. I want to see them all hangin' high, but especially Avery," Brendan growled. "I want mine to be the last face that bastard sees. And I'll be grinnin' from ear to ear."

Severn nodded. "We'll see what we can do about that. Meanwhile, my friend, I can't help thinking only two of us should work our way into Avery's outfit. You look like you could use one of us nearby to guard your back."

Bren hadn't told them about the way the raiders had concentrated on him that night. "What has you all so damned cautious? I'm not plannin' to get myself killed."

"We know you," Ted James said. "Are you trying to say you're not so pissed you're being reckless? Are you claiming to be objective about this, hombre?"

Of course he couldn't say that, dammit!

"All right," Brendan admitted. "I can't promise at this point I'm at all objective. We'll play it your way, Severn."

"I'm going into the Bar A," Ted declared. "One of you can keep an eye on this crazy Irishman."

"I didn't say I needed a nursemaid," Brendan argued.

"Still, Ted's got a point. I'll stay behind," Nathaniel

offered. "If you're gone from Shamrock, someone has to watch your wife."

"You keep your hands off my wife," Bren warned, only half in fun.

Nate grinned and spread his hands in surrender. "I take it the marriage is working out again?"

"It is," he said. "But I want you in at the Bar A with Ted. If someone stays behind, it should be Severn. I was never sure you'd get hired anyway, Severn," Bren said, turning to the blond man. "Like I was tellin' you, they've always attacked dressed as Comanche. We let the newspaper know there were twenty dead Anglos left behind at Shamrock, so there's no reason for the disguises to continue, but who knows?"

Brendan shrugged, thinking how Avery had endangered the lives of the Comanche who now lived on a reservation. The army could have decided to retaliate with a raid of its own. Maybe a just punishment would be to turn Avery and his minions over to the chiefs and let them handle the manner of execution.

No maybes about it. His objectivity was shot to hell.

Getting his mind back on Severn Duvall, Brendan continued, "Besides the disguises, you're pretty damned distinctive looking, and you're gettin' to be well known, too. That could disqualify you in Avery's eyes. Also, a set of ears might be a good thing at the Golden Garter. There's a new place in town, too. It's called Connor's Saloon and Gamblin' Den. You'd fit right in there. And Avery's regular men might let slip some information they don't realize is important."

Duvall looked mighty pleased with the change in his assignment. "So these two should head to Mountain Home and look up this Tolliver hombre, and I'm off to move into Reiman House to get established in the saloons."

"Well, I'm glad to have made your day," Brendan stated, and turned to Harry to tighten the cinch. He mounted and said, "Wait a bit for me to be on my way. I'll see you in town, Severn. Don't take anyone's last dime and go gettin' yourself shot. Keep an eye out for Quinn, too. His deputy is an idiot—the mayor's nephew, unfortunately."

He waved and left his friends behind. With any luck this plan would prevent any more raids, and they'd find enough hard evidence to arrest and convict those responsible.

Chapter Eleven

At the sound of boots on the wooden floor, Helena looked up to see Brendan stroll around the corner of the porch. He smiled broadly as soon as his gaze fell on her. "There's my girl. Still enjoyin' the air, are ya?"

When he got close, she rested her head back against the chaise and smiled up at him. He was so wonderfully tall and strong. She wanted his hands on her in the worst way, but he was determined to keep her at arm's length.

With their history, worry had begun to creep into her thoughts. She'd tried to tell herself her problem was having too much time to think, and that she was imagining things. How was she to know if her doubts were valid or if Doc's orders were really the reason Bren held himself so apart from her? Was it only guilt and their marriage vows keeping him at Shamrock? Their feelings seemed so fragile and there were things neither of them had given voice to yet.

"Well, are ya? Or did Maria abandon you out here?"

She blinked, called back from her dark and confusing thoughts. "You're right. About how lovely it is out here, not about Maria. She pops her head out constantly. How was your day so far? Did you meet with your ranger friend and give him his message?"

Brendan dropped his saddlebag on the porch floor, turned away and grabbed one of the chairs. After bringing it closer, he muttered almost angrily, "It's handled."

He seemed to be having a hard time settling, too. Next he took his hat off, then ran a hand through his damp hair. He sighed, dropped his hat atop the saddlebag and shook his head. Even as he sank into the wicker chair, he was still restless.

"What's wrong, Bren?"

"Oh, nothing. Nothing at all. I don't like playing delivery boy, is all. And it was hotter than Hades in the sun. But it's much better here in the shade of the porch. So how was your day, lovey?"

"Too quiet," she complained, wondering if he was truly so tense because he was annoyed over having to pass a message to another ranger. That didn't seem at all like Brendan. Was he dissatisfied with the day-to-day life at Shamrock? Had delivering that message reminded him of the excitement he was missing?

"I shouldn't complain," she went on. "At least there's a view of the place from here. There was a time I wanted nothing but one day with no work to do and no need to look at a saddle, let alone mount up into one. Now I can't wait to be strong and capable of a long day's work."

"I'm here now. There's no need for you to be slavin' at a man's job if you don't want to, lovey. If you're wantin' that, though, you'll get there. Gettin' healthy takes time, is all. You lost a lot of blood, then you had that infection to beat. Maybe the next time you see Doc, he'll lift a few of his mean-spirited and coldhearted regulations." Brendan's voice was gentle. Then his lips curved in a smile so sweetly teasing it brought tears to her eyes.

Were Doc's restrictions really all that kept Bren's touch so impersonal, his words so careful?

She looked away, blinking furiously to clear her vision. What was wrong with her? Since the raid her emotions had been tenuous at best.

Helena sucked in a shocked breath and her thoughts fled as Bren tunneled his arms under her thighs and back to lift her. But not to take her to her room and confine her in those same four walls. Instead he moved her against the arm of the chaise, then slid onto it next to her. He was so wonderfully close as he wrapped her carefully in his embrace.

Strange. Even though he lived a completely different life from when they'd met, there was still the same lime and bay essence to Brendan's scent. He'd had a nearly religious fixation on daily baths back then because he so hated the mines. But after going from miner to Texas Ranger—pickax to gun, coal dust to gunpowder—there was still that clean, tangy scent about him.

Despite all the outward changes the West had made in Brendan, he was the same handsome, teasing, sensual man she'd unwisely tumbled in love with. Those twinkling green eyes were still lit with mischief, able to tease or arouse with a look. His humor made her laugh. His stinging remarks could make her cry. His grin made her want to either slap him or kiss him, depending upon his intent. No wonder she'd never been able to evict him from her heart. Who could?

Certainly not her.

She took a deep breath and rolled a bit to her side to face him, then rested her cheek against his chest. "Just hold me for a while," she breathed, and sighed when he eased over to his back so she could settle against him. Tired of her conflicting thoughts, she realized she didn't need words. *I love you* hadn't held him before. Neither had their vows.

He had to want a life with her enough to stay.

He took her chin and tipped her face to his. "You're lookin' and soundin' a little lost, lovey. Try to buck up. It's killin' me to see you so down. Now tell Bren what has tears fallin' from those pretty blue eyes of yours."

She was a mess. She hadn't even realized she was actually crying, until he mentioned it and wiped her cheeks with his thumbs. The whole truth wasn't something she was ready to admit, so once again she told herself a partial truth was better than nothing. "I feel useless and unsure, Bren. All I do is lie around, with people waiting on me. It's like my old life has come back to haunt me." She sniffled. Her partial explanation made her feel silly and childish.

She'd worked hard to build this new life. Her old life was haunting her? What drivel. It was the uncertainty between them that was haunting her. Dare she ask why he'd been so standoffish since she'd begun to heal?

The physical side of their relationship had never been a problem, but now it seemed to be. She had to at least address that. "You say you're afraid to come near me, but I don't think it has a thing to do with Doc Clemens and his orders."

Brendan caressed her arm. "Of course it does. It's all that's stoppin' me from carrying you off to your bedroom, then…" He paused and gave a half groaning, half annoyed sigh. "Maybe what you're sensin' is that I'm…I'm a bit afraid."

She stared at him, growing more certain that what she saw was regret and not fear. He'd never been afraid of anything. Bren had even poked at Franklin Gowery, taunting the powerful man with lies that were sure to infuriate him and have him vibrating with impotent anger.

Then again, fear wouldn't be easy for Brendan to admit. "Nothing scares you," she said finally. And in spite of her certainty, she prayed he'd told the truth.

Bren kissed her forehead. "Did ya know I was scared witless every day I was in the mines?"

She raised her eyebrows in disbelief.

"No. Truly. I didn't only hate the work and disrespect, I hate closed-in spaces. They make me sweat bullets and make my skin crawl. Just as it's true I'm tryin' hard to be careful of you. As careful as I can be, Doc's threats notwithstandin'. Try to understand, lovey. I thought I'd lost you. I was soaked in your blood by the time Mallory found us. And I was responsible for your gettin' hurt."

Was this the regret she'd seen? "No, Bren. Don't take that on yourself. You had me safe with Alex and Patience. I came back of my own accord. It was my choice."

"You came back because you thought I was defendin' Shamrock even though I'd never wanted it. And now you know that wasn't true. So you came back because I'd lied to you for three years."

"Bren, you know what I think? I think we have to stop looking back and worrying about the past. Please. I can't keep doing that. It'll come to no good." She feared he'd discern the panic in her voice.

"But I feel responsible," he countered, obviously more centered on his own guilt than on her fretfulness or the reason for it. "Do you remember when I told you I was afraid the raiders were ready to move on Shamrock?"

She nodded.

"And do ya remember I thought they were comin' before I could strengthen Shamrock's defenses?"

She caressed his jaw, a bit stubbly despite his early morning shave. "You said they'd have come after us eventually, anyway. Wasn't that true?"

He shrugged. "I suppose. Your Shamrock is quite a prize."

"*Our* Shamrock, remember? You haven't been avoiding me to get me ready for you to leave again, have you?" That fear in one way or another caused all her apprehension.

He looked so stricken that his expression alone drove a lot of the worry from her heart. She no longer needed reassurance, but he reiterated all his promises, anyway. "Of course I'm not leavin', lovey. I told you, I'm resignin' from the rangers as soon as we arrest the one responsible for the raids, along with his hired guns. I'm stayin' right here to work Shamrock and give you lots of babies. I'll still be right here on this porch to rock beside you when our sons run Shamrock. I've just been worried."

He was worried… She smiled up at him, but as her mind replayed his words, she frowned. *Lots of babies.* "No more looking back," she exclaimed, then took a deep, calming breath, realizing she'd been the one who'd looked back. "Right? We move ahead. Look ahead," she said, as she laid her head back on his chest, closed her eyes and breathed him in. That calmed her.

"Forgettin' what an idiot I was is a mite hard to do."

Helena looked back up to see that same tortured expression in his eyes.

He continued, "When I found you—" But his voice broke and he had to clear his throat. "I was afraid I'd waited too long to make everything right. When I look at you, still so fragile, that night comes bursting back every time. Think how you'd have felt had it been me so grievously hurt, and if you'd come out of the battle with just a few scrapes."

She poked his tight belly. "You had more than a few scrapes and you know it. And I for one am glad those were your only injuries." She stretched a bit to kiss his jaw, but he looked down at the same moment and her innocent kiss landed just next to his lips.

He moved a fraction and caught her mouth in a kiss that was anything but innocent. As he slanted his head to take her mouth more completely, she gloried in his tortured moan. It vibrated through her, calling out to her in an elemental way that defied definition.

She rejoiced in the knowledge that he was as helpless to escape this attraction between them as she was. Again she told herself this was enough. Then his tongue traced the seam of her lips and she opened to the demand, which spoke even louder in the silence that had suddenly fallen over their little corner of the world.

Brendan was her other half. She was his. They needed each other and were only half-alive when they weren't together. Words had always gotten in the way and put distance between them in the past.

Their tongues wrapped around each other hungrily. The rough texture of his had tremors zinging through her, making her stomach flip, her head spin and her body melt into his. She prayed she affected him the same way.

His hand moved to her breast and his thumb found her nipple. He rolled and kneaded it gently, driving her happily mad.

She made a noise in the back of her throat born of the best kind of frustration she'd ever felt. She was suddenly thankful she'd only ever felt this in Bren's arms.

This was theirs.

When he moved on to her other breast, his fingers brushed her bandage and he sucked in a quick, startled breath. *Oh, no, not again,* she thought, as his groan rumbled against her lips and his hand withdrew.

He planted his knee on the chaise and started to push himself away from her. "Dammit!" he growled out, then turned the air blue with words she'd only ever heard by accident. And never from him.

She grabbed his shirt. "Don't you dare. Not again," she repeated, aloud this time.

Braced over her, looking both frustrated and stricken, he said, "I have to, lovey. I have to. Doc says—"

"I don't care what Doc says. At least hold me. Please just hold me. It feels so good to have you close."

He sank back down and took her face in his big hand, pressing his forehead to hers. "Yer killin' me. You know that, don't you?"

She stared into his darkened eyes and smiled. "Come to my room tonight and I'll help you out with some of this frustration."

"I'm not frus—"

"Don't deny it," she interrupted, and let her hand drift below his belt, finding all the evidence she needed to prove her point. She pressed her palm against him, hoping to tempt him beyond his worry for her.

"Jaysus! Are ya really tryin' to kill me?"

She laughed. Even in her own ears it sounded deep and more enticing than she'd hoped. "I'm not asking you to break Doc's antiquated, overprotective rules. I'll—"

"I get what you're suggestin'." He shuddered as she continued to knead his erection. "For God's sake, don't actually say the words or I'll lose the rest of my mind, minx. Wonderful as it sounds, I don't know if it's a good idea. I want more than that. I want you so bad I've been walkin' bowlegged for a week."

She laughed again. "My goodness." He grinned, but the smile faded and his jaw dropped when she added, "Now I know what Maria meant this morning."

Flags of embarrassment appeared on his cheeks. "Maria?"

"Apparently the positioning of your hat didn't fool her, Ranger Kane."

"Women talk about things like that? Jaysus!"

Helena laughed and he cursed again, maybe because all she could think about was her plans for later that night. And those plans were alive in her laughter.

Evening had progressed toward night while Helena reclined on the parlor sofa. She felt better, her energy restored by a long nap.

She heard his footfalls coming in through the dining room doors from the porch. The setting sun glowed orange behind him as he walked toward her.

"You're awake," he said when he saw her. "I didn't wake you, did I?" His tentative, careful tone was a worry. He was terrified to even touch her.

It was as if she'd lost all the ground she'd gained, showing him she was a changed woman. A strong woman. "I'm fine. You're making me feel like I'm an invalid."

"It's only that I'm terrified of you slippin' backward. Of the fever returnin' if you overdo. Or of the wound openin' up if you fall. And you have to admit, you're so weak you could easily fall."

"Bren," she began, trying to hold his gaze, trying to make him see how much what she had to say meant to her. "You know that old saying, to kill someone with kindness? I suddenly understand exactly what that means. The longer I'm confined to bed, or you haul me from place to place, the weaker I get. I know myself. I don't care what Doc Clemens says. Listen to *me*."

Brendan moved closer, squatted down next to her and rubbed the back of his fingers across her cheek in a heartbreaking caress. "I'm sorry. Damn Doc and his rules from now on. We'll start buildin' up your strength tomorrow. And I'm haulin' the mattress from the bed I've been using into your room."

She sighed. "That would be wonderful. I'm still so lonely."

He looked confused. Hadn't she ever told him about how lonely she'd been? No. She'd thought about it, but had never gotten around to saying it.

"Lonely?" he asked. "You've been lonely, too?" He raked a hand through his hair again. "Agh. Of course you have. Sometimes I thought I'd rather die than spend another night alone. It made me a mite reckless now and again. Apparently worried some of the other rangers I've worked with."

What better reason could there be to seduce him?

Tonight he wouldn't be lonely. And neither would she. But tonight had to be mostly about Bren. Even Helena didn't really think she was up to lovemaking. "Would you mind taking me to bed now?"

"Sure, lovey," he said, carefully scooping her up in his arms, then carrying her upstairs. When he stepped through the doorway of her bedroom—and now his, if she got her way—she nipped at his ear. He turned his head to stare down at her, his teeth set, his eyebrows drawn together.

She giggled, her heart feeling lighter than it had in years as she slipped one shirt button after another loose, exposing first his throat, then letting his chest hair peek out. She rubbed the backs of her fingers over the crisp strands, remembering the feel of that deliciously sensual pelt grazing her nipples, ramping up her excitement. Oh, she'd missed him. Missed his touch. Missed touching him.

"Forget that extra mattress," she whispered against his ear, her voice raspy. "There's plenty of room in this bed. We could cuddle up to each other. We are married, after all."

She watched his throat move as he swallowed hard. "I'd not get a wink of sleep."

She stared into his clear green eyes. "That sounds promising."

She rejoiced to see those eyes darken.

"Doc says no. This is entirely different from building your strength."

"Being a lawman has had a detrimental effect on you. I remember a man who loved courting danger and flaunting rules. We made love in a bed of high, late-summer grass that first time and all the following

Sunday. The only thing we used our clothes for was a blanket. We were naked in the woods for hours."

"We're flaunting Doc's rules," he told her, sounding a bit desperate.

"Ah, still worried about your anatomy?"

"You're playin' with fire. Again. Be careful or you might get burned," he warned.

She waited until he put his knee on the bed to lay her down before she replied. "I'm not the one about to be set on fire," she whispered against his ear, keeping her good arm hooked around his neck.

He overbalanced, as she'd hoped he would. He had to drop her legs and put his hand down to keep from falling on her.

She grinned up at him and slipped the last shirt button free. Then she ran her fingers through that delightful crisp hair sprinkled across his hard, well-muscled chest.

"Are you tryin' to torture me?" he growled, but his voice shook a bit and he didn't try to pull away. Instead he sank down over her, caging her while supporting most of his weight in his arms. She reveled in the feeling, but longed to have him closer still. Especially that bulge pressed to her belly. But some things had to wait. Others didn't. "I won't tattle to Doc if you don't."

"No." He slid to the side, leaving his leg bent over hers.

"Then at least kiss me. The way you did this afternoon. You stopped then." She licked her lower lip and pouted. He'd once told her he couldn't resist that expression. That he always wanted to kiss it off her face.

Apparently he'd been serious. In a blink, he'd sucked her lower lip between his teeth. Then came the scrape of those even white teeth, sending shivers coursing through her. She rejoiced in the sensations, while somehow managing to remember her mission. She carefully worked at his fly buttons and he soon sprang into her hand.

Bren sucked in a breath and moaned. He nipped her lip again, then groaned, "You're *killing* me. You understand that, right?"

She smiled against his mouth. "But I can't think of a better way to die. Can you? Let me do this for you."

He dropped his forehead against hers. "I can't let you—" She circled him, her thumb caressing the tip, giving no quarter. She could feel the tremors of need coursing through his body. He tossed his head back, gritted his teeth and gasped for breath.

"Oh, Jaysus," he shouted. "I give in. For God's sake, don't stop now. It's been so long. Too long, dammit."

"I know," she crooned. "So many lonely years for us both."

He curled into her, his face tucked against her neck. She touched and caressed and stroked him until he shook and peaked to a shuddering end, her name on his lips. Then he took her head in his big capable hands and covered her lips with his in a kiss as desperate and devoted as any given any wife in history.

As his breathing quieted, and his pounding heartbeat slowed, she wished he'd shouted out his love and not just her name.

She held those words in her heart, unable to bring herself to be the first to say them. After all, suppose he didn't reciprocate? Once that happened, there'd be no forgetting.

But maybe he feared heartbreak as much as she did.

He called her "lovey" all the time. For now that and his obvious desire for her were enough. They had to be. She closed her eyes and followed him into sleep.

Chapter Twelve

As he came around the bend on the ranch road, Brendan cursed when he saw Doc's buggy parked in front of the house. He sure as Hades didn't need another damned lecture. Bren wasn't as big an idiot as Doc seemed to think. Helena had forgiven him for the hash he'd made of their marriage, so who was Clemens to pass judgment?

Still, he was a husband again and he wanted to be there to hear what the doctor said about Helena's troubling weakness. Bren urged Harry to a faster pace, anxious to be at her side.

He'd gone into town to check with Severn Duvall for a progress report. He and Severn had settled at a back table in the Garter, using poker as a front for their meeting.

Brendan was elated with the headway all three of his friends had made in only a week. Unexpectedly, Severn had managed to befriend Avery over cards, giving Brendan full access to many of the enemy's movements.

Avery was reinforcing his depleted ranks, so with an introductory letter from Tolliver, Ted and Nate had managed to get on his payroll as guards. As a condition of employment, neither was allowed to leave the Bar A. Ted, patrolling with another seasoned guard, had escorted Severn to Avery's home when the gambler stopped by at the invitation of his new friend. Ted had managed to pass Severn a note outlining their duties, and their worry that a new hire was wanted for murder. To them that said Avery intended more raids. Brendan agreed.

He'd stopped to catch Ryan Quinn up on the progress. The sheriff had been watching Severn from afar, unaware that he was a ranger, and not happy having a stranger in town who'd cozied up to Avery. Brendan had next stopped at the bank to check in with Josh, then gone on to the general store to see Abby. He'd picked up a gift for Helena there and headed home.

Dismounting in front of the house now, Brendan looped the reins over the hitching rail and gave Doc's horse a pat. After loosening Harry's saddle, he took the book he'd bought Helena out of his saddlebag. Then he headed to the house, hoping she'd understand why he'd bought this particular volume.

He stepped inside, where the warm feeling of the home Helena had created settled around him like a cozy blanket. It stunned him that she'd continued to hope he'd come back to her as she'd been furnishing the house.

He couldn't help wondering what had changed that hope into the near hate she'd greeted him with the first time their paths had crossed, in town. She hadn't spoken a word that day. The look in her eyes had said it all, even though he'd been instrumental in saving her friend Patience days before. Had it only been time, and the pity or disdain of the people she encountered in town?

The deep rumble of Doc's voice coming from their bedroom washed the questions away. Helena wanted the past forgotten, and Bren would give her what she wished. He'd forget the anger, but not the good memories. They were the reason their crazy wedding had happened in the first place.

He walked down the hall at a quick clip, wondering if Helena had convinced the doctor to lift some of his restrictions.

"Afternoon, Doc." Brendan strode into the room as if it was his own. He grinned. Actually, it was. For the last two nights and for the rest of his days. Just thinking that felt good. As if all was right with the world. "How's my gal doin'?"

Helena's smile was wide and excited. "Doc says I can be up and around, as long as I don't overdo."

Brendan nodded, walked past the doctor and sank to his heels next to her chair. "I've brought you a present." He handed her the package. "I was hopin' this would make restin' a bit easier to handle. I remember you enjoyed *My Wife and I*."

Her eyes bright, she tore into the package. She looked back up as her hands caressed the tooled, red leather cover. Her happy smile spoke volumes. "You remembered."

He ran the back of his fingers over her cheek. "Not a moment of those days has ever left my thoughts." He pivoted on the balls of his feet. "So, Doc, how much can she safely do?"

"She's to keep that arm in the sling for at least a week longer. You can begin a little easy movement a few times a day this week, then it's back into the sling. As for being up and around, she's to do a bit more each day, slowly building her strength. For the next month, no mounting a horse on her own and no hard riding. And absolutely no driving a carriage. Certainly not—"

"Doc," Helena interrupted, exasperated. "I'm not a child. And Brendan isn't my father or my keeper."

"I'm well aware of that, young woman. I also know you won't be happy with half measures. Which is why your husband here needs to know how careful you have to be. And how careful he has to be of you." Clemens looked at Brendan. "No bed play for at least another week. Understood? And nothing rough or adventurous for at least a month."

"Doc!" Helena squealed.

Brendan's laughter bounced off the walls. Still grinning widely, he glanced back at Helena, who'd blushed to the roots of her hair. She looked so sweet. The top part of her shining blond hair was tied up in a ribbon, with the rest hanging around her shoulders in a cascade of silky waves.

"I'll be careful of her," he declared, staring into her pretty blue eyes. "Don't worry, there's no one I'd be more careful with." He said this to Doc, but spoke mostly to her, and she gave him a shy smile. He stood and turned to the older man. "Is there anything else I need to know about?"

Doc glanced at Helena and frowned. "No, I suppose your wife can relay anything else she thinks you should know. I'm going to go check on Regina Mallory, since I'm out this way. Save her a trip to town. Dangerous damn times."

"I'm doin' my best to see them done with."

"Try doing it without getting your fool head blown off." With that, Doc grabbed his bag and disappeared.

"I actually think he cares," Bren teased. Turning back to Helena, he couldn't help grinning when he saw she had her eyes shut and her hands pressed to her hot cheeks. "Are ya a bit embarrassed, lovey?"

She opened her eyes and narrowed them again in less time than it would take to blink. "I'd strangle him, but he'd probably threaten to use a switch on me if I took my arm out of this darned sling," she grumbled. "Man treats me like a child." Then she looked up at Brendan, her lips curved upward to match his grin. "But I think you may be right. You're winning him over. Come sit with me."

Instead of taking the other chair, he hunkered back down at her side. "What is it? You're not really upset about what Doc said, are you? Is this the same shameless seductress from the other night? Do ladies not discuss such things in the light of day? You and Maria were certainly free enough with a discussion of my attributes."

She gave him a light smack on the shoulder. He pretended it had overbalanced him, so fell backward and wound up sitting on his butt, looking up at her. "Ya'd better watch brutalizin' me. You said it yourself. Doc's startin' to like me."

She tried valiantly to keep from smiling, but lost the battle. "Would you stop? It's not the discussion itself, though that part of marriage isn't freely discussed in polite company." Her blush seemed to deepen. "It's that Doc is a man who reminds me of my father. And with my parents both gone, the Clemens have become…"

Terror suddenly flooded Brendan's brain. Her mother had died in childbirth. So had his. He ceased hearing

Helena's words, though he knew her voice was there, behind the other sounds in his mind.

A vision…no, it was a memory he'd thought buried in the long-ago past. It reared its head and had his breath dammed in his lungs. There was his ma, calling out for his da, who was in the mine. Thomas had been crying, clinging to her, afraid of losing her. Abby trying to help, in a panic and afraid. When Bren had found them, Ma was on the floor. And blood was everywhere.

He heard Helena calling to him, and blinked. Her worried gaze locked with his. Her hand gripped his. "Bren? You've gone absolutely pale. What is it?"

"If you were in a family way," he managed to begin, his voice strained and shaken. "The doc is the one who'd be takin' care of you, right? You wouldn't be after trustin' a midwife just because she was a woman, would you? He's a cranky bastard, but he saved you for me."

"Shall we not talk about this yet?" Helena suggested, sounding a bit upset herself.

He'd started out trying to make her laugh, but now that his mind had gone where it had, he couldn't let it go. Her need to forget the bad things in the past wasn't always a good idea. There were lessons to be learned from mistakes as well as from triumphs. He had to know she'd not be foolish with her life again.

"No. I need a promise it'll be Doc Clemens you'll go to. No matter how embarrassed you are. I've always wondered if Ma would have lived if she'd had a real doctor. You'll have the best. Promise me."

Helena frowned, but then he could see understanding dawn in her eyes. She squeezed his palm. He hadn't even known they were holding hands.

"Oh, Bren. I'm sorry. I hadn't thought of your mother

or mine, in relation to our future. You mustn't worry so. But I promise. I'd see no one but Doc."

He nodded and stood. "Sorry. I panicked there for a minute, lovey."

"It's fine, Bren."

"Suppose we take a turn around your lovely court-yard and get our minds on something else? Time to start helping you regain your strength. Got to get you in shape for all that rough bed play I've leave to start in a month."

She swatted him again. "Laugh now, but I was the one getting Doc's permission. Maybe it's you who'd better get his strength up."

Brendan nearly collapsed in the doorway, laughing. Oh, he'd missed his Helena so much.

Chapter Thirteen

Helena waited as Brendan, clearly trying to be as silent as possible, entered their pitch-black room, pausing when the boards creaked underfoot. His movements were so silent she knew he had no intention of waking her.

Fair to a fault, when Brendan had drawn Friday night's first watch, he'd taken it, and promised Helena to make it up to her tomorrow. He hadn't been happy for either of them, but Bren wasn't someone who would ask anyone to do something he wasn't willing to do himself. That attitude stood even when it went contrary to every plan and promise he'd made about the night.

She had no intention of waiting any longer. Tonight was supposed to be their night. So she'd cozied up in bed, wearing her finest nightgown. She'd read for a while, then, as midnight approached, had turned down the lamp and settled in to wait.

Just to see what he'd do.

The big sneak must even be carrying his boots. A supposition confirmed a moment later when she whispered, "Brendan," in her most seductive voice.

"Damn," he yelped. Then in low, halting breaths, accompanied by what sounded like hopping, he went on, "Oh, my poor toe." Next, his boots hit the floor and the chair squeaked. "Damn, woman. You scared ten years off my life. And oh, Jaysus. Who moved the damned chair?"

Chuckling at his rant in spite of feeling sorry for his poor toe, she sat up. "You're back."

"And clod that I am, I woke you."

"I expected you to wake me, Bren. You promised."

"No, I didn't. If I'd meant to wake you, I'd have had somethin' a bit more suave in mind than breakin' my toe and howlin' like a banshee."

She'd swear there was a grin in his tone. "I decided to wait in case you decided to renege. I guess I should have left the lamp burning. I'm sorry about your poor toe. Want me to kiss it and make it better?"

A match flared next to her, illuminating his handsome face as he lit the bedside lamp. He replaced the chimney and the rose-colored shade bathed the room in a warm glow. He grinned and arched an eyebrow. "I've something a bit north I'd rather have your pretty lips ministerin' to."

She laughed and swung her feet off the side of the bed as he straightened to his full, wonderful height. "You are incorrigible," she said, and poked his hard belly. "I can see I spoiled you with that all week."

"A week with those talented hands and wonderful soft mouth on me was bound to spoil me a bit. I can't help wantin' more but, lovey," he said, and took her face in his hands, "it wasn't enough."

"At least the waiting is over." She sighed happily. "No more of Doc's cruel restrictions."

Brendan sank to his haunches next to the bed, skimming his fingertips along her arms, then took her hands and kissed the backs of them. Finally, he looked up at her, his expression serious. "Not touching you has been pure torture, but I gave the old man my word. You're precious to me, Helena. It's my job to take the best care of you I can manage."

"I'm not sure I like being thought of as just a job."

He raised his eyebrows. "Did I say 'just'? Because you're also my pleasure. It's my pleasure to work with you. To sleep next to you. To sit across the table and look at you. Maria's piping-hot meals go cold by the time I get to them because I can't take my fool eyes off you."

He rose to his feet, planted a knee on the mattress and sat facing her. "And since you're awake, tonight it's going to be my pleasure to make love to my wife again. At last. If I wasn't so afraid of tiring you too much, we'd still be at it as the sun rises over Shamrock's hills."

She traced his full, beautiful lips with her fingertips. "Now you're bragging."

He narrowed his eyes and grinned that challenging grin of his. "Is that a dare?"

Oh, how she loved his teasing ways. Helena raised her chin. "Take it however you want."

"Don't worry, lovey. I intend to take you every gentle way I can." He grasped her hands, placed a kiss on the back of each again, then laid them on her thighs. "I don't think you know what you do to me. You steal my breath. You make my mind reel. Make me burn with one touch. You've been using these beautiful, clever weapons on me for seven marvelous, hellish nights when I couldn't handle the temptation of touchin' back. Now it's my turn."

The rough timbre of his voice sent a delicious shudder racing through her. He smiled as if he knew—as if he'd wanted exactly that. "I'm takin' up the challenge. I'll be inside you as the sun rises or my ma didn't name me Brendan Joseph Kane." He cupped Helena's jaw. "Now," he said against her lips, "we'll have to see if you can handle *my* challenge. Keep those hands to yourself, lovey."

He seemed to be all talked out as silence fell. Rather than move closer, he moved away—far enough so he could trace her face with his gaze, feature by feature. Pleasure, dark and steamy, seemed to glow in those darkened emerald orbs. She could have stared into them for hours.

But Bren wasn't a patient man. He leaned in again and she let her heavy eyelids drift closed, enjoying to the fullest the feel of his tongue running along her lips. He drew her moist lower lip inside his mouth, sucking on it, nipping at it, nearly snapping her control. But she wanted to give him what he'd asked for. So she curled her fingers around the sheet on either side of her and let him have his way. She shook in frustration and vibrated in ecstasy at the same time.

"Not easy, is it?" he asked, with a devilish smile.

His teeth sank gently into her bottom lip again, sending sparks of joy showering over her like the fireworks she'd seen once back East.

Then the time for teasing ended. He'd clearly reached the limit of his endurance. His kiss was suddenly a little restless. A bit rough. A lot demanding.

He wrapped his arms around her and pulled her close, lifting her onto the leg he'd bent when he'd sat facing her. His full, rigid erection pressed tight to her hip thrilled her. A secret little triumph burst in her heart. He enjoyed kissing her so much he was already fully aroused.

Now when his tongue sought hers, his hunger for her was in his every movement. Every action. Every reaction. If he could have devoured her, she thought he might have, because the same kind of hunger rolled through her. Oh, how thrilling to be wanted like this!

Tremors raced along her spine to her core. She rocked against his erection—felt him pulse, even as her moist center throbbed in answer.

He tore his mouth from hers and she moaned in protest. But he ignored her objections and traced a path of fire across her cheek to her ear. His hot breath stirred against her. "You make me so damned hot. I swear we could set fire to these sheets."

"Then we should. Don't make us wait, Bren. Not this time."

"Ah, my impatient temptress." He laid claim to her neck, blazing a trail to her shoulder, nipping and licking his way toward her breast, laying her on the bed as he did.

Her entire body pulsated with need and she moaned his name. The cool sheets under her back did nothing to cool her heated senses. When he leaned over her, claiming her breast through the fine cotton of her nightgown, she repeated his name—a refrain of need she sent echoing in the room. Her mind was suddenly devoid of any other thought or word or sound that could express her longing.

Her world narrowed. To him.

His hand captured her other breast, and his thumb played with her nipple. She sighed in relief, knowing there was no big unwieldy bandage that might derail them. No, this time they were on the trip till the end—and beyond.

The temptation of his hair, brushing her chin as he paid undivided attention to her breast, was too much. Forget his challenge. She wouldn't spoil this for him; she'd just touch those soft locks. That was all. She tunneled the fingers of both hands through the thick, silky mane.

He looked up. Grinned. "I win."

She smiled back. "No. I do. I have you right where I want you."

"Do ya now? And here I was thinkin' how brilliant I am because I'll have you under me any minute."

She laughed. "Well, don't let me distract you."

"Ya needn't worry. This is all that's been on my mind. I just wanted to be enjoyin' you a bit at a time."

"I hate to bring this up," she said, using her thumb and forefinger on his earlobe, "but we're both wearing way too many clothes for your plans."

He closed his eyes, biting his lower lip, took a deep slow breath, clearly reaching for control. "And don't I have a very smart woman for a wife?" he whispered, a slight tremor in his voice.

It made her smile, that tremor.

After a deep swallow he admitted, "The trouble is, I don't want to let go of you."

He kissed her again then, his tongue stroking hers, enflaming her need of him. Even as he circled her tongue with his and silently encouraged her to suckle it, she went to work on the shiny, metal buttons of his shirt.

His breathing labored, he broke the kiss. She glanced down at his exposed chest and blew, ruffling the short curling hairs that to her were an enthralling sign of his stunning maleness.

He looked down and saw that she had his shirt unbuttoned to the bottom of the placket. Then he looked back up. "It's a wily fairy I've wed, one with clever fingers."

"Perhaps I'll turn out to be a wood nymph." She tried to go to work on his jeans, but he moved away.

"No more of that now." He pushed himself up, to stand by the bed. Then he paused, staring down at her, his expression so intense it seemed as if he was trying to memorize the moment for all time. He blinked. "Give me your hand, lovey." She did, and he pulled her up beside him. His eyes fixated on her lips for a moment, then he shook his head and, sinking to the mattress, took hold of her hips to pull her into the V of his legs. His long, tapered fingers rose to cup her breast, and he bent his head.

Helena went for that black-as-midnight hair again, letting the satiny strands slip through her fingers as his mouth closed over her. She let out a shocked yelp, completely unready for his moist, clever mouth nipping at her exposed nipple.

"I think you're a *fear sidhe*," she whispered. "It's me who's under your spell. Maybe *far dorocha*, the dark man on the dark horse. They say no one can refuse him. I've never been able to refuse you," she admitted, and gasped as he tongued her nipple, then suckled hard. Her legs turned to jelly. "Please, Bren. I can't stand—"

"Have a little more patience. I know you can stand quite a bit more lovin'. I remember. I remember well."

He went back to suckling at her breast, and the pleasure was too much. It blanked out her mind and her knees gave way.

Bren moved with lightning speed, wrapping his arms around her, pulling her close. "Oh, Jaysus. I'm such a clod. Ya meant you couldn't stand."

She had no idea how, but in a blink he had her naked and was lowering her onto the cool sheets. Then he stripped off his clothes, and he was as magnificent as she remembered.

Dreamily, she said, "You take such good care of me."

"Nothin's more important to me than you," he said, and then he was over her, his hands skimming her body, quietly arousing, worshiping her with his mouth as he knelt between her feet. Cupped her. Kissed her, then looked up along her body, his gaze capturing hers. "What a fool I was. You've gone from girl to woman when I wasn't lookin'."

The way he said "woman" in that lyrical Irish accent, his voice rough with arousal, combined with the hot look in his eyes, was nearly as arousing as his touch. As that intimate kiss.

But he didn't linger there as he often had in the past. She closed her eyes when tears threatened. He moved on, kissing his way up her body, his lips so tender they felt as light as a butterfly landing on a flower. Their mouths mated and their bodies touched hip to hip, chest to breast as he supported his weight, giving her only what she could handle and still breathe.

Without breaking their achingly sweet, achingly deep kiss, he gently pressed himself into her waiting heat, then withdrew. He kept up the infinitely careful advance and retreat until he'd pushed home, finally filling her, and they both sighed long and deep.

She opened her eyes, her gaze locking with his again. It was exactly like the first time. She'd never been told what to expect, and he'd been half out of his mind with need that day. Yet he'd somehow wrestled his desire into submission. He'd offered to stop, though she'd known it had nearly killed him to even ask. When she'd said she wanted to belong to him forever, he'd breathed a relieved sigh and explained what would happen. Then he'd gone ahead—endlessly gentle, sweetly and lovingly making her his.

And she'd been his ever since.

"All right?" he asked now, calling her back to the present.

She smiled up at him through her happy-sad tears. The big bad lawman. Former fugitive from the law he now served so diligently. He was such a fraud. And wonderful. And sweet. Oh, he'd hate her calling him sweet. She chuckled. "Of course I am. I'm always fine in your arms."

He gritted his teeth. Took a shallow, half-shuddering breath. "You were always so small. So tight. It's been a long time. And you're still so damned, wonderfully tight around me." His voice shook with his restraint.

She hooked her legs around his waist, driving him deeper. "I'm wonderful, too."

"Selkie," he growled, and started to move in her, pulling nearly all the way out, then driving forward.

"Far dorocha," she countered, and her body became his and his hers as he drove them both higher and higher toward what felt like the top of a great cliff.

All the talk of folklore and fantasy rolled in her head. She felt as if she could touch the top of the world. Then they were falling. Together.

She called his name as something that felt like the sea closed over their heads, leaving her struggling for air. She didn't want the *selkie's* freedom of the sea. She wanted to stay with the man who'd taken her as his wife.

Bren rolled to his back, carrying her with him, and the world righted itself. His hand stroking her back chased away the rest of the captivating fantasy that had invaded her thoughts. No fairy tale could ever be as wonderful as her real life. She settled her head on his shoulder and sleep called.

Thin light flowed into the room when Helena opened her eyes, to find Bren's face hovering over hers. "Good mornin', lovey." His gaze held her a helpless prisoner as she realized what had awakened her. His clever fingers had found their way into the moist folds of her womanhood.

He massaged her, making her swell at his every caress, stoking the fires of her ardor. She knew he would enter her soon. He'd never fully satisfied her this way, always acquiescing to her need to be one with him. Soon she was gasping, expecting him to mount her, but he slowly, silently shook his head. She didn't understand what was there in his gaze. She wanted to close her eyes, but couldn't seem to look away from those compelling orbs and the message she didn't understand.

Then a second finger penetrated her, finding, stroking the entrance to her womb. She gasped, and panted as his thumb found that magical hidden nub and pressed and rubbed and circled, wringing a wild cry from her. Her body was on fire and she started to quake. Still his kind and serious gaze didn't let her go. "Bren, please. I need you. I need you now."

He didn't stop. Only drove her higher. "But it's good, isn't it, lovey?" he asked. Even his voice was so serious.

She'd never let go with him only touching her. But she realized this meant something to him. Shaking, she called his name, but managed not to beg him to stop. And he didn't. He kept driving her toward singular ecstasy until, tears blurring his image, she shattered. Release, dark and complete, rolled through her, over her.

"Why?" she gasped, when she had enough breath.

"Because I needed you to trust yourself to me. Completely. You never trusted me that way. It always needed to be both of us surrenderin' at the same time. I broke your trust when I left. I woke and watched you sleep. I wanted...no, I needed to know you'd trust me in everything. I wanted you to know I want only good for you. Only happiness."

"I never meant for you to think—" She broke off. How to explain? She took a shuddering breath. "I was so...isolated before I met you, and after you pushed me away, until we came West together. It wasn't about not wanting to surrender to you, about not trusting you. It was about needing us to be together. Me alone meant loneliness. The two of us becoming one meant togetherness. Bren, we said no looking back. You agreed. Can you do that now?"

She couldn't move forward if he kept bringing up the past.

He crawled up and flopped next to her. Nipping at her ear, he whispered, "We look ahead—together. And speakin' of together. How about I offer you a happy little mornin' ride? I've been, uh, left hangin', so to speak."

She rolled to her stomach and glanced over her shoulder. He stood strong and proud. "Hmm. I wouldn't call that *hanging,* except figuratively. So this has nothing to do with a certain challenge and this being nearly past dawn?"

His grin was back in place. "Of course it does. I remember how you like your early morning rides. It's how we met, after all. I went fishin' after six o'clock mass, and there you were." His hand glided from her shoulder to her buttock and back up in a slow, arousing caress. He spoke in an enthralling half whisper, half purr. "I looked up from my fishin' and there, limpin' toward me, was the angel I'd spied in the choir loft, come to earth as my very own lost damsel in distress. How can a man get luckier than to meet up with the woman he'd spent the mornin' fantasizin' about?"

She crawled over him, her light hair falling like a blond curtain around them as she bent forward and kissed him. He used her position to find her and fit himself inside her. She sat back, smiling, her hands braced on his hard muscled chest. "Well aren't you clever?"

"Clever is my confirmation name," he whispered. He smiled, too, his eyes so dark, so compelling and adoring it stole her breath. His hands stroked her. Aroused her. He tunneled his fingers in her hair and pulled her forward for another long, intense kiss.

Then he pressed upward, driving deep inside her. She started to pulse around him, crying out, shocked by the sudden and startlingly complete sensation. She seemed to hang there, the moment turning into five, ten, twenty moments till he went rigid beneath her. Then it was Bren crying her name as she collapsed onto him. They clung together, stunned and satiated, wrapped in ecstasy and each other's arms. United in all ways but one.

The most important three words had gone unsaid.

Again. Sliding toward sleep, Helena said them to her-self as the silence seemed to echo in the room.

She'd been the one who'd driven him away. He had to be the one to say them. And oh, how she wanted to hear the words.

Otherwise how could she tell him what her anger had cost? How could she know he'd be able to forgive? Without knowing that, she couldn't risk her heart.

Chapter Fourteen

Brendan let his horse pick his way along the rocky path leading into the canyon, his mind occupied with Helena and what was still left unsaid between them. He'd had to escape her proximity to gain some perspective, and had figured the best way to get that would be to go looking for something that tied Avery to the raids.

The odor of death pulled him from his thoughts. He stood in the saddle and stared at the desecration spread beneath him. This certainly took his mind off Helena.

Half an hour later he and Harry climbed the last ten feet out of the canyon, where at least fifty head of cattle lay dead on the rocks below. They were Rocking R steers.

Alex and Helena had decided to block off the canyon because cattle weren't the brightest of God's creatures. Fencing discouraged them from wandering where they'd never survive. But the wires and posts had been downed again. Brendan swung out of the saddle and ground-tied Harry. Scratching his head, he walked along the rim, looking for the place where the cattle had gone over.

When he found it, he crouched down. The soil was torn up as if the steers had run to their deaths. Stampede? The weather had been beautiful. Nary a thunderhead in sight. He stood and turned from the rim to start working in an ever-widening circle, checking the ground for some clue about what had happened. He was fully on Rocking R land by the time he found it—tracks from about five horses. They'd been heading straight toward the canyon rim at a full gallop.

The cattle had been run over the edge. He could only assume Avery wanted to discourage either spread from using that grazing land to assure his marauders' secret path to the Bar A.

Brendan sighed. Someone should ride over to the Rocking R with the bad news. But he missed Helena. And just that quick Brendan's mind went to her and the problem that had sent him out there.

He'd longed to tell her how precious she was to him. Well, he had, but only that. He hadn't said he loved her. He couldn't, but not because he didn't love her more than life itself. He didn't think she could go from hate to love in the short time they'd been back together, when she had every reason to doubt him.

He'd said "I love you" often in the past. And he'd walked away, leaving her at the mercy of men like Avery and Gowery. Twice.

No. Those words had to come from her first. Him saying them wouldn't make her believe in him again. His actions would.

He kept seeing something in her eyes that he suspected made her hold the words back. He clearly had to make up for more than embarrassing her.

More than leaving her alone, and worse, lonely.

More even than leaving her to be targeted by a man like Avery.

Brendan couldn't bring himself to risk hearing only silence if he told her how much he loved her. That would hurt more than the simple yet complicated absence of them did. More important, he didn't want to pressure her into saying something she wasn't ready to say. She had too much integrity to lie. But tough as his Helena was, she was just as tenderhearted. Hurting him would hurt her, and he'd hurt her enough already to last two lifetimes.

Brendan had just reached Harry when the sound of horses scrabbling for purchase on the steep hillside rose out of the canyon. He grabbed Harry by the mane and pulled his peacemaker, prepared to fire or apologize, depending on who showed up. The breath stalled in Brendan's chest as he extended his gun hand, ready to fire. He spit out a curse when Ted, then Nate came up over the rim. When no one else followed, Brendan holstered his weapon.

Nate looked at him blandly. "You kiss that pretty wife of yours with that dirty mouth, Irish?"

Brendan ignored him. "You two stuck havin' anythin' to do with that?"

Nate shook his head. "No, but some of Avery's Ghost Warriors talked about purposely stampeding some cattle into the canyon for him."

Brendan nodded, climbing into Harry's saddle. He settled himself as he scanned the area. "I pretty much had that figured out. So is Tolliver findin' enough replacements?"

Ted grimaced. "Two more rode in yesterday. One's a sharpshooter. Not smart riling a rattler, Irish. I get the idea Avery wants you dead in the worst way. Be careful riding out alone."

Brendan nodded. "That it? No names for us?"

Nate shifted in the saddle. "Ham Buford. Ace Whitman."

"I'll check to see if they're wanted." Brendan looked around again. "We'd better head our own ways before we're seen together."

Ted nodded and wheeled his horse back toward the canyon.

Nate waited a beat and started to follow at a slow pace, then turned in the saddle and faced Brendan again. "Seriously, watch yourself. This whole situation bothers me. We're used to dealing with straightforward outlaws. Most of them even expect to go to prison a time or two before they die. Avery—he's unpredictable. And a noose is a hell of a comedown from his palace in the hills."

Brendan watched as Nate turned around and followed the rocky pathway, disappearing into the canyon. Tossing a curse after him, Brendan remembered what the ranger had said about his mouth. Living among the Lyons gang, Brendan had learned a whole new vocabulary.

Helena was a lady and she didn't need a husband she was ashamed of. So far she didn't seem to be, even considering his early life. Still, he'd better clean up his mouth before their child's first words were ones better not repeated in polite company.

Helena came into the barn as he was rubbing down Harry. "I thought you were going to the Rocking R?"

He hated to disappoint her. "The Mallorys and their

brood were headed over to the Rocking R to visit with the O'Hara family. They're all going to church together in the mornin', since Father Santiago is expected here for Sunday mass this week."

Brendan wrapped Helena in his arms. "Maybe we'll make a start on a nice family of our own this evenin'. How about we pack a picnic dinner and go somewhere away from pryin' eyes?" He winked. "Just for old times' sake. Sounds better than visitin' the neighbors and talkin' about his dead cattle, doesn't it?"

She frowned, staring at nothing in particular that he could see, then said, "Maybe we could go to church tomorrow, too."

"Would you be havin' the bell tower at San Rafael's collapse? Father Santiago could get smashed right up there on his little altar. I haven't darkened the door of a church since Rafferty married us at gunpoint."

She looked as if Brendan had shot her. "I'm sorry, I—"

"I was only teasin', lovey." He loosened his arms, only to tap her adorable nose. "Have I ever done one thing I didn't want to do?"

"You said 'I do,'" she mumbled, still looking so sad he wanted to kick himself.

"Oh, I wanted it. I just needed to be kicked into it. Don't apologize. Not again. It'll be a great story to tell the grandchildren, about what a thick head their pop has. Though I suppose we'd have to tone down Abby's reasons for holdin' the gun."

Helena flinched, then pivoted and rushed out of the barn. As she turned away, she looked...well now, he didn't know for sure. Not hurt exactly. Sad, maybe. Like when she'd admitted to having been lonely these last years. Clearly, the wedding wasn't something to tease her about. He needed to show her he was sorry.

"Jimmy, finish up on Harry, would you?" he called to the young stable boy.

Always anxious to please, Jimmy raced up the aisle. "Sure thing, Ranger Kane." The kid eagerly took the brush Brendan held out to him as they passed in the doorway of the stall.

As he strode through the barn, Brendan noticed an apple Helena must have left sitting on top of the feed box. He picked it up and stared at it.

It was the middle of June and she'd brought an apple. For his horse. It had to be nearly the last of her precious store from last fall's crop. The damned apple was worth a good piece of change at this time of year. And she'd planned to give it to a horse.

He couldn't help that his mind went way back. He'd seen an apple in the company store when they'd been new to Wheatonburg, so he'd been pretty young. Ma had had Abby in her arms. Bren had wanted that apple in the worst way. He'd nearly been able to taste it. But no, his ma had said, they had no money for a luxury. He'd cried and cried there in the store. The apple had come home with them, and she'd made a brown Betty with it, to spread the treat through the family.

But he hadn't enjoyed his portion, because young as he'd been, he'd known she hadn't bought her dress fabric. Because of him. He'd known it was his fault. The next day she'd taken him to the trash dump. She'd made a great game of searching for tin cans Wheaton's cook had discarded.

With their bounty in hand, they'd gone home to plant an apple seed in each can. And together they'd watched, day after day, for the little green leaves to appear. Three of the resulting saplings had survived their first winter behind their possession house. The apples from them had eventually become a little source of income for Ma by the time Michael Thomas came along. Then old man Wheaton had learned she'd been selling her apples to his company store. He'd taken a cut of half, claiming they'd grown in his soil.

The day they'd buried Ma, Bren had gone home and hacked down two of the trees before Da could stop him. Not an apple had ever gone to the store again. Brendan took great pleasure in giving them to anyone who'd wanted one, and damn Wheaton.

Harry nickered, dragging him back to the present. Jimmy stood staring at him. "Is that for Harry?" he asked.

"Yep." Brendan tossed the damned apple to the kid. "And he likes his back brushed," he added, to cover up his scattered thoughts.

He couldn't continue allowing the past to affect his marriage. Helena was right. They had nothing to gain from taking their eyes off the present and future.

"Helena?" he called to her retreating back. But she didn't stop. In her troubled state, she'd run almost as far as the house while he'd been getting angry at a dead man about apples. Brendan caught up to her on the porch. "Stop. I'm sorry I upset you."

She whirled to face him, tears rimming those pretty blue eyes.

"Something I said back in the barn has bothered you. What is it, lovey?"

She closed her eyes and the tears fell. "You talk about

children all the time. You must bring the topic up five or ten times a day."

"We've been going at it like rabbits all week. If we keep this up…as I fully intend…well, that'd be the natural result, don't you think? It isn't as if we're not expectin' to be expectin'."

"But what if it doesn't happen?" she said, her eyes troubled. "Abby wanted another baby. She and Joshua have been married three years and it's just happening now."

Brendan wiped Helena's cheeks. *Women.* They worried about the strangest things. Sometimes he thought they were born worrying. Then he remembered his own reaction to memories of Ma's last hours. He guessed it was all in the hands of the Almighty.

Keep marchin' forward, he told himself again.

He took her in his arms and hugged her. "Then we'll have three years to practice. Maybe church tomorrow isn't so bad an idea. You pray for that baby we're both wanting, and I'll handle the part about you both comin' through it perfect. How's that sound?"

Held in the circle of his arms, she leaned back and smiled up at him. "Good." A little sob shook her. "It sounds good. It'll be nice to go again. I've missed it."

He was relieved by that smile, because it was genuine, but he was troubled by her last remark. She'd missed it? He'd noticed she hadn't been going, but thought it was due to her recuperation. Now that he thought about it, he'd lay odds she'd been shunned in some way after he'd taken off. Dammit. He'd even taken the comfort of her new faith from her.

Sure as his name was Brendan Joseph Kane, they'd walk in tomorrow and sit in whatever pew Abby and

Joshua took. "Suppose we get there early enough for confession before mass. That might keep that bell tower up there where it belongs and off the good father's head."

Happy with the chuckle he'd drawn from her, he said, "Let's put that picnic together ourselves, so Maria can go on home early to Donato. I'm not bad at Saratoga chips myself. And since everything will be cold, once we find our spot, maybe we'll get in a little *practice* on that family before we eat." He grinned and waggled his eyebrows. "After, too."

She laughed. "You see, you *are* incorrigible."

Ah, there it was. All was right with the world. He'd sparked that pretty laugh of hers. Like the tinkling bells of Christmas services, it was. "Funny you should mention that," he said. "Incorrigible's my confirmation name."

She eyed him, still smiling. "I thought you said it was Clever."

He shrugged. "Couldn't decide. What does a kid that age know, anyway? I wanted to keep it open-ended, as I had no idea where life would take me."

Some time later, Brendan left Helena packing up the dinner they'd put together and went to saddle Harry and Paint Box. He got the mare all set and lashed her to the corral rail, then went back to see to Harry.

He'd just stepped out of the barn again when someone off to the side shouted his name in a mean tone. He didn't get the chance to see who it was because Harry shrieked and reared, turning from good-natured prince to wild destructive *pooka* between one second and the next.

It felt to Brendan as if the gelding yanked his arm right out of its socket as he reared again, pulling him off his feet and back inside the barn. They weren't quite clear of the doorway when something heavy knocked into the back of Brendan's head and other shoulder. The blow sent him flying forward, to land on the floor beneath Harry's sharp hooves. Brendan instinctively dropped the reins and curled into a ball to protect his head. Fortunately, the big black's feet somehow missed him, and the animal came to a halt.

Brendan's dazed thoughts hadn't even cleared when he heard Helena screaming his name. He couldn't seem to get himself moving. Just as he thought he had his wits gathered enough to crawl out from under Harry's belly, Jimmy approached and the black reared up again. Instinctively, Brendan froze.

Then Helena's voice was coming from somewhere above him, calm and soothing, her skirts flowing as she approached. Harry chuffed to her and the quivering tremor from his knees to his fetlocks quieted. Still, was she daft? Suppose Harry went off again?

Brendan rolled toward Helena and got to his knees, then his feet. Shaking, he waited for his head to settle a bit. Whatever had hit him had his ears ringing. He stepped close to Helena so he could get between them if necessary, then turned to face Harry. He hadn't expected the placid, dreamy look in his horse's eyes as Helena crooned to him. Then the big dumb black turned his head toward Brendan, butted his chest playfully and whickered.

"What in the name of all that's holy was that about, I'd like to know, you lame-headed son of Satan? Helena, sweetie, step a bit away. I'm not in a trustin' mood with him right now."

"I don't know what spooked him, but he probably saved your life. Are you all right?" she demanded. Even in the darkened barn he could see she was pale as a bucket of milk.

"For all intents. My shoulders are burning like sons of a—" Nate's remark about his mouth echoed in Brendan's head, along with the ringing bells. "They hurt," he amended, moving them gingerly. Then his wits cleared a bit more and he realized what Helena had said. "What is that about him saving my life?"

"Bren, look," she said, and stepped aside, gesturing out the door. A big pile of hay bales lay tumbled in the entrance, almost blocking the way. "They'd have broken your neck if they'd hit you."

"Who in hell was so careless?" He looked at the two men who'd followed Helena into the barn. Jimmy was there, too.

There was something hanging around on the edge of Brendan's memory. "Wait. Someone called my name. But it sounded more like a challenge than a warning."

"I heard it, too," Jimmy said. "I thought it was what scared Harry."

"I just heard Harry. I was halfway here, coming from the house." Helena was still awfully pale. "Then the bales fell."

"I heard the voice," Hodges interjected, "but I was too far away to recognize it. When I saw those bales fall, I thought you was a goner."

"All I heard was a horse squealing. I ran this way because I knew something was wrong," Yates said. "Did anyone see who was in the loft? I went up to look, but it's empty. Just a broke rope and the pulley assembly sticking out the window up there now." He shook his head. "Damnedest thing. How'd any fool think he'd lower that much weight even using the pulley?"

Brendan reached down and picked up his hat, smacking it against his leg, then putting it back on. His head swam again and he reached for Harry's halter. After patting the black on the neck, he blew in his nostrils. "Thanks, boyo. I appreciate the hand, even if my shoulder is a bit tender."

"We'll stay home," Helena decided, touching his shoulder. "Have our picnic in the courtyard."

"Not necessary. We'll stick with the—"

A shot rang out.

"Both of you stay in the barn," Brendan ordered her and Jimmy. Leading Harry, he raced with the other two men out the door, through the narrow space among the tumbled bales.

Brendan had a head start on Yates and Hodges because they each had to grab one of the horses from the remuda and saddle it. Considering there were a hundred fifty available it shouldn't take long.

He was probably a quarter mile from the home place when he saw a man lying in a gully. One of their horses stood not far away.

Rather than ride down there, when he had no idea where the shot had come from, Bren stopped under a big old sycamore and dismounted. He ground-tied Harry and, using the dense foliage and substantial trunk of the tree as cover, took a long look around for whoever had fired that shot. He wouldn't do the man lying down there any good by getting his own fool head blown off.

Cautiously, he moved down into the gully. No shot

rang out. Still in a crouch, Brendan ran through the brush, keeping his head down. When he reached the man, he quickly realized two things. First, that Jud Kirkwood never knew what hit him. He'd died instantly. And second, Avery's new sharpshooter had already earned his month's pay.

Brendan turned at the sound of hoofbeats. One of the men had been damn quick saddling a mount. But when he looked up out of the gully, he spat a curse. Dammit! How in hell was he supposed to clean up his language if Helena wouldn't stop putting herself in danger?

He hustled up the hill toward her and grabbed her by the waist, dragging her out of the saddle to make her less of a target. "Woman, are ya daft? Didn't I just nearly lose ya last month? I told you to stay put in the barn."

"I was worried about you. How come you're the only one allowed to put yourself in danger?" Then she looked past him. "Oh, dear Lord!" She turned away from the sight of Kirkwood's body and buried her face in Bren's chest. Moments later, she gazed up at him. "Is that one of our men? Bren, he's dead, isn't he?" Tears had flooded her eyes, making them glitter in the filtered sunlight.

He hugged her close. "He never knew, lovey. Never felt a thing. Jaysus, but this has been one hell of a day."

"Shamrock is still a target, isn't it?" she asked.

He nodded.

"Maybe that picnic isn't a good idea."

"I'd have been distracted for sure. Not safe with a killer around. The courtyard'll do fine."

She nodded, then asked, "Who—who is it down there?"

"It's Jud Kirkwood. How long has he been with you?"

"He started right before you came back. He kept to himself mostly, but he was always respectful. He rode with me into town a few times. I don't know if he had family."

"I have to scout around down there. I doubt I'll find anything, but it's still my job. The other men should be along soon. Sit yourself down. You've gone pale again."

He helped her settle under the tree, then grabbed the canteen off his saddle. Theirs was supposed to have been a leisurely ride, and he'd intended to help her into the saddle and out, as Doc had ordered.

Settling on his heels in front of her, Bren passed her the water and she took a drink. Kirkwood was gone. Nothing in that gully was going to change in the next few minutes. And she was badly shaken. "Are you doin' a bit better?"

She nodded.

He reached out to brush back a lock of her hair that had come loose from the cluster of curls at her neck, hooking it behind her ear. "Doc said you weren't to mount or dismount on your own, Helena. You could have hurt yourself."

"Why do you persist in thinking I'm some foolish ninny without the sense God gave a goose? I climbed up on one of the hay bales."

"Oh. I suppose the idiot who dropped them did us a favor, then," Brendan said, keeping his voice light. He no more thought that pile of bales hitting him was an accident than he thought Kirkwood had blown that hole in his own head. "But even if you found a safe way to mount up, you still shouldn't have come out here."

She looked away, out over the hills. "I came because I was worried about you," she repeated. "I never thought one of the men would be shot, just riding along. I feel so responsible."

"Lovey, ya didn't fire the rifle. Someone else did. It's the raiders and their boss who are responsible. Either that or Kirkwood had an enemy."

"I don't understand why they'd be doing all this if it was the same people who attacked Shamrock."

"Well now, when I make an arrest, I'll be askin' that exact question, and I'll let you know the answer. How's that?"

Before she could respond, hoofbeats thundered up over the rise. Hodges and Yates pulled up and stared into the gully before swinging down from their saddles.

"Kirkwood?" Yates asked.

Brendan nodded and stood.

"Never knew him well," Yates said, hat in hand.

Hodges shook his head. "Me, neither. Kept to himself. Not real friendly, you know?"

"Hodges, suppose you ride back for a wagon, and take Mrs. Kane with you," Brendan said. "Help her dismount onto one of those hay bales. Maybe you could stay with Jimmy, lovey. Or go over to Maria and Donato's. I don't want you alone right now. But I sure don't think you need to be here for this."

She nodded. Looking sad and unsettled, she let him pull her to her feet and boost her into the saddle. "Be careful. Please," she told him.

Brendan patted her thigh. "I'll be along soon. Don't worry."

As they rode away, he thanked God she hadn't gotten a good look at Kirkwood up close. Head wounds weren't pretty.

The ground around the body revealed nothing, as he'd assumed it wouldn't. The shot had come from a pretty fair distance. Finding the spot the sharpshooter had sighted from would have to wait. Bren needed to get the body out of the gully, and himself back to Helena. He and Yates worked together and had the deed done quickly.

They would bury him in the morning. This was still Quinn's jurisdiction, but Bren wasn't leaving Helena here without him, to go into town to inform the sheriff tonight. And he wasn't putting one of the hands on the road to town, either. Bad enough some of the men had gone in to blow off some steam. He'd get word to them through Quinn tomorrow, to wait in town as an escort home for him and Helena. There'd be safety in numbers.

One thing was for sure. Brendan wouldn't be getting much sleep this night.

Chapter Fifteen

Helena had a sad duty that bright and beautiful Monday. She had to pack up Jud Kirkwood's things. Both Bren and Mallory had offered to do it, but she'd been the one to approve his hire. She felt it was her responsibility, even though she'd cried out some of her guilt at his graveside yesterday.

Resolutely, she stepped onto the bunkhouse porch and marched inside. It wasn't the first time she'd done this, but the last time had been her father's personal property. This would be easier, she told herself. But then she remembered she hadn't felt responsible for her father's death.

The men working the day shift were already gone, and the others were still asleep, their snores resounding from the smaller room. Mallory had suggested including two rooms when she'd had the bunkhouse built. Later, if he decided to move on, it would do for a foreman's quarters. For now, and hopefully for a long time to come, the men who stood guard at night used it. They seemed to appreciate not being awakened by the day shift's comings and goings.

She counted the bunks and stopped at the third one on the bottom—Jud Kirkwood's. She hoped something in his belongings would point to family somewhere. She was sure they'd appreciate word of his passing, and the return of his few possessions as mementos.

And there looked to be very few. His saddlebags were hooked over the foot of his bunk. She started there. They contained only the usual trail items, such as safety matches, an oilcloth poncho and a roll of twine.

After she put them in the crate Bren had left for her to use, she noticed a pretty leather-covered box on his shelf. It was a bit heavy, giving her hope that she might find an address book inside. She sat on the bunk to look through it, but as she sank down, the mattress crinkled.

She stood and put the box back on the shelf before lifting the mattress. A copy of the *Sentinel* rested there, and when she lifted it, a thick envelope fell out from between the folds. She discarded the newspaper and picked up the envelope. There was nothing written on the outside.

Eager to see if it contained the name and address of someone she could contact, she flipped open the back flap. Perhaps there would be the beginnings of a letter home or, considering how thick the envelope was, maybe a letter he'd intended to answer.

She'd expected anything but a large number of silver certificates. They weren't all dollar notes, either. Her curiosity turned to worry as she thumbed through them. There were a few ones, but the rest were tens. She paid in tens. She started counting, but stopped at seventy-five. There were just as many, if not more, left to count. Where would a cowhand get this much money?

She sat back down on the bunk and stared at the

notes in her hands. Shamrock certainly hadn't paid him this much, even if he hadn't spent a dime. And if he'd had so much money, why come to work for her for fifty dollars a month? This was enough to buy the small spread he'd told her he wanted someday.

Helena shrugged. There were stranger things in Texas than a man who saved his wealth in his mattress. She noticed a piece of paper on the floor at her feet that must have fallen out of the newspaper, or out of the envelope when she'd pulled out the money. Leaning forward, she picked it up.

She unfolded it. And her hands started to shake as she read the note:

Kill Kane Saturday. Make it an accident. You get the other half when it's done. We'll be watching. Meet my paymaster in the usual place. Burn this note.

She stared in horror, then jumped when she heard footsteps. She looked up as Brendan sauntered in.

"Jimmy's waitin'. Did you— Lovey, what is it?" he asked. "Where did all this money come from?"

"It was Jud Kirkwood's." She held the note up, her hands still shaking. "This was with it."

Bren took the note, read it and looked back at her. "Well, I'm not surprised—those bales weren't an accident." He sat next to her. "No one tries to lower that much weight on their own. The rope wasn't so much frayed as cut. And the night of the raid, Mallory agreed they'd targeted me. Which probably saved my life. I was in the barn with Kirkwood. He'd volunteered to stand with me. I'm luckier to be alive than I thought."

Wrapping his arm around her shoulders, Bren said, "It'll be okay. I for one feel a lot better about you goin' about now that I know Kirkwood was the sharpshooter's target. As I said, I've known *I'm* a target for a while."

"I don't feel better. He was supposed to kill you. And something still doesn't make sense. Why kill him before he'd succeeded?"

"I'd say whoever wrote this decided the cost of a bullet was the cheaper second half of the payoff."

"But Harry reared. You weren't killed. He didn't succeed."

"From up on the hill it must have looked like he'd hit his mark." Bren gave her a little squeeze. "Now you have no need to feel guilty. Come on, you're done here. This is now my problem, as he'd committed a crime, so there's no need for you to do something you were dreading. You and your escort can get on the road."

Disheartened, she shook her head. "I don't feel like going to town." Looking down at all the notes spread at her feet, she felt anger surge through her. "Sometimes I hate money so much. I cried for him, and he'd tried to kill you for that blood money!"

"If you don't want to go, I'll walk you back to the house and you can take it easy today. Laze about on the porch. Or bake a pie with Maria, if doin' something feels better."

Brendan stood then and pulled her to her feet. They walked to the house, his arm around her waist, her legs feeling leaden.

How had their westward dream turned into such a nightmare?

It was nearly noon on Wednesday when Helena, Maria and their escort reached Tierra del Verde. With no desire to dawdle, they went straight to Abby's general store. Brendan rode on to the sheriff's office.

Helena walked in and caught her sister-in-law balanced on a chair, putting cans on a high shelf. "Abaigeal Kane Wheaton, what on earth do you think you're doing?"

It struck Helena that she'd instinctively done that three-name thing she'd always envied. Abby had become her sister. The one she'd always wanted. Warmth spread through her to her soul. Once again Bren had given her something deeper and more meaningful than anything money could buy.

Abby got down in a hurry and, through the blur of tears, Helena watched her rush toward her. All the danger and fear for Bren and their men, plus her own disappointment in Jud Kirkwood, had bubbled up from deep inside and there she stood, blubbering in the busy store. Then Abby's arms closed around her, hugging her tight.

"Come with me," Abby ordered, and pulled Helena into the back room. "Now you sit there and calm down." She stuck her head out the back door and shouted for Daniel to get into the store and help Maria with Shamrock's supplies. Then she rushed back to Helena and poured a glass of cool tea. "I can see you heard. Josh and I hoped I'd be able to silence all this nonsense before you came into town again."

Helena sniffled. "What are you talking about? I'm upset over Jud Kirkwood. He was always so nice to me."

"We saw it in the *Gazette*. I'm sorry you and Bren lost a friend."

"But he wasn't," she cried, and the story spilled out of her. In the telling, though, Helena's tears stopped. Her strength and a good dose of healthy anger took over.

"I wish I'd gone through his things before we buried him. I swear I'd have spat on his grave instead of crying over it. After being nice to me for months, he tried to kill my husband!"

"Oh, good sweet Lord, that brother of mine and this job of his with the Texas Rangers are going to be the death of me."

"This is about the raids, not the rangers. Bren's quitting the rangers as soon as he has the man ordering these raids behind bars. Now, what was all that about something you thought I'd heard, and you trying to end it?"

"Oh, me and my big mouth. I suppose you were bound to find out anyway. Suddenly the gossip about you and Lucien Avery is everywhere again. I've tried to tell them you would never betray my brother and that him leaving the way he did was all his fault. That you'd done nothing to drive him away. That you've been a saint to forgive him as easily as you have.

"I've been terrified that Bren would hear it and, hothead that he is, call him out. No one's seen Avery in weeks. Some say that proves you and he had an affair, because he's terrified Bren will kill him if he sees him. I think he's staying home because that big-time gambler who blew into town has been organizing poker games out at the Bar A. Avery has little need to come to town. Usually he gambles, or has a meal with you, or very occasionally stops in at the bank."

"I have to talk to Lucien. I'm sure he doesn't realize he's made the gossip worse by staying out of town."

"Listen to me, Helena. Brendan will have a cow if you go near Avery's house without him, and he'll not go there with you if he hears more of this. Maybe even if he doesn't. Just the mild talk before bothered him."

"Well, he's just going to have to pretend at Alex's summer social."

"Oh, sweetie, Alex and Patience aren't the ones having it this year. Patience isn't up to all the organizing, and she's a bit ungainly. They backed out. But to make matters worse, Josh heard Lucien Avery will host it at the Bar A."

"Actually, that may be perfect. Brendan and I will go, he'll chat with Lucien as if nothing's amiss, and the gossip will die its natural death."

Abby shook her head. "I know my brother. That isn't going to happen. He'll never go. Josh says the only way the gossip could have gotten this bad is if Avery himself started it somehow. Bren'll see it that way, too."

Helena thought back to that last luncheon she'd had with Lucien. How he'd touched her in a way that made her uncomfortable. Had he continued to hope for something between them even after she'd told him over two years ago it would never happen? He'd seemed to understand—until that last luncheon.

She needed a strategy. A foolproof one. She smiled. Brendan was a goner. "I need a new dress. One Bren will really like. Something a little more revealing than I usually wear. He has to go to this, so I have to make him want to go. Need to go. If we stay home, the talk will only get worse. If he won't go, I'll have to go alone. But together would do more good."

Abby shook her head. "I think you're wrong. He won't go. But it's necessary for one or both of you to put in an appearance."

Helena opened her mouth to ask if she had made anything lately that would do the trick. But Abby called out, "Daniel, your aunt and I are going next door to Cassie Abbot's shop. Now," she continued, turning toward the rear door, "you're in for a treat."

"You're taking me next door? I thought I'd buy something you'd made. Your smaller dresses are usually a close match for my figure. Abby, I can't give my business to your competitor."

"Well, aren't you sweet? Don't worry. She's not a competitor. With the baby coming, I'm not going to have time for such things, and I haven't felt up to all that work, either. I've given it up except for personal sewing. But don't worry, you're going to love Cassie. She belongs in Paris, not Tierra del Verde."

Helena followed Abby out her back door and into the one leading to Abbot's Ladies Apparel. Two hours later, Helena's lovely new silk gown was all boxed up, after a few relatively quick alterations. Helena was so fascinated with Cassie's Singer Model 15 sewing machine, she had Abby order her one.

The gown was the most special and daring dress Helena had bought since her father died. And it was all to tempt Brendan to attend the summer social, if only to publicly renew his claim to her.

"Are your eyes covered?" Helena called from the hall just outside the parlor, where Brendan waited to see her new dress.

"They're shut tight," he replied.

She crept quietly into the room. He didn't react, so she knew he wasn't peeking.

"Am I finally allowed to see what this dress looks like?" he demanded.

She took a deep breath. "You can open your eyes now."

He did. Then he blinked. "Jaysus. You're a vision. All pink and pretty." He stood. "We'll have a party so you get a chance to wear it."

"I bought it for the summer social. You will go with me, right?"

"Well now, you wouldn't be goin' dressed that way alone. Wild horses couldn't keep me from walkin' in with you on my arm. I suppose I'd better be prepared to defend my territory. Should I bring along my old baseball bat?"

She fought back the guilt. This was a carefully baited trap, but she needed every advantage. Helena wasn't looking forward to the next sentence, when she told him where the social was being held.

But when she'd made the full turn, about to say the dreaded words, Bren was there, taking advantage of her open mouth with his. He stepped back, his hands trailing down over the bodice. "It's soft. But not as soft as that skin of yours," he whispered, his fingers moving to caress her neck, then her breasts. He took her by the hips and pulled her against him, his substantial arousal pressing against her stomach.

"I say we call it a night. I have a hankerin' to have my hands full of the woman this dress shows off so nicely. So perfectly." His lips were back on hers, brushing them lightly as he purred, "Perfect. You're the perfect woman."

She didn't feel so perfect at that point, but he would be stubborn. Helena was as sure of that as she was that she'd be out of her pretty dress as fast as he could get the buttons undone. He was halfway there already. Maybe the rest of the news about the social could wait. What harm could come of waiting?

Chapter Sixteen

"You lied to me," Brendan said. Helena sat across the table from him, trying to look innocent. And failing. She might have beguiled him with that Easter parade of hers last night, but he was thinking straight again.

She looked up from playing with her food. "I didn't lie. I never said the social was at the Rocking R. It's the town's social. Alex doesn't have the exclusive right to hold it. You assumed it was there because he's done it the last two times. All I said was the dress was for the summer social, and I asked if you'd be going with me. You said something about needing to go to defend your territory. Then you said you'd have to bring your baseball bat. Sound a little familiar?"

Brendan crossed his arms. "You *won't* be goin' alone. You won't be going at all."

She smacked her hand on the table so hard she winced. "We have to attend. You don't understand. That gossip about Lucien and me is worse. Abby can't seem to quell it. Everyone seems to want to brand me a fallen woman. I've gone from an object of pity or a bad wife who drove you away, to a woman of questionable character, and now to an adulteress. And all I did was try to give you your dream, and have lunch with someone who respected me."

"Going is sure to stir up more gossip. Especially if I catch the bastard eyeing your—"

She jumped to her feet, stopping him from saying a word he knew he shouldn't. "I have to go to that social. We need to go together. You have to smile and shake Lucien's hand. Talk about cattle with him and pretend you don't hate him. Please."

Brendan gritted his teeth. "I won't step foot in his house. He might not have got you where he wanted you but believe you me, he wanted you, under him any way he could manage it."

Her eyes widened in genuine shock. "That was crude!"

Jaysus, did she think Bren didn't know he'd put his foot in it by letting his temper get away from him? She wanted him to chat with the man who'd nearly had her killed. "Well, you wanted to marry a dirty stinkin' miner, and you got the mouth to go with him."

She clenched her small hands into fists and leaned toward him, her tone lowered, her gaze accusatory. "Remember something, Brendan. When you talk about yourself like that, you talk about every miner who ever went down into the earth to earn bread for his family. Every miner who never came back out, or who almost didn't. Your own father included."

Between what she'd said and the tears rolling down her cheeks, he felt about two inches high. And that made him even madder. He steeled himself against those damned, irresistible tears. She was crying, but she was also screaming like a banshee. He tried to take comfort in that. She'd started the yelling. But he hadn't seen her this way since that first day he'd gotten here.

She took a shuddering breath, clearly trying to calm herself. He longed to reach out to her and explain that he was 99 percent sure Avery was the leader of the raiders. But he knew her. She'd be doubly determined to go, so her name wouldn't be linked to his when hell rained down on Avery's head. And Brendan knew himself. He was very likely to weaken and agree to go—and those tears were making that a near thing. Then she'd be facing Avery with knowledge of his deeds right there in her eyes for him to see.

"He's just a friend," she said, so patiently it was as if she thought she was talking to a daft lad of six. "You said you didn't believe I'd done more than go to luncheon with a friend. Why do you hate him so much?"

"I don't hate him," he lied smoothly. "I just don't trust his motives where you're concerned. And I won't accept his hospitality, feelin' like I do."

"How can you be so stubborn? I need your help, Brendan. *I'd* help *you*." She paused as a sob shook her.

He took advantage of the break to say again, "Ask anything of me but not this. I'll not be changin' my mind."

"Fine. Don't go. I'll go by myself. But remember this—you're making me walk in there and face this situation alone. A situation you already admitted is partially your fault in the first place. I guess it's fitting some of this is spilling onto you. Because thanks to this gossip, you, Ranger Kane, look like a poor cuckolded husband to everyone in town. How's your infernal pride feel now?" She whirled and stomped toward the front door.

He yelled after her. "If I go I'll look like the poor

stupid cuckolded husband." He winced as the door slammed behind her. He tossed his napkin to the table and sank back to his chair, stunned.

He needed to go after her. But maybe he'd be better off letting the storm pass. He'd go find her after she'd had a bit of time to cool down. Then he'd see if he couldn't get her to listen to reason.

Maria stormed in and picked up Helena's barely touched plate, then grabbed his meal from in front of him.

"Hey, now. I'm not finished with that."

"*Sí,* you are," Maria snapped. "When your belly gnaws at itself before noon, you remember. Lonely feel same pain, but it eats…eats the soul. I no like Señor Avery, but she was not sad the days she go meet him at hotel to talk to neighbor." The housekeeper shrugged. "Friend. But you on those days? Far, far from her."

"Do ya think I don't know that?" He jumped to his feet. "I've work to do. Tell her what you told me about your sister. Maybe she'll start to see him for what he is."

He worked like the devil after that. He started off cleaning stalls, because Jimmy had hurt himself trying to stack those damned bales that Kirkwood dumped. Another wrong to lay at Avery's feet. "I swear, I'm goin' to dance at the bastard's hanging," Bren muttered, dumping yet another barrow full of manure into the pile of horse dung out behind the barn.

With the barn as clean and sweet smelling as a barn ever got, he went to work on Blaze, the half-broke sorrel he had his eye on as a second horse for Helena. That stampede Doc had told him about was always in the back of his mind. If she insisted on riding with the herd, this little sorrel would be her horse.

The mare was sweet tempered, though still skittish. She had four perfect stockings that matched her wide blaze—distinctive enough markings to set her apart from the rest of Shamrock's working stock. He hated the idea of Helena grabbing just any mount out of the remuda, where it was easy to mix up the best and the worst.

Blaze danced away from him as he approached her, but warmed up quickly. Needing to keep her calm helped him tamp down his anger.

By the time he was done with Blaze for the day, he'd started to see the social more and more from Helena's point of view. She saw what Avery wanted her to see—a fellow rancher who'd been her friend when she most needed one. She knew nothing of his savage misdeeds. If she did, she'd be calling for his blood, same as Brendan.

Helena also knew Brendan had lived among a notorious gang and had managed to avoid being found out. He could lie with the best of them when he needed to, and she knew it. Which meant he should be able to hide his feelings from Avery. No wonder she'd been crying while she'd screamed at him. She'd all but begged him, and he'd turned her down at the cost of her reputation.

Damn. Was she right that the simple act of them putting in an appearance as a couple would end the gossip? Hell, what did he know about how society worked? Except, of course, he knew how damned mean some women could be, and how inappropriate men could be to a woman with a damaged reputation. He'd watched his sister and nephew being picked at for years by members of one of the lowest levels in modern society—the wives of miners. Brendan sighed. Would he ever learn not to let his temper get the better of him?

He left the sorrel in the corral and rushed to the house and Helena. He sure as hell hoped Maria hadn't told her about what happened to her sister. Because it looked as if he was going to be shaking hands with the devil himself come Saturday, and he didn't want Avery questioning what it was that had changed Helena's opinion of him. Walking into the snake's den was going to be dangerous enough.

When he couldn't find Helena in the house, he went to the kitchen, where Maria told him she'd gone riding.

He stalked back out of the house. Maybe Helena hadn't had such a bad idea. He needed to clear his head, too, and nothing did that better than having the wind in your face and a lively horse under you.

Brendan returned to the corral and got a saddle on Blaze. Then he mounted up and gave orders for the gate to be opened. After a few halfhearted bucks, she settled a bit and he gave the mare her head. Off they went, galloping over hills, leaping a few streams and scaring more than a few head of cattle. She finally slowed and obeyed his direction to head back toward the house.

He let his mind wander then to the Helena he'd first met, as lost in the hills of Pennsylvania as she was in life. She'd been a sad, naive girl grieving for her murdered father. But when Brendan had purposely looked away, she'd developed a will of iron and become the woman who'd borrowed a priest's gun to force Bren to do what he most wanted to do—marry her.

Texas had changed that impulsive young woman into one she'd had to become to survive without him. He wished he knew if she could look sweetly at Avery and hate the air he breathed, which she would when the truth came out. But Bren couldn't take that chance with her life.

Trying to sort out his raw feelings and think past them, he let the sorrel drift along toward the home place, until he realized they were in the low meadow behind the house. It was overlooking this piece of land that Helena still started and ended her days.

Something Doc had said the night of the raid filtered back to the forefront of Bren's thoughts. He'd mentioned that Helena had already picked out a pretty spot for a family cemetery.

Brendan stood in his stirrups, looking for fencing or anything out of place in the wild landscape. Then he realized what was wrong with that. If she'd picked out land for a cemetery, why hadn't she mentioned burying Jud Kirkwood there, considering how hard she'd taken his death at the time?

Bren saw it then—a marker sheltered under the low-hanging branches of a big old live oak. The branches all but hid the well-tended grave. He'd stood up there at the top of the hill, wondering what it was she saw when she looked out over the valley. Had she lost a member of her original group of cowhands in that stampede?

Curious about that lone marker, he dismounted and led the sorrel over to the small but intricately carved stone.

Kathleen Kane * Beloved Daughter * December 3, 1876 * The best of us * Always loved * Never forgotten.

"Oh Jaysus, no." Brendan's knees hit the dirt hard enough to rattle his teeth. But he barely noticed. Her child. Their child. When she'd been hurt in that stampede, this had been part of it. When he'd left, she'd been carrying their baby. And lost it.

He touched the stone. Traced the words. Trying to wrap his brain around it all, he blinked back the blur of tears. Here lay a babe, one he'd never known about. A babe he'd never held. A babe whose grave he'd not dug, though it had been his duty. A sweet little girl robbed of life because her mother had been doing the job of her father.

All because he'd left.

And what was worse, at that time no one had known where he was. What had Doc said? The only ones who'd known Helena had been hurt were the Mallorys, Shamrock's men and the Clemenses.

She wouldn't have wanted to force Bren to come back to her. He'd have welcomed the excuse, but she couldn't have known that. Who was he trying to fool? She'd probably, and rightly so, blamed him for Kathleen's death. Why would she have wanted him back? Wanted him to know? In fact, she still hadn't told him.

Calling on Abby for support would have put his sister in a bad spot. She'd have been forced to betray one of them. Which had left Helena in the midst of strangers while she'd grieved for her lost child.

Alone.

Again.

If the thought haunted him, what had it done to her? She'd lived alone for so long. To go through so much heartache and loss, all alone?

No wonder she'd never said she loved him. He'd wondered why her love had turned to hate. He had his answer. He'd broken more than her heart. He'd inadvertently killed their child.

How could she forgive him for the loss of their baby, when it would never have happened if he'd been where he should have been?

When he was young and his temper had got the best of him, Da would say, "You can't unring a bell, son."

No, you couldn't unring a bell. Still clutching the stone marker, Brendan closed his eyes. You couldn't undo most life-changing mistakes. You'd think he'd have learned that by now.

The first thing he intended to do was beg her forgiveness again—for all of it, this time. And he'd happily go to the damned summer social. He'd lived with Lyons and his gang, dammit. He would shake hands with Avery, smile sweetly and chat. He'd get the point across to every neighbor that after he'd been an idiot, she'd taken him back, anyway.

And if Doc told him there'd be no children, he'd get himself to the orphan train and bring her back an apple-cheeked baby. Maybe one with siblings. She'd have a family to love and cherish.

He opened his eyes again and stared at the stone. "I'll make up for this, Kathleen. I swear I will." An unexpected sob racked him. Before he could keep his promise, he had to find his Helena.

Helena rode Paint Box full-out, heading to town and Abby's arms. Once there, she turned from tying her horse to the hitching rail in front of Abby's store and bumped into Lucien. He looked impeccable as always in his tan summer suit.

He caught her lightly by the arms, a marked change from the last time he'd touched her. "Helena, what a wonderful surprise. I was checking on my order for Saturday. Your sister-in-law has everything well in hand. She's very good at running her husband's store, but I confess I don't understand why Joshua Wheaton allows his wife to do such menial labor. Do you know she actually made the clothing she used to sell?"

Helena could only stare. Had Lucien only recently become a blowhard, or had she been so starved for companionship she'd ignored it? Now his judgmental attitude infuriated her. "Unless the fairies were in there sewing every night, how else would all those dresses have been available? When I ride herd on Shamrock's cattle, is that the distasteful menial kind of work you mean?"

"Of course not. You know how much I respect all you've done with that derelict ranch. You've worked wonders."

How did Brendan have her doubting a man who'd been her friend in really dark times? "I'm sorry. I'm in a terrible mood."

"So it wasn't me who's upset you? That husband of yours? I can see you've been crying." He took her hand. "He won't be around to hurt you much longer. I promise."

She blinked. "Lucien, what goes on between Bren and me is not your problem. I don't need your influence with the governor. I don't want Bren transferred. I was upset, yes. But it's mostly that Bren's furious about all these awful rumors. I'm trying to convince him that if he comes to the social with me a lot of this nonsense would go away, but he doesn't understand how society works."

"Rumors? What is all this about rumors?" Avery asked, clearly confused. She supposed he hadn't heard.

She felt a blush heat her face that she'd inadvertently put him in this position. "They're saying there are improper feelings between you and me. And that we… well, that we did, were doing, something about them before Brendan came back."

Lucien's eyebrows rose in surprise. "And of course that's preposterous. Between us, I mean. It's always been Kane, hasn't it?"

She'd heard something in his tone again. Anger? At her? Or the gossipers? "Lucien, we've always understood that, haven't we? I told you that years ago."

He held his hands up, palms facing her. "Heard and understood, my dear. It's these scandalmongers I'm annoyed with. I'll see what I can do to quell some of it."

She breathed a sigh of relief. "Oh, thank you. And please don't be so scarce around town. Apparently even that is suspect. You can't simply be busy. No. They think you've been hiding from Bren's gun."

Lucien smiled. But his dark eyes seemed too serious for a smile. "Well, I do hear he's fast," he said.

Now she understood. "Bren's a lawman, Lucien. He'd never shoot an innocent man over rumors he knows are false. Bren's integrity means a great deal to him, as does being a Texas Ranger."

"Yes. He left you to pursue that path, after all." Avery pulled his watch out and popped it open. "Goodness, I have to get moving, Helena. It's been an interesting chat. I do hope you make it to the social, with or without your husband. But I won't be surprised not to find you there."

With that said he hurried off. As accidental as it was, Lucien had challenged her. She *would* be there. With or without Brendan. Mad all over again, she stalked up the steps and into Abby's shop. "I'm going to strangle that brother of yours," she shouted without preamble. Luckily, to an empty store. "Abby?"

"I'm back here with my feet up," her sister-in-law called out. "Won't go to the social, huh?" she said when Helena reached her. "Have a seat. Don't feel too bad about Brendan. Josh won't go, either, which is odd, as Lucien Avery is one of the bank's bigger depositors."

"I don't know how to convince him. I talked. I screamed."

Abby gestured to Helena's face. "You cried."

"He makes me so angry. He won't listen."

"I told you. My brother is pigheaded."

Helena started to feel a little weepy again. "I'd do anything for him and I have. But he refused. I have to go. You know I do."

"I don't like you going alone. Not in that dress, especially."

Helena dropped into the chair on the other side of the small dining table that Abby kept in the back room. "No, if I go alone, that gown won't convince anyone Lucien is just a friend. I'll wear something else. That dress was for Bren."

"Well, at least tell me my brother enjoyed it."

Helena nodded, then shrugged. "But not enough to convince him to go."

"If I see him before Saturday, you'll be on his arm at that social," Abby promised.

Helena hoped she was right.

After they chatted for a while, Helena left for home. But she'd just mounted up when Doc Clemens rushed around the corner. "Helena, this is a miracle. My dear, I need your help and you're the perfect person. I've been called to the bed of a young woman. It sounds as if she's losing her baby."

Her heart cried for the poor woman. "How can I help?"

"I've had to leave Georgia caring for Amanda Green. She's in heavy labor. But you should know the other young woman I'm going to see has been savagely beaten. She works above stairs, my dear."

"Above stairs?"

"At the Golden Garter. She's sixteen and all alone in the world. There are back stairs, so you wouldn't be seen going in."

Helena felt her heart squeeze. Sixteen. At sixteen she'd been reading Shakespeare with her tutor and excelling at embroidery. Overwhelmed with charity for the girl, Helena nodded. "I'll follow you there."

Helena spent three hours with Lucy Ortiz. The soiled dove wouldn't tell anyone the identity of the customer who'd beaten her. She feared reprisal. Helena extended an offer of help once she recovered. Lucy wanted to run as far from the man as her meager savings would allow. So Helena offered an education and the safety of a boarding school back East. She didn't know if Lucy would take her up on the offer or not.

Helena finally left her, when Georgia arrived. As she rode home, Helena thought about the man she'd met, the one who'd gone for the doctor. He was a big-time gambler, new to town, and Lucien's new poker-playing friend. He seemed very nice, a decent sort who was quietly furious at what had happened.

She had also met the woman in charge of the business above stairs. Darla, the madam, was rough around the edges, but despite her occupation, was genuinely nice. She could easily have been the wife of a farmer. Helena left, her head filled with thoughts of how one decision could change someone's life.

Hers had been her decision to take advantage of being left unchaperoned in Wheatonburg. She'd gone riding alone in the hills and met a handsome, green-eyed man named Brendan Kane. And had fallen hopelessly in love.

Chapter Seventeen

"Maria," Brendan called into the kitchen, "have ya seen Helena?"

"No. She says she need time away to...think or... maybe not to think. I learn new word from her. She want to *strangle* the *señor?*"

Brendan sighed and nodded. Could he feel any lower? "Were you here in the beginning?" he asked. He needed to know if Helena had at least had Maria when the baby died.

"I come a few weeks after the *señora* was hurt. She sad. Very sad. Why you leave sweet *señora* alone?"

"Reasons that don't amount to a hill of beans. This thing with the social at the Bar A—*that* I have good reasons for. For her I'll do what feels wrong, and trust she knows best.

"If you see her before I do, don't tell her about your sister. I don't want that knowledge in her eyes if we go to the bastard's house. And it would be."

He left then and crossed to the main house, checking the entire place once more. As he opened the front door, he found Sheriff Ryan Quinn ready to knock. "Ryan. What can I do for ya?"

"It's what I can do for you." He held up a piece of paper. "Wire from your major. I figured you'd want this as soon as possible. It's marked urgent."

Brendan took it. Read it. And cursed. "Jaysus, why now?" He raked a hand though his hair. "I have to get to Mountain Home. There's a witness to the Belleza massacre. He was gut shot this mornin', but he's alive. His chances wouldn't be good, I suppose. I have to get there fast or I might miss the chance to talk to him." And he had to get back by Saturday or Helena would go to Avery's social alone.

"You want to throw your gear together?" Ryan asked. "I'll ride as far as town with you. If I had a decent deputy I'd go along. There's no sense pretending Avery hasn't got a price on your hide."

Brendan stepped back to admit him, but Ryan shook his head. "Is that black of yours likely to let me saddle him?"

"Should, but have Jimmy help. Harry likes the kid. Once he's saddled, could you bring him up to the house? That'd save time. I'll be all set in a few minutes."

Brendan took less time gathering what he needed than he did trying to compose a note to Helena. He finally started writing, and said what was in his heart.

Lovey,
I waited for you to come home, but I have to leave.
I'm ordered to Mountain Home to talk to a wit-
ness of the attack on Belleza. The witness likely
won't live long or I'd have gone after Saturday.
I apologize for being so stubborn about going to

*Avery's. I'll move heaven and earth to get back
in time to take you to that social. If I am delayed,
please don't go alone.
With all my love,
Bren*

He stared at his unconsciously written closing. He
picked up the paper to tear it up, but stopped and read
the words again.

No. He'd leave it.

She did have all his love. He loved her. He'd never
stopped. He'd been captivated from the moment she'd
come into view that day in the Pennsylvania hills. She'd
had the sun at her back and it had turned her golden
tresses into an angelic halo.

Then she'd smiled and said, "I'm lost, Sir Knight.
Are you free to save a damsel in distress?" And he'd
tumbled helplessly into love with an American princess.

It had become their place, that little fishing spot.
He'd rarely fished there again, because he'd soon been
too busy making love to her.

Then had come the day she'd arrived upset and shaking. She'd said her guardian had run out of patience with
her insistence on mourning her father for a full year.
Her guardian was taking her to New York, to start to
introduce her to men he'd called "worthy of an heiress."
She'd said he wanted her well and truly wed, and her
affairs her husband's problem.

"What was it you were waitin' for, if not to mourn
your father?" Bren had asked carefully, worried what
she'd say....

"Love, Bren. A love like I've found with you. We

could run away. Get married the way we planned. But not next year. Now. Then I'd be shut of him."

Brendan had hesitated, unsure if he had the right to take a wife. He and his family had been scrimping and saving for years to pay their debt to Wheaton mining, so they could all head to Texas. To add Helena to the mix would mean working even longer in the mines to earn enough to get them all West.

"You're an angel," he said, instead of beginning to make plans to run off with her. "How much of a problem could an angel be to an angel's guardian?" he asked, hoping to tease her into one of her beautiful smiles. If she continued to refuse the men, she and Bren could stick with their plans.

She'd shrugged, looking uncertain, worried. "Well, it's really my father's investments and the way Daddy handled them that are driving him mad. He's constrained by the way loans and such are written. Daddy did business much differently than Uncle Franklin does. He finds it distasteful, which is really—"

"Franklin?" Brendan interrupted. His stomach turned to stone. It couldn't be. Fate couldn't be that cruel. "Jaysus, not Franklin Gowery?"

She rolled her eyes. "One and the same." But she'd seemed to be fighting tears. "I think I hate him. I don't understand how Daddy could have left me in his care." She'd looked up then, blue eyes sparkling with tears, and worry—real, terrible worry—took over her features. "Bren, what's wrong? You won't let him scare you, will you? We'll still go West. You, me and your family. Right?"

Her voice was filled with fear. Sounded small. He ignored any sympathy bubbling up, and kept it stuffed behind his anger. She'd hidden a terrible secret from him. "How much of a problem are you for him, Helena? How much money did your father leave to you?"

Had he not been sitting, he'd have staggered at the sum she named.

"Why do you care?" she cried. "We love each other. You didn't want me for my money. That's how I know you love me. Not like all the rest. They'll fawn and kowtow to him, and smile at me no matter how rude I am to them. They'll care nothing for me. They're just worshiping at the shrine of money. I've seen it for years while I traveled with Daddy."

"What would happen if we ran off? You know your guardian will never condone you marrying me."

"As if I care one whit what he likes and doesn't." She was angry now, her blue eyes flashing.

"What would happen?" Bren demanded.

"The money is mine on my twenty-first birthday no matter what, or sooner if I marry a man Uncle Franklin approves of. I don't care. Daddy was probably killed over money. I don't need it as long as I have you."

"But what would happen to it?"

A little frown drew her eyebrows together. "Later, when I turn twenty-one, in March of '76…well, life would simply get easier for all of us. It's not that long to wait. Of course, if he refuses to turn it over to me, I wouldn't have the money to fight him. So I might have to let him keep it. Or pay him off with a big share of it." She must have gotten an inkling of how Brendan felt, for she added, "It won't matter to us, anyway. We'll have each other."

But it would matter to him no matter how it went. He knew himself that well, anyhow. His heart breaking, he stood. Backed away. "I can't do that to you. I won't. You should live as you've always lived. I can't give you what you were meant to have. Go home to your uncle. Go find a man who can give you all the things you've always had."

She knelt up on the quilt and extended a hand to him. "Bren, please. You're scaring me. You don't know what you're talking about. You don't know how he—"

"I know all I need to know now. All of it. I'd never realized who your father was. *Harry* Conwell, right?" He'd said her father's name like the curse it surely must be. "It has to be him."

If she got her inheritance, how could he use such blood money on their future? But how could he cost her the life she'd always had? "What is it you think I could ever give you that you couldn't get on your own?"

"You're talking about *things*. I don't care about things. I care about you. I love you. Not the dollar signs Franklin Gowery and his ilk care about."

"You say that now, but you have no idea what it is you'd be signin' on for. Look at you, in your fine, pretty dress. Abby hasn't had the material to make a new one in years, and she's never had a shop make one for her. Can you even thread a needle, Helena?"

"I'm wealthy, not stupid. Have a little faith in me. Is that too much to ask? Please, Bren, don't be this way."

"The problem is you seem to have too much faith in me. I'm nothin' to a man like Franklin Gowery, and I'd have been nothin' to your father if he were here. I'm a dirt-poor, Irish mine worker. I do the same work as the German and Welsh miners, yet I get paid less. I toil at a job I hate and don't even get the respect of their lowly status."

"What has status to do with love? I love you. I gave myself to you. We've made love. Did that mean nothing to you?"

"It did. But you've made a bad bargain with your love and your body. And apparently, it meant more to you than the truth, as you never told me. I never had a chance. We never had a chance...."

Now, Brendan squeezed his eyes tight, trying to banish the memory of his idiocy. Enough! Enough memories of what a fool he'd been. And was still being. Enough of letting pride stand in his way. After seeing that sweet little grave, he knew how lucky he was to be in Helena's life at all. Enough of waiting for her to love him again before he told her how he felt. He needed her to know his every thought, word and deed were colored by his love for her.

Brendan folded the note in half, leaving it as he'd written it, and placed it on her pillow, where she was sure to find it.

Then he hurried to get on the road. The quicker he left, the sooner he'd return home. Having Ryan Quinn ride with him until he got through town was worth the rush. Ryan was right. Bren knew he couldn't be too careful.

On the ride to town he and the sheriff decided Brendan's obvious murder would invite an investigation by even more rangers. Avery wouldn't want that, so they figured his new sharpshooter might be less a danger to Brendan than they'd first thought.

Severn Duvall walked out the back door of Connor's Saloon and saw Brendan and the sheriff talking. Moments later, Irish wheeled that big black of his away and rode out of town in the opposite direction to Shamrock. The sheriff rode toward Severn down the alley.

"He's going to Mountain Home. Dying witness to the Belleza raid," the sheriff murmured as he stopped his mount. A bit louder he said, "Thanks for your help with Lucy Ortiz this morning. Are you sure you don't know who it was who beat her?"

Of course, they both knew it had been Avery, but appearances had to be fostered, so it would look as if Severn had lied to protect the rancher.

The undercover ranger shook his head, then tipped his hat. "You have a nice day now."

As Quinn went off to do his job, Severn figured he should get to his. He had a nice little winning streak going at Connor's expense. Two hours later, with his pockets full of tens and a new gold watch, Severn walked toward the Garter, hoping for information and perhaps another lucky streak.

He'd just reached the corner of the business district when a couple shots rang out. Severn pulled his Remington and ran toward the bank. Through the open window he could see Ryan Quinn on the floor, bleeding.

The masked man with his gun trained on the teller wore black, had black hair, and his shirt sported silver-colored buttons. He also spoke with a poor attempt at Brendan's mild Irish accent. This was a setup. A damn clumsy one. It was probably meant to look as if Brendan had suddenly taken up bank robbery. Severn had little doubt money from this robbery would be found somewhere at Shamrock.

He heard quick steps coming his way and looked back as Joshua Wheaton charged toward the bank.

Severn pulled him into the alley. "Stay here. You get yourself killed, Irish would have my head."

"*Ranger* Duvall?" Wheaton asked.

Severn winced. "Keep that under your hat and stay right behind me," he ordered, then moved back into position outside the bank. If the robber made a move on Quinn, Severn would put one right between his shoulder blades. The nervous teller handed over an old carpet bag ostensibly full of money. The robber checked it and nodded. "Now that was smart of ya." He turned and aimed at Quinn. Severn fired and the robber dropped like a rock.

Turning to Joshua Wheaton, Severn handed him his short-barreled, pocket Remington. "Now get in there, unmask the dead man and be the hero of the day. By now they all probably think Brendan is the one dead on the floor. Go along with anything I say."

Wheaton nodded and hurried forward, Severn trailing slowly behind. When no one congratulated him on his shot, he figured he was still just the new gambler in town, and his cover was intact. He followed Joshua Wheaton into the bank, where the man did as ordered—sent someone to go for the doctor, then checked the dead bandit, unmasking him.

The small, bespectacled teller who'd handed over the bagful of money gasped. "I'd have sworn that was your brother-in-law, Mr. Wheaton."

"Brendan's a ranger. He'd never take a cent that wasn't his. Even if this man had gotten away, I'd have known it wasn't my brother-in-law."

Some prune-faced woman said, "I'd have sworn it was him."

"And you'd have been wrong, Mrs. Bradley," Wheaton replied.

A nicely dressed woman knelt next to the sheriff, unmindful of her lovely dress. She held a delicate handkerchief against Quinn's wound.

Severn handed her his larger one and turned to Wheaton. "The sheriff was fortunate you came along."

Brendan's brother-in-law took his cue perfectly. "Lucky, Mr. Duvall. But it looked like the robber was intent on killing the sheriff. I had to fire."

The doctor rushed in then and Severn took the opportunity to fade into the crowd.

Helena rode to Shamrock's barn and hurried inside, to find Harry gone. It scared her. She prayed Bren had only gone riding to expel his demons, as she had. She looked toward the house, but Jimmy followed her into the barn to take Paint Box. She needed to know if Bren had left her again without a word.

"Jimmy, how long has Brendan been gone?"

"A few hours, ma'am."

Maybe he was out looking for her. "Did he say where he was going?"

Jimmy nodded, his eyes alive with excitement. "Sheriff Quinn came to the barn and had me help him saddle up Harry for the ranger. He said Ranger Kane got a telegram from Major Jones. Ranger Kane had to hurry to some other town about the raids."

Despite Jimmy's exhilaration, and her own relief that business had taken Bren away, Helena felt disappointment blossom in her heart. "He had to leave?"

"In a real rush!"

Mindful that Maria would have the evening meal

ready soon, Helena set off for her room, to change out of her riding clothes. And there, propped on the pillows, she found a letter from Brendan. She held it for a moment, afraid to read it. Suppose he'd left for good again? Was one argument really all he would stand? Each time he'd left her that was all it had taken.

Finally, her need to be sure pushed her past her fear of what the letter might say. She unfolded the note and read the short missive, then read it again. She didn't know what to think. He seemed sincere about the urgency of the trip, his reluctance to go and his promise to try to get back for the social.

Then her heart quickened as the closing words sank in. "All my love, Brendan," she read aloud. He wouldn't have written those words carelessly. Bren was anything but careless. She sat there, stunned. Just that morning she'd thought her world had ended. It had felt as if he'd chosen to care more about his ferocious jealousy than her desperate need to repair the damage she'd foolishly done to her reputation. Then, after hours of brooding, of accepting that her problem was as much her fault for having continued her weekly lunches, as his for leaving her, she'd returned, to find it all not only fixed, but changed. Oh, she couldn't wait to see him, to tell him she loved him, too.

In the light of his declaration, she wished she could back down about attending the social. But if she didn't go, the gossip would get even worse. If it affected only her, she might not care. But if a miracle happened and she was blessed with children, they'd have to grow up and go to school in this town. She had to put a stop to this gossip once and for all.

But she would wait as long as possible for Brendan.

Even the gossip and her obligation to walk among her detractors and smile sweetly couldn't dull the words he'd written.

With all my love.

Helena sat there like a young, love-struck girl, tracing those precious words and silently reading them over. And over. And over again. And she smiled, feeling younger. Lighter. Happier than she had in a long time. Because Brendan loved her.

Chapter Eighteen

Helena stopped the gig under the portico of Lucien's home, surprised at how palatial it was. She'd grown up visiting houses as ornate, but here in the Tierra del Verde area such lavish architecture was out of place. She shrugged. Lucien was free to spend his money any way he wanted.

A young cowhand stepped out of the shadows created by the stairs, and tipped his hat. "Evening, ma'am." He held out his hand to help her down.

"Thank you," she said. "Please leave my rig easily available. My husband is due back at first light, so I'll probably be leaving earlier than nearly everyone else."

"Suppose I park it right over there at the head of the ranch road?"

She smiled. "Splendid." Fluffing her skirt, she waited there at the foot of the ornate stairs to make sure she knew where he'd left the gig. She didn't intend to stay longer than she had to. She was at the social for one reason only— to prove she'd never been more than a friend to Lucien or less than a wife to Bren.

She'd even worn Brendan's favorite dress. It was a

lilac voile frock with a modest, square, lace-edged neck-line and a fitted waist. A six-inch-wide lace ruffle fes-tooned its elbow-length sleeves and the full overskirt. Bren always winked and said she looked sweet enough to devour for dessert. Helena hoped for sweet and rela-tively innocent, tonight.

She wished Bren had made it home, but that wasn't to be. After waiting for him as long as she could, she'd left for the social.

Dreading the coming ordeal, she advanced upward toward the front door. Right then she'd rather be any-where than entering an oppressively sumptuous home she feared was hostile territory.

The social seemed to be in full swing as she entered the house and turned into what appeared to be an elab-orate parlor. She was about to say hello to Martha Bell when she heard Ophelia Bradley, the mayor's wife, say, "I think she must have had a hand in decorating this place. She's an heiress, after all. I hear her father's for-tune rivaled that of John D. Rockefeller's.

"Like the rest of those rich folks, she apparently thinks money gives her leave to climb into *b-e-d* with anyone she wants, and escape the consequences. One wonders what it is she came to Texas to avoid. She cer-tainly drove that sweet Ranger Kane away quick enough after he brought her here. Imagine her shock when that husband of hers came back."

Helena longed to inform the mayor's wife that John D. Rockefeller was a staunch Baptist who gave God credit for his wealth, as had her father.

She nearly spoke up when Martha said, "But Abby Wheaton absolutely adores Helena, which she wouldn't if Helena had treated her brother shabbily. Abby lays the blame for the estrangement on her brother. She says this gossip is wrong. And that Brendan and Helena are deliriously happy."

"You mark my words, Martha Bell..."

Helena turned away, her cheeks burning. She couldn't say much more to defend herself than Martha had said on her behalf. And she would never convince Ophelia Bradley. Needing to regroup, Helena backed out of the room.

She moved to the doorway across the hall and peeked in. The music was much better than their ragtag group of local talent ever sounded. At the far end of the unexpectedly large room what looked to be a professional orchestra played. Helena found it ironic that Lucien would go to the trouble of bringing them in when the homegrown group Alex usually used had been good enough for Alex, a British aristocrat.

She quickly decided this was the wrong place for her at the moment, as well, but before she could retreat, Lucien's voice boomed, "Helena, my dear. You've finally arrived."

She blinked as all heads turned toward her.

"Ladies and gentlemen," Lucien was saying. "Here is my hostess for the evening, the lovely Helena Conwell." Everyone gasped.

As had happened in front of the hotel the afternoon Brendan had come to town looking for her, Lucien grabbed her wrist in a tight grip that felt impossible to break, and ushered her toward the bandstand. The dancers parted and the orchestra stopped playing.

"Lucien, what are you doing? Have you forgotten I'm a married woman?" His grasp only tightened more, making her wince. She would never break his hold.

She told herself to think her way out of this situation. Helena allowed him to request a tune of the orchestra, but as he let go of her arm to move to a dance position, she stepped back and patted her hair. "You could give a lady a moment to freshen up, Lucien. I only just arrived. Excuse me," she said, and stepped farther back.

Free at last, she started to walk away, but noticed she still had everyone's attention. May as well make the best of a bad situation, she thought, and turned back. She didn't know why, but the band stopped playing again.

"Lucien, a bit too much refreshment seems to have gone to your head. You're clearly confused. My name is Helena Conwell *Kane*. A name I wear proudly and have from the day I took it. I told you that the first day you asked me to share your table at the hotel, and that has never changed.

"I don't know why you would announce me as your hostess when I was supposed to arrive with Brendan. He's been delayed in Mountain Home or he'd be at my side. As for you and me, I'm not even sure we're friends anymore. Since the day Shamrock was raided we've seen each other exactly once—Thursday, in front of the general store. A true friend might have stopped by Shamrock to see how I was faring, after being shot. Now, if you'll excuse me…"

"My," Lucien said, a smug tone to his voice. "I suppose I should be used to her difficult moods."

Helena ignored the embarrassed little titters from the crowd and walked out of the ballroom on the other side from where she'd entered.

She was going home.

She and Brendan would have to find another way to

suppress the gossip. She'd been a naive fool about tonight and about Lucien's intentions toward her.

A hall off to the right beckoned. She rushed down it and around a corner, looking for an exit. Unfortunately, the hall ended at a large library and office. Lucien's, she assumed. Helena gritted her teeth. She certainly didn't want to go in there. She might smash something valuable. Something very valuable! She whirled and retraced her steps before her temper got the best of her.

Nearing the turn in the hall, she heard two men talking, and froze. She was so uncontrollably angry at that point she was liable to say or do anything if she encountered more gossip.

"Embarrassing him like that was foolish," a man said. "He has a hell of a temper with women."

Another man's voice reached her next. She recognized it as the gambler's she'd met in town. "You forget I witnessed it firsthand. When I saw all the blood, I thought Lucy Ortiz might die. I'm glad I got suspicious and went upstairs. After I found her I knew why Avery had gone out the back way."

"You sure it was him who beat her? Chancy, showing himself like that."

"I saw him go up, but he must have left by the back stairs. And really, how chancy was it?" the gambler asked. "No dove ever tells who beat her if the local law asks. Besides, men don't convict other men of that kind of treatment of a whore. It's wrong, but there it is."

Helena couldn't believe her ears. She'd like to say she couldn't believe Lucien was capable of using his fists on a woman, but she could still feel the burn of that iron grip on her wrist.

As if a facade had begun to crack, in the last months

she'd begun to see hints of a different man than the one she'd thought she knew. But she hadn't imagined he could actually be a bad person.

"I've seen it with the doves he brings us here from Mountain Home. The one he picks for himself always looks scared."

As if to confirm what she'd finally realized, the gambler said, "Avery isn't the man Helena Kane thinks he is."

"Something else," the other man said. "From what I've heard around here, he's wanted Shamrock since it was the Circle O. He thought he'd wait for it to go completely derelict and pick it up for a song. Then she bought it out from under him. She couldn't have known who she'd gotten the better of."

Helena heard the sound of a match being struck, and then smelled tobacco smoke before the man continued, "I hear tell a few months later, Avery had some of his hired guns cause a stampede at Shamrock, and that she was nearly killed."

Managing to stifle a gasp, Helena put a hand to her stomach. Lucien had ordered the stampede. He'd killed her precious baby, perhaps her only one, if Doc's dire warning came true. Fury boiled through her. She'd blamed herself and Brendan, when all along it had been a man she'd called friend.

The stranger talking with the gambler continued the conversation. "The men I've talked to since I got hired tell me he changed his plans for her a while later when he got a look at her and heard who her father was. He still wants the ranch, but he wants the money, too. Now he means to get Kane out of the picture and talk her into becoming his wife."

"You'd better get back out that side door before he realizes you're mixing with his guests," the gambler said.

"Yeah, you're right," the other man said, his voice growing nearer her position. "Keep in touch. It was good to see you again."

Hurrying back down the hall, Helena forced herself to step into Lucien's study. She was just as unsure of these men as she was of Lucien. His pungent cologne permeated the room she'd stepped into. The odor turned her stomach as she started to ease the door shut.

Before she got it latched, she had to freeze because the two continued down the hall nearly to the study.

She peeked through the crack and saw they had stopped at the door on the left. "There was one other thing I thought you needed to know—"

Afraid to keep the door open, she eased it shut, closing off their voices. She'd heard enough ranch gossip to haunt her all the way home and beyond.

Pacing silently to the windows, she found what she expected. The house sat too high on this side for an escape that didn't involve a possible broken neck. Which meant, until the men moved on, she was trapped.

Trying to take her mind off all the disturbing information she'd overheard, Helena stopped at a bookcase and noticed *Voices in the Night,* the book of poetry she'd given Lucien.

He probably didn't even like Longfellow. In an act of spite, she reached for the volume, tempted beyond measure to take back the gift. But as she tipped it forward from the top to grasp it, she felt a vibration through the spine, and a click echoed in the silent room. Then the bookcase swung toward her, pushing her back a couple steps, as it seemed to float toward her.

Curious, she peeked behind the bookcase, and her stomach turned over. Illuminated by a nearby sconce, a painting hung on the wall of a secret room. It was a painting she'd seen in the home of Don Alejandro Varga. A house the raiders had burned to the ground, after murdering the wealthy sheep rancher and his many employees.

Lucien wasn't only after Shamrock. His greed went beyond that. He was behind the raids. Helena looked at the painting again and shivered. She had to get out of there.

As quickly and silently as she could, she put everything back the way she'd found it. Then she moved to the door, praying the men had moved on.

And they had.

What was better, she now knew how to leave the house while avoiding Lucien. If she saw him, he'd know. She was tempted to lift a pistol from one of the men, press it to Lucien's chest and blow his cold heart to smithereens.

He'd killed their Kathleen.

She peered up the hall and saw no one. Then, creeping to the door of the room Lucien's informative employee had used, she held her breath and looked inside. Empty. But there was the door the two had talked about.

Helena rushed through the room and out the door, slowing only as she reached the front corner of the house. As if nothing was amiss, she waved to the cowboy who'd parked her gig. She patted Gray, then climbed in and wound her way down the Bar A's ranch road, heading home.

As she rode along, wishing with everything in her that she'd brought an escort, her mind started replaying and analyzing all the facts she'd learned. Something popped up into her memory, stalling her heart between one beat and the next.

When she'd bumped into him in town the other day, Lucien had taken her hand and said something about not having to worry about Bren being around for much longer.

Not an offer to influence the governor, after all?

When added together with all she'd learned that night, the true meaning of his words on Thursday became sinister, clear. They'd been a threat, pure and simple.

Another memory surfaced: the way the raiders had gone after Brendan the night of the raid. Lucien had been furious with him that same afternoon, and Bren had been sure the raid was coming that night.

She slapped the reins on Gray's rump, pushing him faster. She had to get to town. Had to wire Bren and warn him. Because she'd stupidly said that in the near future he was due to travel between Tierra del Verde and Mountain Home. And now Lucien knew exactly where to get to him.

And Bren…Bren had known about Lucien all along. No wonder he hadn't wanted to go tonight. He must have been so frustrated with her and the lack of proof against Lucien. There was only one reason he'd have stayed silent: he'd been trying to protect her. Considering that she'd felt it necessary to sneak out of Lucien's house rather than face him, she could hardly fault Bren's instincts.

She'd learned the truth and that the proof he needed existed. And she knew exactly where it was. Nearly in town, she heard the thundering of horses behind her.

Panic set in. "Yah!" she shouted to Gray, and snapped the reins. The speed of the gig went from a quick pace to breakneck. When she saw the shadow of the school come up on her left, she reined the horse in and turned so she could hide the gig on the far side of the building.

The question was, who were the men riding by? She had to find out.

She left her gig where it was and went on foot toward Sheriff Quinn's office. But just as she was about to step out of the shadow of the alley, she saw them. The street was being watched. The men were strangers. There were no strangers in Tierra del Verde, except for the twenty dead raiders, of course. They'd been strangers, too. It wasn't a far leap to figure out these were Avery's men. Men he hid.

Helena melted back into the alley, desperate to get to the sheriff. But when she tried from two other spots along Main Street, she faced the truth. It wasn't possible to cross Main. She had the feeling that if she circled town she'd find the back door being watched, too.

Maybe she could warn Bren by a wire to the sheriff in Mountain Home. But at Sam Houston Street she faced almost the same problem at the alley across from the Western Union office. Sitting in one of the chairs in the shadows of the front porch, his feet crossed at the ankles and propped up on the railing, sat another cowboy who probably worked for Lucien. Once again Helena backed into the cover of darkness.

Then came the clomp of feet on the boardwalk of the building next to her. She scooted behind a rain barrel. Two men stopped out on the nearly empty street near the mouth of the alley, terrifyingly close to where she crouched. Praying the light of the moon wouldn't reveal her lilac dress, she clung to the barrel, hoping they'd move on.

And as she waited, she planned. Where to go next? Whose help to solicit? Joshua was brave and trustworthy. He'd get involved. But he was only a banker, schooled in mine engineering. With Abby expecting, Helena couldn't endanger him. Bren wouldn't want that, either.

Then one of the men spoke. "Ain't nobody seen Kane in town yet. He'd stay here, being the sheriff's all shot up. So he's gotta be betwixt here and Mountain Home. Away from here, he's fair game. Him getting killed out there won't cast no suspicion on Avery, or have more rangers snoopin' round here."

"We wait for Ace to get back. Boss tells him we go, we go."

"Chicken shit," the first man groused.

"Rather be a live chicken than dead as shit. Make a bad step and the boss will put you six feet under sure as Monday follows Sunday."

"Then I'm waitin' at the Garter."

"It's your funeral if Avery finds out you were parading around town and risked being seen. We were supposed to be careful not to be."

With Ryan Quinn out of the picture, Helena fell back on her new plan B, and moved through the alleyways to the back steps of the Golden Garter. She crept up to the second floor and slipped into the hall. She was only four or five steps from Lucy's room. Outside the door, she stopped, relieved to see a slight glow from beneath it. "Lucy?" she whispered.

"Sì?"

Lucy looked worse, her face swollen and purple,

when Helena stuck her head in the door. "How are you?" she asked.

"Much pain, but better I think, *señora*. But I am… how you say…confused. I mourn my baby, but I am relieved to have no ties to the father and not to have another to care for. Maybe alone I can be more than a whore."

Helena winced. Such a judgmental word. She would never automatically think poorly of women with no resources for survival but their bodies.

"You can put all this behind you. I'll help. You didn't want what you called charity, so we could trade one deed for another. I need help. Do you think you could help me?"

Somehow a bargain struck in desperation for both of them performed some sort of magic.

Within minutes Lucy had summoned Darla. And on hearing the tale, the madam turned into what amounted to Helena's fairy godmother. The speed with which Helena's problems were solved was truly bewildering.

Dressed as a man, she soon sat as tall in the saddle as she could, with Darla walking next to a horse from the livery. In her saddlebags Helena had ammunition for the rifle in the scabbard, and for Brendan's Winchester and Colt.

Mr. Dowdy, the man Bren used to work for at the livery, was on his way to the Rocking R, and his son was headed to Shamrock, to gather a posse to ride to Brendan's rescue. But both women knew they'd be too late if Bren didn't know trouble was hunting him.

At the far edge of town, Darla patted her on the thigh and called out, "See you next week, pilgrim."

Helena didn't even chance a glance back at Darla,

who'd turned back to the Golden Garter. She just picked up her pace and left the town behind.

As far as Helena was concerned, no one could outdo Darla as a fairy godmother.

Chapter Nineteen

"Whoa, old son," Brendan told Harry, as he steadied the big black. Then he stepped down out of the saddle to check the gelding's fetlock and knee. He looked back, but didn't see anything Harry could have stumbled over. "You're just tuckered out, aren't you, boy?"

Brendan sighed. Exhaustion tugged at him, too. He'd known his chances of being home in time to take Helena to that damned summer social were slim. But a man could hope. It had been hours since he'd left Mountain Home, and now it was well past dark. Poor Harry had kept on going to please him, but it was time to give up.

They both needed sleep. But that wasn't going to happen till Brendan dealt with another problem. Someone had been dogging him since he'd left Mountain Home. He found a little clearing nearby, dragged the saddle off Harry and built a small fire. Brendan moved back to the gelding to rub him down, waiting for his eyes to fully adjust to the darkness again. Then he melded into the dark woodlands to do a little hunting. But not for dinner. His purpose was to ferret out a two-legged variety of predator.

Within minutes he had nearly closed in on his target. Whoever was out there apparently didn't like being the prey, and suddenly galloped off, hell-bent for election.

Brendan went back to his camp, made coffee, pulled out some jerky and settled on his bedroll to eat his puny meal. His actions were pretty much done by rote, his mind numb with exhaustion and no small amount of disappointment. He'd wanted to get home for Helena's sake. He'd wanted enough evidence to be able to walk into Avery's place and slap cuffs on him and his band of marauders.

Bren tried to empty his mind so he could sleep, planning to set out for Shamrock at first light. He hoped to at least be there when she woke. Or maybe he'd wake her himself. He was sure she'd understand why he hadn't made it home despite their last words. The delay couldn't have been helped.

The man he'd gone to see had been in very poor condition, and unconscious for a long time after Brendan arrived. Unfortunately, waiting had earned him very little in the way of help or information. The victim had apparently seen a man carrying Alejandro Varga's watch, and been shot for his trouble. Bren had done a drawing of the shooter as the man described him. Other than this image for a Wanted poster, all Brendan got was a description of the raid on Belleza that the tracks had already revealed.

Brendan reached for his saddlebag and pulled out his sketch. Staring down at the face he'd drawn, he muttered, "I'll get you, ya bastard. He had a young wife, five little ones and a fine life you took from him."

"Hello, the camp," a female voice called. Brendan

had his Colt in his hand before he registered the fact it was Helena's.

"What in the name of all that's holy are you doin' all the way out here in the middle of the night, woman?"

She came into view, dressed like a man, a beat-up old Stetson pulled down over her ears, and leading a huge gelding behind her. "I came to save you," she told him, her tone grim but a touch triumphant.

"Have ya now?" She could draw a smile from him no matter how crazed she made him with the chances she took with her safety.

"I know, Bren," she said, sounding dead serious. That sobered his mood real quick.

"Ya know what, lovey?"

"I know about Lucien and the raids. In fact, I may know more than you do."

Now that was some statement. "How is it you know all this?"

"It doesn't matter. Smother the fire. We need to get away from here. They're not far behind me."

Without a thought of questioning her, he tossed dirt on the fire and set about throwing the saddle on Harry. "We'll have to walk. These woodlands through here are too thick even with the full moon. Harry's tuckered out, too. Who is it we're runnin' from, lovey?" Bren asked, even though he was pretty sure he knew.

"Lucien's men. At least some of them. I don't think they're all bad. I went to the social…" She held up her hand. "You don't have to tell me how stupid it was. You were right about his intentions toward me. I rejected him in front of a ballroom full of guests."

Bren's breath stalled in his chest. "Jaysus, Helena," he gasped. "He could have—"

"I don't want to think about that, thank you very much. Remember, I didn't know how dangerous he is. The worst part was he made me so angry I said the only reason you weren't with me was that you hadn't gotten back from Mountain Home in time. So he knows where you're coming from. In town, I overheard the men who followed me from the Bar A say that Lucien plans to have you ambushed out here, thinking if you're killed so far from Tierra del Verde, it won't draw rangers to town."

"It's a bit late for that," he told her, hurriedly tossing his things into his saddlebags. "I've three other rangers there already. Two infiltrated Avery's raiders. One's living in town and befriended him."

"The gambler? That would explain a lot."

Bren nodded and tossed his bedroll behind his saddle. "If you can guess, Severn's gettin' sloppy."

"Another long story," she muttered, half under her breath.

"Which I'm sure I'll hear about later. All set?" he asked, and reached for the reins to Helena's mount, tying them to Harry's saddle. "Let's go. We have to get deep into the cover of the trees, and move fast." He took her hand and pulled her into a loping run. "There's a high cave and a ledge where we can hide, or make a stand if necessary."

They'd been running for a few minutes when she squeezed his hand. "It'll be okay, Bren."

"How? You're in danger. And this whole damned trip was a waste. I got nothing."

"I did."

Brendan blinked and looked down at her, running next to him in the darkness. "What?"

She sucked in a big breath, panting fast. "I found something." She took another gasping breath. "Tell you…when we get…where…we're going."

He wrapped his arm around her waist to lend her support. If she'd found something tangible, she'd done in one night what a U.S. Marshal and four Texas Rangers hadn't. At least if either Ted or Nate were among the men coming after him, their testimony would count as evidence. They might come in handy, as well.

No sooner had he thought that than thundering hooves sounded out on the road, about a quarter mile away. He pulled Helena to a stop as the force of men rode by. "Come on," Bren said, once they'd passed, and pulled on her hand to start running again.

"I don't understand. The raiders went by us," she protested. "Maybe we could make it to town before they realize they missed us."

He saw her worried expression in the dappled moonlight. "I'm sorry, lovey. Someone was doggin' me, until I stopped and did a little doggin' of my own. I figure it was Perez's killer. He's connected to Avery, and he's headed toward Tierra del Verde. He knows where I stopped. They'll be back once they find I'm not there. It'll be okay. We'll make our stand at the cave."

About a half mile beyond, he slowed at the base of a large outcropping, where he'd camped on his way to town in February. "Time to climb."

He grabbed the rifles and handed her the one from her scabbard, then pulled his saddlebags off Harry. When he dragged the saddlebags off Helena's borrowed horse, he damn near dropped them. He looked at her in surprise. "What the hell's in these things?"

"Darla packed ammunition for the rifles and your Colt."

"Apparently enough to start another revolution." He hefted the weight onto his shoulder. "Darla? Upstairs at the Garter, Darla? How in hell do you know her? Yet another long story?"

Helena nodded. "And she got Mr. Dowdy and his son to go for help at the Rocking R and Shamrock. They'll be coming, but not for a while."

"We need to have a bit of a talk when we get home tonight. I want to hear all these long stories." *If we get home,* he thought, but refrained from saying.

He gave Harry a hard slap on his flank. "Go on. Get lost. Not too far, fella," he ordered, and the black, leading the other mount, faded into the darkness of the surrounding woodland.

Bren had slept in the cave near the top in February. They'd hide there and if necessary defend the position until help arrived. He hoped the men from Shamrock and the Rocking R reached them in time. And he hoped Ted, Nate and maybe Severn would find a way to help. Jaysus. If anything happened to Helena…

"We're heading up along this trail. Keep close to the high side."

Luck was with them. Before Avery's men found them, they'd made it to the ledge overlooking the crescent-shaped clearing below. He dumped the gear in the shallow cave there. "This is as close to a perfect place as we could hope for," he told her, trying to put a good light on a bad situation. "This ledge and the cave are in shadow by this time of the night, but anyone coming will be visible below. I'll be able to pick them off one at a time if they try to follow us."

"We, Bren," she said, a quaver in her voice. "There are two rifles." Her tone was less confident than her brave words. "Besides," she went on, "how will they track us in the dark?"

He'd been watching the torches off in the distance. "Because, lovey, they aren't tryin' to hide. We are. Or were." He pointed. "They're comin'. Remember, like you said, we have help on the way. We just have to hold them off awhile."

The torches got closer and closer. Brendan was tempted to open fire, but any of those men could be Nate or Ted.

"Boss, we got tracks heading up thataway," one torchbearer shouted.

"Here we go, lovey," Bren whispered. "If you don't want to fire, you can keep the rifles loaded for me. I'd rather you were a bit behind me and out of the fray."

"No." He heard a round chamber in the Winchester. "They've killed my friends and neighbors. Like the night they raided Shamrock, they started this."

He nodded and chambered a round himself. "Let's get 'em, tough gal." They both fired at once, and the torchbearer and another man nearing the base of the cliff trail fell.

They continued firing for what felt like hours, until Brendan's shoulder ached. He could only imagine how Helena felt, stretched out on her belly next to him, firing while he loaded, and loading while he fired.

Jaysus. Why hadn't she gone home, and sent Mallory with the men? Big brave Texas Ranger that he was purported to be, he was afraid to ask why she'd come. What if the answer she gave wasn't what he hoped?

He shook his head and took aim. All that could matter was keeping the bastards pinned down in the trees and behind a few scattered boulders in the clearing below.

With the ammunition Helena had brought along they could probably hold off Avery's raiders as long as his and Helena's strength didn't give out. But help would arrive before that. He had to believe it.

All at once dirt and pebbles showered down from above, to prove him wrong. Brendan rolled to his back, ready to fire, when a man dropping down from above landed on him.

Helena yelped. The thought of her in the hands of those monsters down there chilled Brendan's blood and gave him strength.

"Keep firing," he shouted to her as he grappled with the attacker. "Keep them pinned down." He pushed the man off him and sprang to his feet. He wanted to stay between Helena and the outlaw, but had to draw the man toward the cave so Bren couldn't be pushed off the ledge. And so gunmen below couldn't get a good shot at him.

Brendan fought with the raider, who managed to shove him backward, then made a move for his sidearm. *Big mistake,* Brendan thought as he pulled his Colt and fired. The man tumbled backward off the cliff, not even screaming as he fell.

Helena, meanwhile, had continued to fire at the shadows beyond the moonlit clearing.

A few moments later, more dirt rained down, but this time Ted's voice called softly, "We'll defend the ramparts, Irish. Help shouldn't be much longer." Three shots fired simultaneously, telling him all three of his friends had arrived. Brendan's confidence rose. Five against twenty or so, with the high ground advantage. Not bad odds.

"Who's up there?" Helena asked, as she stopped to reload the Winchester.

"Rangers. Ted James, Nate Richards and Severn Duvall, the gambler you already met."

"Welcome, gentlemen," she called out, and fired her rifle. A man in the darkness below cursed in pain.

From behind the raiders, rifles boomed and flashed into the sky. "You're surrounded. Drop the weapons or we'll save the hangman a day's work," Alex Reynolds shouted.

"It's over, lovey," Bren said at her side, and breathed easy for the first time since Helena had showed up.

"No. It isn't," she said, her tone grave. "You still have to arrest Lucien. I don't want him killed in a shoot-out. That's too easy."

"Granted," Brendan said, as he got to his feet. He reached out his hand to help her up, then held her in the circle of his arms. "We aren't going to make it easy on him, I promise. Are we, gentlemen?" he said to his fellow rangers as they finished the climb down the face of the cliff, to join them on the ledge. He introduced them to Helena, who politely thanked them for their assistance as if they'd helped clear away the china after dinner.

"How did you find your way up there?" he asked, trying not to chuckle.

"We followed the clever bastard you tossed off the cliff."

"No, Bren shot him. He fell on his own," Helena said.

Brendan chuckled this time. "She's turned utterly bloodthirsty. I think I should be terrified." He stepped back and grasped her shoulders, feeling worried. Her anger at Avery was beyond what he'd expected. Something had occurred he'd yet to hear about. "What is it you want to happen at the Bar A, lovey? We can't lynch him, you know."

"No. Again, too easy. I want to be there when you arrest him."

Whoa. That wasn't what he'd expected. But he didn't have the heart to say no. Had it not been for Helena he'd be pushing up daisies by that time tomorrow. But taking her back to the Bar A didn't sit well, either. Reluctantly, he nodded. "And?"

"I want to be the one who retrieves the evidence. I found it, after all. But mostly, even though I don't want to watch him die on the gallows, I want him to know I'm the one sending him there."

"It would be an unusual end to my career," Brendan hedged. She clearly knew of a way to bring down Lucien Avery. "You never did say what it is you found in Avery's house."

She trailed a finger down the buttons of his shirt. "I'll show you when Lucien's watching his fancy life come to an end. It would be too hard to explain where it's hidden. Oh, and I'd like to stop in town to change. If I show up looking like this, it might alert someone at the Bar A that something isn't right. I've had my fill of shoot-outs."

That was a relief to hear. "Me, too, lovey," he said, and put his arm around her again. "Are ya sure you wouldn't rather wait at home? Between the four of us we could find about anything with the right instruct—"

"I'm coming along, Bren," she interrupted, her tone as determined as he'd ever heard it. He sighed in defeat and his friends chuckled.

* * *

It was an hour past midnight when they arrived at the Bar A. Through the windows they could see a few guests still dancing. Severn Duvall walked up the front steps and into the ballroom. Lucien, off to the side, held court with the mayor and the circuit judge.

Brendan, having entered with Helena from the side door she'd fled through earlier, watched from the hall, and backed away from the archway as Severn asked Lucien if he could speak to him privately.

Nate, Ted and several members of the posse were waiting for the signal to round up the rest of the Bar A's men. No one knew how much any of them had known, but they had to be questioned. As far as Ted and Nate could tell, all of Avery's so-called guards had been killed or arrested out at the clearing.

Brendan had left Helena waiting just inside the side door. He patted her arm as he walked back out to signal the posse, and squeezed her hand after latching the door so she'd be safe again. He stepped back into the hall and proceeded to the office Helena had already pointed out as Avery's.

Bren sauntered inside and leaned against the desk to await the other ranger and Avery, who walked in a moment later. Severn pulled his gun as he cleared the doorway. When Avery saw Brendan, he stopped and backed into Severn's weapon. Avery's expression went from shock to horror. Brendan couldn't wait to see his reaction to Helena's appearance when she exposed whatever it was she'd found hidden in the room.

Brendan pulled his own gun when he noticed the man's hand start to move. "I wouldn't," he said, and strolled over to relieve him of his weapon. "Ya look a mite sick, Avery. I'd have thought you were made of stronger stuff, considering the savagery you've ordered time after time."

Brendan searched him—admittedly a little roughly around the family jewels—and found a deadly little chrome-plated Derringer tucked in a vest pocket.

"Ranger Duvall, suppose you cuff this bastard. I don't trust him not to have more of these stashed in the furniture somewhere."

"I'd be only too happy to, Ranger Kane."

"I thought you were my friend," the rancher growled when Severn pulled his arms behind him.

"I have much better taste, Avery," Severn replied, and squeezed the cuffs good and tight.

Avery bellowed,. "This is an outrage!" His shout was as loud as it was indignant. Bren imagined the murdering bastard probably expected someone to come to his aid. As everyone in his employ should be sharing a locked storeroom by then, help was unlikely.

Brendan pushed everything off the desk onto the floor, took Avery by his lapels and shoved him against the big piece of furniture. "Don't move a muscle," he told him, "or you'll be even less comfortable."

"I'm going to make you pay, Kane," Avery growled.

"I was just about to say something along those lines to you. And I promise a long drop before the rope snugs around your scrawny neck." Brendan turned to Severn. "I'll be right back. No matter how annoying he gets, don't shoot him. You'd spoil our surprise." Then he walked down the hall to get Helena. He still didn't like this, but without knowing what they were looking for they were as powerless as Avery.

"Lovey," Brendan said a moment later, as he stuck

his head into the room across the hall. "Would you come along to the ballroom? There's a circuit judge in there. I think havin' him as a witness to you showin' us what you found would be best."

"Is Lucien handcuffed?" she asked, taking hold of Bren's arm.

He grinned and managed to nod without laughing at how fierce she looked. "You're reminding me of a spittin' kitten again, lovey. I'm just glad those long sharp claws aren't goin' to be layin' me open this time."

She looked up and patted his arm. "Just remember how much kitten scratches hurt, cowboy."

"Yes, ma'am."

They walked into the ballroom and up to the judge. "Judge Stevenson, would you mind coming with us? We need an unimpeachable witness in Mr. Avery's office."

The judge frowned, then nodded. "Of course, Ranger Kane. If you feel it's necessary." They proceeded down the hall.

Helena followed the men into the library, and Avery popped to his feet. "Helena, you have to talk to this lout husband of yours."

"I talk to him all the time, Lucien. He's my husband. I suppose you're wondering why I've come back after the way you embarrassed me earlier. I came to show these gentlemen something I stumbled upon. Do you remember that book of poetry I gave you Christmas last?"

Avery looked as if he'd swallowed his tongue.

"I see you remember. It was *Voices in the Night,*" she told everyone else. "A Longfellow volume. I ran across it in here earlier tonight. Oh yes…" She sauntered over to a bookcase on the left side of the room. "And picture my surprise when I tipped it forward, like this."

A mechanical click sounded and the bookcase swung into the room.

"You can imagine what a shock it was, Your Honor, when I looked around and saw this." Her voice had gone deadly and hard, and she disappeared behind the bookcase.

She emerged with a smallish painting of a ram trussed up for slaughter. *"Agnus Dei,"* she said. "It was painted about 1635 by Zurbarán. It's a little unusual, as it's a ram and not a spring lamb, but fitting for a shepherd. I know all this because Don Alejandro Varga invited me to see it one day. He was very proud of this painting."

"He sold it to me," Avery said quickly.

Helena handed the painting to the judge and went to stand in front of Avery.

Brendan moved with her and shoved Avery back to perch on the desk.

"No, he didn't, Lucien," Helena said. She had Avery dead to rights and she knew it. "He'd never have sold it. It was his proudest possession. The don's father gave it to him to take to America, hoping it would bring good fortune to his son and bride. Farrah Varga mentioned how sad it was that it had burned with the house after having been in the family for so long. And because it had meant so much to the don."

Helena's voice went cold as death when she suddenly switched subjects in the blink of an eye. "Tell me about the stampede, Lucien," she demanded. "The stampede you had your men start at Shamrock when we finally got to a place where we could gather the herd. Was it your success that night that gave you the idea for your

Ghost Warriors? Do you know what happened to me in that stampede? What you did to me?

"You didn't just hurt me. You killed my baby, Lucien," she hissed, inches from Avery's face. Brendan stood there, stunned. And before he could act on any instinct of his own, Helena swung her arm and punched the bastard in his face. Avery fell back onto his big, important desk. His head hit so hard he was knocked senseless. And if Brendan wasn't mistaken, she'd broken Avery's pretty nose.

Then she stepped back, the deep breath she must have been holding rushing out of her. Bren's own fury at what she'd said—at what Avery had done—scared him. He had never been so close to becoming judge, jury and executioner than he was at that moment.

Brendan looked at Helena. All thoughts of his own reaction left him as he watched silent tears run freely down her cheeks. She began to shake. He had to get her out of there.

He nodded to Severn, leaving him to handle Avery, ending a career that mattered not at all now. Brendan wanted nothing but to be able to care for his wife. He wrapped her in his arms. "Feel better?" he whispered as he guided her out of the room.

She sucked in a sob and put her head on his shoulder. "Take me home, Bren," she begged, as they walked out the side door and into the summer night. Afraid she'd crumple, he scooped her into his arms, carried her to the gig and set her on the seat. "I guess we have a lot to talk about," she whispered as he climbed in and pulled her close. He set Gray into a trot.

Brendan wrapped his arm around her waist, holding her there where she belonged. He didn't think he'd ever forget the sound of her grief and anguish when she'd spoken in that deadly whisper to Avery. *"You killed my baby."*

Brendan wasn't sure if she realized what she'd said. Even in the midst of unleashing her anguish and anger, he'd been shocked to his core that she'd curled that dainty hand of hers into a fist and knocked Avery six ways from Sunday.

"Yes. We've a lot to talk about, lovey. And we will. But it's nothing that can't wait. Let's get you home first." And then he spent the time between the two spreads trying to formulate the words of a heartfelt apology. As he drove them home—on roads safe for the first time in years—a few thoughts gave him courage.

She'd never hated him as he'd thought. He'd heard hate in her voice now, unleashed at Avery. She'd allowed Bren back into her life. She'd come to save him. And he was already one lucky son of a bitch, even if she never loved him again.

Chapter Twenty

Helena stirred and sat up, lifting her head from the comfort of Brendan's shoulder. Her mind a bit fuzzy from sleep, she looked around. He'd brought the gig to a halt in front of the house. When she looked at Bren she found him studying her.

"You killed my baby," resounded in her mind. She'd finally said it aloud, but confronting Lucien hadn't put an end to the grief and loss she felt.

And now Bren knew, because in a moment of fury the truth had erupted. That wasn't the way she'd wanted to tell him.

"Did I grow a second nose?" Bren teased, with a sweet smile.

She blinked. Damn, she'd been staring at him, trying to discern answers to questions she wasn't ready to ask. But she had no choice, and maybe that was for the best. Not talking had brought them nothing but strife.

"I have to take care of the horses. Myself," Bren added, his voice hesitant and as quiet as the night. He looked toward the house. "I don't want to wake Jimmy.

So it's, uh, it may take a while. And you need to get to bed. You're exhausted," he said.

Seeing him so uncertain gave her pause. Did he blame himself? Her? Tonight had shown her the truth. The tragedy could be laid at only one person's feet.

Lucien Avery's.

Suddenly sure of herself—of them—she put her hand on Brendan's and squeezed. "We'll put up Harry and Gray together. You're no less tired than I am. I'm helping."

He sighed. "I'm not trying to take over or—"

"Brendan Joseph Kane, I'm not misunderstanding your motives. You wanted to take care of me. I get it. I wanted to take care of you earlier, even though I put myself in danger to do it."

He nodded.

She touched his arm. "I'll help with the horses. I refuse to see another day end until we have a real heart-to-heart talk. There's time enough to rest later. I want to wake in the morning at the beginning of a new life. Not in limbo the way we have been since you moved back in with me. So let's care for these animals."

He gave her a weary half smile, nodded and flicked the reins for the last leg of the trip home. The thud of hooves, the jangle of harness and creak of leather seemed to play a peaceful, hopeful tune as they rode down the hill to the barn.

Once there they worked in harmony the way they always had before she'd ruined everything by ignoring his feelings. She'd made that mistake twice now—once three years earlier, when she'd bought the ranch, and Thursday over the social. Maybe she'd even done it when they'd first met, by holding back more than the most basic facts of her life.

By God, it was an error she wouldn't repeat.

The horses all tucked in, they walked back up the hill toward the house. Bren took her hand as she broke the companionable silence that had fallen between them. "I've been thinking about a lesson I learned a long time ago. Lies can hide behind soft words and fine-looking faces."

"Like Avery's."

She couldn't hold in a deep, regretful sigh. "I was so lonely when you left. I had no one to turn to, and then I lost the baby. So when Lucien offered his friendship, I forgot how devious people can be. I didn't question his motives."

Brendan stepped in front of her, then cupped her shoulders. His eyes locked with hers. There was an innate gentleness about him; there always had been. It always surprised her when she felt it in his hands and saw it in his emerald eyes. He was so masculine and pretended to be so tough, but she knew his vulnerabilities.

"Helena, lovey." He swallowed. Hesitant but determined, he went ahead. "You were right. We do have to talk. I can't go on with all this bursting inside me." He trailed his palms down her arms, took hold of her hand again and led her inside, to the sitting room. "I'm sorry," he said. "I know you're dead on your feet but…"

"No. It is long past time." Helena sank onto the sofa, her exhaustion physical only. Her mind was alert, her heart unguarded.

Bren sat to her right, his left knee bent on the cushion so he faced her. He tucked a curl behind her ear. "I'll start, as I caused most of our problems. I'm sorry

I judged your father so unfairly. It was small and mean of me, and I'm ashamed to have been such a bastard about your inheritance.

"And there's the note I left when I went to Mountain Home that needs explaining."

"Oh, Bren, you don't—"

"Yes. I do. Let me say this. After you rode off on Thursday, I went lookin' for you, to apologize."

"But you were right."

"I had information you didn't. I should have told you the truth. I realized that. I was going to explain when I got home instead of dictatin' what you should feel and do. I wrote that note with a damned heavy heart."

"I know you were trying to protect me," Helena replied. "I couldn't have talked to Lucien without showing my contempt. I never meant to blurt out the truth about the baby in front of you." Her voice faded to a whisper. "I never meant you to learn about what happened that way, but I lost control. It must have seemed so callous."

He grimaced. "The worst part was seeing how much grief you still feel. You see, lovey, I already knew. When I couldn't find you on Thursday, Maria said you always come home through that low-lying meadow behind the house. I remembered you lookin' off in that direction. It always seemed like you were prayin' so I'd never wanted to intrude."

He took her hand and stared down at it, caressing it with his fingertips. "I found Kathleen's grave. I knew you'd been hurt in a stampede a while after I left. I put that together with the date on the stone. It was my fault. Doc said I should've been here—"

"No!" she exclaimed. Brendan looked up. His grief was new and fresh, not dulled by the years as hers had been until tonight. Her pain had all come rushing back when she'd learned Lucien had caused the accident that had ended the promise of Kathleen's life. "I should have told you before, Bren. You shouldn't have had to find out that way."

"I'd have thought you would have tossed it in my face and ordered me off Shamrock, the lies I'd told in town about moving home be damned."

"At first when you came here, I was still so angry I didn't think you deserved to know about her. After the raid, when we got back together, I didn't know how to tell you."

"You should never have been riding herd."

She stiffened. "You aren't thinking anything I haven't."

He winced and looked down. Could he be so disgusted with her carelessness he couldn't even look at her? Was it the last straw for him?

"I'm sorry, Bren. Believe me, I've felt such horrible guilt about losing her that way. I've been so worried you'd hold it against me. Especially what it might mean to any hope of a family."

"Jaysus!" He squeezed her hand and looked up, his eyes wide with some emotion she couldn't name. He stared at her for a long moment, clearly gathering his equilibrium. "What in hell do you have to feel guilty about? It was me who should've been ridin' with that herd. In your condition you should have been safe at home knittin' booties."

"I told myself that same lie for a long time. But I made the decision to go with the men that day. The undeniable fact is it was my fault."

Bren pressed his lips together and for a protracted

moment stared at her. Then he kissed her hand and in a gentle tone said, "Tell me. Tell me about that day. Why did you go with the men?"

"We'd found more mavericks roaming Shamrock than anyone had expected. It left us shorthanded. We'd gathered them in small groups along the route Mallory had planned, and added each herd to the next as we drove them along. I was riding drag. It was dusty, but supposedly the safest position."

He nodded, as if encouraging her to get it all out. To show him what was written on her heart and mind.

"We knew we were heading into a storm, so Mallory kept the herd pretty well stretched out along the valleys lying between the hills as we added group after group. It was a good plan."

"Aye. The hills would've directed the flow of the cattle. So what went wrong?"

"We heard a crack of lightning and thunder up ahead. Then it was on us in seconds. The rain fell in sheets and the thunder was…well, wrong. It felt wrong."

"Because it was weapons discharging," Brendan stated.

She nodded. "We were short of men, considering the size of the herd, and no one was riding point. Consequently, we never knew why the herd turned on us. Mallory said it was like the waves of an angry ocean pressing in on the men who were in the thick of it. The memory of those sounds still gives me chills." She shivered.

Bren pulled her across his lap. His nearness, his touch gave her the courage to continue.

"The sound was deafening. The rumble of hooves and cracks of lightning and thunder. Panicked cattle.

The men shouting, but they couldn't turn the steers back. And I was suddenly right in their way." She paused. Drew a breath. "I turned Brownie to run with them, but Yates got to my side and pointed upward. Since we were headed toward the canyon, climbing seemed a much better idea. I turned toward the hill.

"We got pretty far up, but the rain made the grass slippery, I guess. S-something went wrong. We fell. I don't remember anything until I woke up in labor. Within an hour Kathleen died in my arms, and what was left of my world crumbled." Tears welled in her eyes and fell.

"I'm so sorry," Brendan choked out. "If I'd been there…"

"Bren, look at me." He did and his green eyes glittered with unreleased tears. "It wasn't the fault of either of us. I know that now. And you have to believe it or Lucien wins. It was his doing. His fault. I heard Ted James tell Severn Duvall that Lucien had sent his men to start the stampede."

"You said as much in his office, remember?" Brendan's mouth kicked up into a grin. "Right before my fierce wife broke his nose."

"I did not."

"Oh, aye. I think you did." He stroked a fingertip across her knuckles. They were sore. "It helped me contain my anger. That and my concern for you. But I'm going to be sore pressed not to drop him where he stands when he appears in court," he told her. "Though I won't. I promised you he'd swing for the deaths of all his victims. Our Kathleen's included."

Helena had to tell him. Doc had been right about that. Bren had a right to know all the consequences of that day. "Bren, there's one more thing. You keep talking about the family we're going to have. You said I was enough if we don't have children."

He smoothed a hand over her hair and down her back. "You were thinking of Kathleen then, right?"

"I was thinking about Doc's warnings. He says I may not be able to carry a baby long enough. Apparently, it isn't uncommon, when a woman shows a tendency to go into early labor, that it will happen every time."

Brendan nodded, his expression grave. "Would it put your life in danger if that kept happening?"

"No." She sighed, sad and unsure of her purpose in life if she wasn't to be a mother, and now Bren was there to run Shamrock. But at least she was secure in his arms. "Everything has changed," she said. "We're all safe again, but the harm Lucien caused is irrevocable."

"Ah, lovey. I remembered something recently. It was a lesson my da tried to drum into my thick head. You can't unring a bell. Nothing will bring Kathleen back, but dammit, I'm going to try to at least unring all the bells I've rung between us. I love you. I meant it when I wrote it in that note. I love you more than life itself."

"I love you, too. So, so much."

"I'd hoped you did. Though I don't know if I deserve it. And yes, I want children with you if the Lord provides them." He swept a finger down her cheek, following the track of her tears. "How about this plan? If we find it isn't to be, we'll go meet that orphan train and pick us up the family we both want. Two or three nice kiddies ought to fill this place with noise and laughter."

His smile encouraged her to smile back at him. "I wouldn't mind adopting, Bren. But I want to prove Doc wrong. And I want what Lucien took from me. I won't let him win so easily."

Brendan smiled. "Now there's my girl." He cupped the back of her head and drew her forward till their lips touched in the gentlest of kisses.

Then it altered.

Changed.

Grew. And she knew it would be all right. They were finally together. No more secrets. No more things unsaid. No more misunderstandings.

Still holding her tight to him, he leaned back and grinned. "What say we call it a night and go see what we can do about makin' that little Kane?"

She sputtered a laugh.

He grinned back and winked. Then he carried her to bed and did exactly what he'd set out to do.

Green-eyed, black-haired Henry Michael Kane was born ten months later. And proving all the naysayers wrong, Brendan and Helena Kane had three more children and lived happily at Shamrock until well into their eighties.

* * * * *

REQUEST YOUR FREE BOOKS!

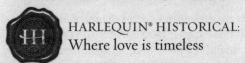

HARLEQUIN® HISTORICAL:
Where love is timeless

2 FREE NOVELS PLUS 2 FREE GIFTS!

YES! Please send me 2 FREE Harlequin® Historical novels and my 2 FREE gifts (gifts are worth about $10). After receiving them, if I don't wish to receive any more books, I can return the shipping statement marked "cancel." If I don't cancel, I will receive 6 brand-new novels every month and be billed just $5.44 per book in the U.S. or $5.74 per book in Canada. That's a savings of at least 16% off the cover price! It's quite a bargain! Shipping and handling is just 50¢ per book in the U.S. and 75¢ per book in Canada.* I understand that accepting the 2 free books and gifts places me under no obligation to buy anything. I can always return a shipment and cancel at any time. Even if I never buy another book, the two free books and gifts are mine to keep forever.

246/349 HDN F4ZY

Name	(PLEASE PRINT)	
Address		Apt. #
City	State/Prov.	Zip/Postal Code

Signature (if under 18, a parent or guardian must sign)

Mail to the **Harlequin® Reader Service:**
IN U.S.A.: P.O. Box 1867, Buffalo, NY 14240-1867
IN CANADA: P.O. Box 609, Fort Erie, Ontario L2A 5X3

Want to try two free books from another line?
Call 1-800-873-8635 or visit www.ReaderService.com.

* Terms and prices subject to change without notice. Prices do not include applicable taxes. Sales tax applicable in N.Y. Canadian residents will be charged applicable taxes. Offer not valid in Quebec. This offer is limited to one order per household. Not valid for current subscribers to Harlequin Historical books. All orders subject to credit approval. Credit or debit balances in a customer's account(s) may be offset by any other outstanding balance owed by or to the customer. Please allow 4 to 6 weeks for delivery. Offer available while quantities last.

Your Privacy—The Harlequin® Reader Service is committed to protecting your privacy. Our Privacy Policy is available online at www.ReaderService.com or upon request from the Harlequin Reader Service.

We make a portion of our mailing list available to reputable third parties that offer products we believe may interest you. If you prefer that we not exchange your name with third parties, or if you wish to clarify or modify your communication preferences, please visit us at www.ReaderService.com/consumerschoice or write to us at Harlequin Reader Service Preference Service, P.O. Box 9062, Buffalo, NY 14269. Include your complete name and address.

HHI3R

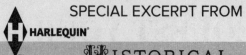
*From Bronwyn Scott comes the incredible new quartet
RAKES WHO MAKE HUSBANDS JEALOUS, featuring two
fantastic full-length Harlequin Historical novels and two
very sexy Harlequin Historical Undone! ebooks. Read on
for a sneak preview of our first hero, Nicholas D'Arcy...
the talk of the* ton *for all the wrong reasons!*

"I'm going swimming. How about you?"

Annorah drew her knees up and hugged them. She used to
love to swim, but that was before she grew up and swimming
was ruled as something ladies didn't do. A lady couldn't very
well swim in her clothes, which made the activity lewd *and*
public. "The water will make my skirts too heavy."

Nicholas grinned wickedly. "Then take them off."

He was going to have to debate with her about it.
Nicholas heard the regret in her voice, as if she was merely
making the appropriate answer. Well, he'd see what he
could do about that. He rose from the blanket and shrugged
out of his shirt. It was perhaps not as gracefully done as
it might have been. The shirt was wet and it stuck to him.
He threw it on a hanging branch and his hands went to the
waistband of his trousers.

"What are you doing?" Annorah's voice barely disguised
a gasp of excitement mixed with trepidation.

"I'm taking off my trousers. I don't mean to swim in
them," he called over his shoulder.

"What *do* you mean to swim in?"

"In my altogether. You could swim in your chemise if
you preferred," he suggested.

"I couldn't." Annorah hesitated, biting her lip.

"Then take it off, too." He pushed his trousers past his hips and kicked them off, leaving only his smalls—a concession to her modesty. He turned around and Annorah blushed, her gaze looking everywhere but at him.

"Don't tell me you're embarrassed by my natural state." Nick spread his arms wide from his sides and sauntered toward her. He couldn't resist having a bit of fun. If he'd learned one thing about her this afternoon, it was that she could be teased—the wildness inside was very much alive once she let down her guard. He rather enjoyed getting past that guard, as he had in the river.

"It's not that."

"It isn't? Then is it perhaps that you're embarrassed about your natural state? I think your natural state would be quite lovely." He reached a hand down to her and tugged, letting the teasing fade from his voice. "Come on, Annorah. It's just the two of us. You've been eyeing that swimming hole since we got here. You know you want to." *You want to do more than swim, and if you'd look at me, you'd know I do, too.*

He had her on her feet and then he had her in his arms, kissing her—her throat, her neck, her lips. She tasted like wine, her body all compliance beneath his mouth. A soft moan escaped her. His hands worked the simple fastenings of her gown. He hesitated before pushing the dress down her shoulders, giving her one last chance to back out. If she resisted now, he'd let her. But she didn't. He smiled to himself. Sometimes all a person needed was a nudge.

Don't miss
SECRETS OF A GENTLEMAN ESCORT
available from Harlequin® Historical January 2014

HHEXP1213R

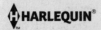
HISTORICAL

Where love is timeless

COMING IN JANUARY 2014

Rancher Wants A Wife

A marriage to save them both...

Among the responses Cassandra Hamilton receives to her advertisement as a mail-order bride, one stands out— Jack McColton's. Since she last saw him, tragedy has made her a cautious woman.

Jack is mesmerized by his new bride—Cassandra might bear the scars of recent events, but she's even more beautiful than he remembers. They both have pasts that are hard to forget, but can their passion banish the shadows forever?

Mail-Order Weddings

From blushing bride to rancher's wife!

Available wherever books and ebooks are sold.

www.Harlequin.com

HH297